Dying for a Taste

Chapter One

At least twice a week, I have customers tell me how lucky I must feel, having been born into this family. Bellies tight from their lunches of clam chowder and *osso buco*, they'll gesture out Solari's picture window at the flocks of brown pelicans soaring up the coast, wing tips just grazing the waves.

"I can't even *imagine* a better place to work than this," they'll exclaim, and pull out their phones to take shots of the fishing boats bobbing up and down in the Monterey Bay.

They truly have no idea.

But then again, they've never had to talk down a rabid waitress on the verge of walloping a busboy over the head with a serving tray, which happened to be the delightful task occupying me at our family's restaurant this Monday lunch shift.

Giulia, a hefty gal in a black skirt and form-fitting white blouse, had cornered Sean in the alcove separating the wait station from the now-busy dining room. Animated voices rose above the clatter of cutlery on ceramic dishes, and the pungent aroma of garlic and fried fish hung in the air.

"Put that down this instant," I said to Giulia, placing myself strategically between her and the cowering busboy, "and tell me what in God's name is going on here."

"It wasn't my fault!" The teenager emerged from behind a rack of soup bowls and stuck out a chin sporting the beginnings of a fuzzy, blond beard. "The man just stood up all of a sudden and threw his arm out, right as I came up to his table."

"Sean managed to knock three orders of cannoli onto the guy at table nine," Giulia retorted, "smearing cream all down the front of his fancy suit. He's been in before and was a huge tipper. That sure won't happen today." She glared at the busboy, and he backed up a step. "What the hell were *you* doing bringing out the dessert anyway?"

"Mario told me to. He said it had been sitting at the window for like ten minutes, and he wanted it out of the way." There was a hint of triumph on the boy's face: one point for his side.

Giulia knew she'd been bested, and her eyes blazed. Raising the tray once more, she started forward, but I blocked her way with my tall, lanky frame.

"Hold your horses, sister. Is the table still here?" She nodded. "Right," I said. "We're all three going out there right now to make a formal apology. How much did they order?"

"Three specials is all. And the desserts. Which of course never made it to the table," Giulia added with another glare in Sean's direction. "No bar tab."

"Good. So you, Giulia, are going to inform the man that the entire meal is on the house and that we'll pay for the dry cleaning for his suit as well. That should appease him a bit. Okay, let's march."

I followed Giulia and Sean into the dining room and then immediately ducked back into the alcove. But it was too late; he'd already spotted me.

"Why, Ms. Solari," a deep voice boomed across the room. "Fancy meeting you here!" I slunk back in and crossed to his table, *the* table: number nine. It was Jack Saroyan, senior partner of Saroyan, Davies & Lang, one of the biggest law firms in Santa Cruz, California.

And my boss from a past life.

"Uh, hi, Jack," I said, managing a weak smile. "So sorry about all this." I nodded at the wet splotches down the front of his pale-gray suit. "Do let me know what the dry cleaning bill is, and we'll cover it for you."

I glanced at Giulia, who was clearly taken aback by the fact that I knew the gentleman. But she recovered quickly and launched into her spiel about comping the meal. Ever the suave politician type, Jack just laughed it off and assured us all that his clothes would be fine.

After Giulia and Sean had gone back to their duties, Jack introduced me to his tablemates: a pair of expert witnesses he'd hired for a land-subsidence case. "Sally used to be one of our very best associate attorneys," he informed the two men. "But sadly she left us a few years ago to return to the family business." He turned back to me. "You know," he said with a glance down his front and a wink, "perhaps managing waitstaff isn't the vocation you were meant for after all. You might want to consider coming back to work for us."

*   *   *

Right, I thought as I headed for the tiny office behind the dry storage room that I shared with my dad. *Like that'll be happening anytime soon.* No matter how much I might bitch about being back at Solari's, the thought of returning to the grind of pumping out endless billable hours was far worse.

I sank into the folding chair and reached across the metal desk for a brown paper bag sitting atop a stack of time sheets. My lunch—a ham and Swiss on Jewish rye with lots of mayo and Dijon mustard—was inside. Yes, I did work at a restaurant, but after a while, you get tired of fried zucchini and spaghetti carbonara every single day. It was past noon, and I'd had no breakfast. I unwrapped the sandwich and took a large bite just as my phone went off: the *Hawaii Five-0* theme song, Eric's ringtone.

"Sal, thank God I got you."

"This better be good," I said, mouth full. "I'm in the middle of lunch, and I have not had a great morning."

"Oh, Sally . . ." There was a pause and labored breathing on the other end of the line.

"What?" I finished chewing and sat up. Eric's my ex-boyfriend, so I know the guy pretty darn well. It wasn't like him to be short on words.

"It's your Aunt Letta." Another pause. "She's dead."

"Wha—?"

"I'm down here at her restaurant. That's where it happened."

"What? A heart attack or something?"

There were loud voices in the background. Eric spoke briefly to someone else—I couldn't make out the words—and then came back on the line. "She was stabbed, Sally. It looks like a murder."

"Oh my God." I jumped up out of my chair and just missed knocking over a mug of yesterday's coffee.

"That's why I'm here. One of the cops on the scene is a friend of mine, and when he realized who the victim was, he gave me a call."

"Oh my God," I said again, sliding back into my chair and slumping over the desk. "Does my dad know?"

"Not yet. You're the first person I've told."

"I better get down there with you."

"I dunno, Sal; it's pretty . . . grisly. And they're not going to let you in anyway. It's a crime scene. They even kicked me out of the building, and I'm a DA."

"I don't care. I'm coming." I shut off the phone and took a few deep breaths, trying to slow my rapid heartbeat. Then I ran out into the hall and grabbed the first person I saw—Emilio, one of the line cooks—by the arm. "Where's my dad?" I shouted.

"He ran out for some polenta. They shorted our delivery yesterday, and we don't have enough for tonight. What's the big deal?"

"Tell ya later." Retrieving my purse from the office, I hurried outside to my beat-up, green Accord, slammed the door, and backed up, nearly colliding with a Stagnaro Bros. seafood delivery truck in the process. The driver hurled some choice words in my direction and then continued on.

Okay, girl, calm down. I waited a moment, made sure no one was in my rearview mirror, and then finished backing out into the road—more cautiously this time.

As I made my way down the length of the wharf, I tried to wrap my mind around what Eric had told me: Aunt Letta's life, which had always seemed so exotic and glamorous to me, was over. Finished. Gunning the accelerator, I cruised through the roundabout and headed downtown. No, it simply didn't make any sense.

In order to make a left off of Pacific Avenue, I had to wait while a gaggle of pedestrians streamed through the crosswalk. This street, which bisects the Eastside and Westside of Santa Cruz from the ocean almost to the hills, is lined with shops, movie theaters, and restaurants and is a magnet for all aspects of our community: university students, moms with strollers, aging hippies, suit-clad professionals, and grizzled men with backpacks and bedrolls.

I finally managed to dart across the road between a pair of adolescent skate punks and an elderly gentleman walking an even more elderly looking chocolate lab and then cut over to Cedar Street, turned left, and drove past my aunt's restaurant, Gauguin. A half-dozen squad cars occupied all the spots in front of the place, but I was able to find parking around the corner on a street lined with brightly painted Victorian homes and trees just beginning to leaf out.

Buttoning up my blazer to ward off the brisk April wind, I walked down the sidewalk with a growing sense of dread. It was easy enough to act all brave and cavalier with Eric on the phone, but was I really up for this?

I mean, even though my dad's sister had left town when I was only a kid, we'd actually ended up fairly close. Violetta, who'd always been known simply as Letta, had returned to Santa Cruz to open Gauguin right when I was starting law school and had been my strongest ally when my dad was so furious about my leaving Solari's—just as she had done, turning her back on the family business, years earlier.

Once back in her hometown, Letta did her best to keep an emotional distance from the rest of the family, rarely even making it to my grandmother's house for Sunday dinner—the only one of us who didn't religiously attend Nonna's weekly ritual. But the two of us had forged a special bond: that of outcast sister and daughter. And even after I'd caved and quit practicing law to return to the family restaurant, she'd still supported me.

But now she was gone.

As I rounded the corner, I looked up to see a swarm of gawkers in front of the restaurant being restrained behind yellow crime tape, and suppressed a shudder. Even if she hadn't been my aunt, the prospect of seeing the actual scene where *anyone* had been stabbed to death would have been exceedingly unsettling.

Well, I wasn't going to turn back now. Pushing my way through the crowd, I tried to get the attention of the policewoman standing guard at Gauguin's intricately carved front door. It was made of koa (Letta had made sure everyone knew this), and as I waited for the cop to shoo off two young men trying to peer through the restaurant window, I studied its Polynesian designs. The swirls and geometric shapes had always reminded me of exotic tattoos, but carved into reddish-brown wood rather than inked into flesh.

I was about to explain who I was to the policewoman when Eric came striding up from behind. "She's with me," he said and, gripping me by the arm, steered me under the crime tape and around the walkway to the side of the restaurant. As always when I was with Eric, I found myself immediately tending to slouch, ever conscious of the several inches in height I had over him, even in flats.

We stopped near the side door. Letta's '57 Thunderbird was parked next to the building, its creamy yellow paint job glaring in the midday sun. Eric unbuttoned his suit jacket and leaned his wiry frame against the stucco wall. Once again, my brain focused on the minutiae—how his pale-blond hair and starched, white shirt took on the hues of the bright-orange wall and the pale-violet trim around the windows. "Mango" and "orchid," Letta had called the colors. Was this some kind of defense my mind was constructing, obsessing over the details to avoid having to concentrate on the big picture?

"They won't let you in," Eric said. "The body's been taken away, but they're still doing their investigation. My guess is, it'll be the better part of the day before they're done."

Through the partly opened door, I could see people milling about inside. Most of the activity seemed to be going on in the *garde manger*, the cold-food-prep area. "Is that where it happened?"

"Yeah. She was discovered on the floor there, near the sink. It was one of the waiters, Brandon, who found her. He'd come in to pick up some books he left here last night. I guess he's a student up at the university?"

"Right. I've actually worked with him a few times. You know, when Letta needed someone to sub at the last minute."

"Musta been pretty horrible for the guy," Eric went on, "finding her like that. Hey, you okay?"

"No," I said, fists and jaw clenched, trying to control the wave of fever that had swept over me. I wiped away a bead of sweat that had formed on my forehead. "I'm not."

"Hot flash?" Eric knew all about this recent phenomenon, which had a habit of plaguing me at inopportune moments.

I nodded, though I knew it was more than just that. "But go on," I said, focusing my attention on a man I could see through the window taking photographs. "I want to know what happened—how she was found."

Eric removed his horn-rimmed glasses to clean them on his silk tie, held them up to the light, and then replaced them. "Okay. So here's what my cop friend told me. She was lying on the floor, like I said, on her side." He paused and glanced at me. "Fully clothed, in case you were wondering."

I hadn't been. Having spent five years as an attorney working for a civil firm, my experience with the criminal side of the law was limited to the classes Eric and I had taken together in law school. So my mind didn't tend to jump to the gruesome as might that of a district attorney like Eric. But even though his tact might be lacking, I did appreciate his frankness. Biting my lip, I motioned for him to continue.

"Anyway, there was a lot of blood—on the ground around her and on her body and clothes. And stab wounds—three or four is what they're saying. It looks like it happened where they found her, that the body wasn't moved."

"Did they find the . . . uh . . . weapon?" Christ, how clichéd that sounded.

"They found a knife next to her. It had some blood on it but had been wiped clean of any prints."

"What kind of knife?"

"I dunno. A big one. One of those, what'd-ya-call-ems, chef's knives? Oh, and the cabinet in that prep room, the one that holds the knives—it was open. Looks like it came from there."

The man with the camera came out the door at this moment, and we stepped aside to allow him to pass. "Afternoon, Stu," said Eric. "You off already?"

"I'm just heading back to the station to get these downloaded, but the other guys will probably be here the rest of the day. See ya later." He nodded to me and headed for his car.

I watched him walk down the path. "You know," I said after a moment, "I think only a few people have keys to that knife cabinet: Aunt Letta and the sous-chef, Javier, and maybe one of the other cooks."

"Yeah. That's what the waiter, Brandon, said. Just those first two, in fact. No one else has a key. He said the cabinet is always locked up as soon as all the food prep is done. I guess the knives in there are pretty valuable. And he identified the one they found by the body as being Javier's and said Javier won't let anyone else touch it."

"You don't think—" I whirled around to face Eric. "No, it couldn't be Javier; he *adores* Letta. Well . . . adored." I knew Javier as being soft-spoken and even-tempered and couldn't imagine him raising even his voice, much less a chef's knife, against anyone.

"I don't think anything, at this point," Eric said. "But I can tell you that Detective Vargas—the lead investigator on the case—is thinking he's our man as of right now."

"Just 'cause he had a key and it was his knife? That seems awful simplistic to me. I mean, how can they be sure the cabinet was even locked? Letta could have opened it for some reason. Maybe when she was attacked, she tried to get a knife to defend herself."

Eric shook his head. "They found her key to the knife cabinet on her key chain in her purse. So unless Letta unlocked the cabinet and then put the key back into her purse while she was being attacked, that theory doesn't fly."

"The killer could have easily put it back there," I protested. Perhaps I was being irrational or naïve, but everything inside me rebelled at the thought of Javier committing such a crime. How could he have, when Letta had practically picked him up off the street to give him a job and then mentored him, as she did all these years?

"Yeah, maybe. They're going to see if they can get any prints off the key, which could answer the question." Eric consulted his watch. "Shit. Look, Sal, I'm really sorry, but I gotta go. I've got a court appearance at one thirty. You gonna be all right?"

"I'm okay. It's just so . . . weird." I followed Eric down to the street, and he pointed his remote at his black Lexus and unlocked it. "Maybe I'm in some kind of shock, but it all seems so surreal. Like I'm watching this whole thing from afar. I dunno . . ."

Eric squeezed my shoulder and walked around to the driver's side and opened the door. "I'll call you later. Let me know if there's anything I can do."

As he shut the door, I called out, "Wait—Eric!"

"What?" He rolled down the passenger-side window and leaned over.

"My dad'll want to know: what will happen with her body? So we can make funeral arrangements. You know, Italian family and all."

"Well, they'll have to do the autopsy before they'll release the body to the family. It's routine in homicide cases. And that'll take a few days."

"Oh, right."

"You can call the coroner to find out exactly how long it'll be," Eric added. "Or I can if you'd prefer."

"That's okay. I can do it. See you." I waved good-bye as he pulled out and, with one last look at the cop on guard at the front door of the restaurant, headed for my own car. No point putting it off. I had to go and break the news to Dad.

Chapter Two

Solari's is out at the very end of the Santa Cruz Municipal Wharf. Though the name "wharf" is misleading, since the wooden structure isn't built along the edge of the shore but rather sticks out into the sea—more like what I would call a "pier." Perhaps my ancestors, the newly arrived Italian fishermen who constructed the thing, didn't speak English well enough to know the difference between the two words when they named it.

Pulling into a spot across from the restaurant, I climbed out of the car and then just stood there, steeling myself for the task ahead. It had been only two years since Dad had lost his wife—and me my mom—to cancer. Another death in the family so soon was going to be hard.

For a couple minutes, I stared out across the water at the Boardwalk and the green hills and dark clouds rising up behind. Then, with a deep sigh, I pushed off from the car and crossed the road toward the front door.

Solari's looks like any number of establishments out on the wharf: a blocky, one-story, white, wooden building with its name painted in red script over the door. Neon Budweiser and Amstel Light signs hang in the window, through which I could see the lunch crowd still working on their bowls of *cioppino* and plates of crab sandwiches. Had it really only been forty-five minutes since I'd mediated Giulia and Sean's spat?

I pushed open the door and blinked, letting my eyes readjust from the bright sunlight outdoors. "Hey, Sally!" called out a waitress coming through the swinging red door into the kitchen. She was bearing a tray loaded down with cups of minestrone soup and baskets of bread sticks.

"Hey, Elena. You know if my dad's back yet?"

"Yeah, he's in the dish room." As she passed close by, she leaned over and added in a low voice, "They're having problems with the drain. It's been backing up. He's not in a good mood."

Great. I took a deep breath and walked through the kitchen to the back of the restaurant.

My father was standing next to the pot-wash sink in the corner of the dish room, cell phone at his ear. Next to him, a young man was busy filling peg racks with plates and loading them into the stainless-steel dishwasher.

Dad looked up from his call when I came into the room and nodded. After listening for a moment, he responded to the person on the other end of the line. "I don't give a rat's ass if you have to send your mother to clear it out! Somebody better get their butt down here *now*. I'm in the middle of a lunch rush!" He listened again; said, "Fine"; and snapped the phone shut.

"Goddamn grease trap is backed up . . . *again*," he explained, shoving the phone impatiently into the pocket of his checkered chef pants, "and they supposedly cleaned it out last Friday." He shook his head and pushed the sleeves of his blue sweatshirt up over his beefy forearms. "Emilio said you were looking for me earlier. What's up, hon?"

"*Papà*." I looked into my father's eyes, deep blue and set off by leathery skin and rows of wrinkles—the result of age, but also a lifetime of long hours in fishing boats out in the sun. "Oh, *Papà*," I said again and then started to cry.

I hadn't meant to; I'd convinced myself I could do this, that I could hold it together and be strong for my dad. But now, standing there in front of him, it hit me: I was about to tell him that his sister had been viciously murdered.

"What is it, *bambina*?" He took me by the shoulders and looked back at me, concern in his weathered features. Though I lack several inches on his six-foot-three frame, my dark hair, big bones, and full face mirror those of my father.

Taking him by the hand, I led him to a small table in the alcove between the dish room and kitchen. We sat down, me still holding onto his hand.

"It's about Aunt Letta," I began after getting control of my tears.

"What's she done now?" my father asked, with more than a hint of exasperation in his voice.

"She's dead, *Babbo*. Someone killed her—stabbed her to death."

His grip tightened on my hand. "No."

After filling him in on what little information I had, I let him digest the news. Although his relationship with Letta had been strained, I knew that deep down he cared for his baby sister.

15

"Do they know . . . who . . . ?" he finally asked.

"They don't know anything yet. But they found Javier's knife lying by her, and it looks like that's what whoever did it . . . used—"

He stood up, knocking over his chair. "Javier!"

"But he couldn't have done it, *Papà*. You know how much he adored Letta."

He sat back down and put his face in his hands. "When did it happen?"

"I guess sometime last night. I don't know for sure. They found her this morning, at Gauguin."

"I gotta tell Nonna. Before she hears it from someone else." He groaned and ran his fingers through his closely cropped, salt-and-pepper hair.

"I'll go with you." I got up and held out my hand again.

* * *

When the Italian fishermen and their families first arrived in Santa Cruz in the late nineteenth century, they settled on the Westside of town in the area next to the sea. This Little Italy neighborhood—which came to be known as "*la barranca*," after the cliffs above which it perched—was where my great-grandfather Ciro chose to build a small, single-story redwood house. It was still in the family, and Giovanna, the eighty-six-year-old widow of Ciro's son Salvatore, now lived there.

It was just a few minutes' drive from the wharf up Bay Street and left onto Columbia to my grandmother's house. Nonna was standing out front when my dad pulled up to the curb in his Chevy pickup truck. She was dressed in a yellow housecoat, hosing down the red volcanic rocks that covered the yard.

"Ma, you're wasting water. The rocks don't need to be washed," Dad scolded her affectionately as he walked up and kissed her on both cheeks. He had to lean down to reach her face. The two of us had inherited our height from Salvatore's side of the family, not hers.

"They's dirty," she retorted in her thick Tuscan accent. "Those kids next door—they let their nasty dogs go pee-pee all over my yard. Gotta clean it off." Nonetheless, she dropped the hose and shuffled over to the spigot to turn it off. "I got some *pappardelle* wit' *ragù* in the *frigo*. You want some? You should eat more, Mario. You looking so skinny."

"No thanks, Ma. Listen, we have something to tell you. Let's go inside, okay?"

We got Nonna settled on the faded, red velveteen sofa by the window, sat down on either side of her, and broke the news about her daughter as gently as we could. She didn't fully understand at first and thought we were talking about my mother, Susan. When she finally did get that it was Letta who had been killed, Nonna didn't say anything. She just turned and stared out the window.

"Better call Father Camillo," she murmured after a bit. Her hand went to the gold cross around her neck. "Another funeral . . ."

"I'll call him, *Mamma*." My dad took his mother's hand. "Don't worry, she'll have a proper Catholic mass."

We sat in the dimly lit living room discussing arrangements for the wake and the burial, my father and I both doing our best to downplay the grisly aspect of Letta's death. I agreed to make sure the body was transferred to the funeral home as soon as possible and to help with contacting extended family

17

and friends. After about an hour, Dad phoned Nonna's good friend Adella, who agreed to come over and sit with Nonna for the afternoon. When she arrived, Dad and I left, both promising to stop by again later on.

"I wonder if Tony knows," my father said as we drove back down to Solari's. This was the guy Letta had been seeing for several years.

"Yeah. Good point. Someone should tell him, I guess." I tapped my index finger on the armrest and looked over at my dad, who remained silent. "Okay, I'll do it," I said with a sigh. I knew that he and Tony didn't get along all that well. They were too alike, I figured—both softies at heart but both trying to prove to the world how macho they were.

"What's going to happen to Gauguin?" I asked, changing the subject.

Dad stopped at West Cliff Drive and signaled for a left turn. "Well, I sure as hell can't take it over. I have my own restaurant to run." After a beat, he added, "But at least I've got you now." He reached over and squeezed my leg. "I do appreciate all you've done in the past few years. Really."

I smiled back and then looked away, afraid he might detect some kind of truth in my face. For though I had indeed come back into the fold, it wasn't at all like I figured he believed it to be. I hadn't been visited by some sort of revelation: Oh my god, my life has been *empty* without Solairi's; how could I have possibly even *considered* any other vocation?

No, it definitely wasn't like that. But I had been supremely unhappy as a lawyer—a lowly associate spending my days, as well as many nights and weekends, on mind-numbing tasks such as answering interrogatories and summarizing

medical records, trying desperately to make my yearly bill-
ables. So unhappy that I had started looking for other work,
maybe even with a nonprofit like my friend Nichole up in
San Francisco.

But then my mom had died. And now here I was, doing
her old job at Solari's. I turned back to my dad, who was
negotiating the traffic at the entrance to the wharf. "I guess
Javier will have to run Gauguin," I said. "At least until we can
figure out what else to do."

"Javier?" Dad stamped on the brake and honked at a boy
on a cruiser bike with a surfboard under one arm who had
darted across the street in front of the truck. "But he's gotta
be the number one suspect, right?"

"So what if he is? You can't really believe he did it, can
you? C'mon, this is *Javier* we're talking about; we've known
him for years. He's like family to Letta. He'd do anything for
her. You know that."

My father set his jaw and shrugged, and I wished I could
take back my comment about Javier's being "family" to Letta.
It couldn't have been easy for Dad, how she'd pretty much cut
him out of her life.

"But what if he gets arrested?" he asked after a moment.
"And even if he didn't do it . . . I mean, it just wouldn't look
right for Javier to be taking over the restaurant."

"I don't know who else we can turn to, *Papà*."

We drove slowly out to the end of the wharf, the old truck
rattling as it passed over the ancient wooden boards set atop
barnacle-encrusted pilings. Dad stopped in front of the restaurant. "I gotta go home for a few hours before the dinner
shift," he said. "And just . . . I dunno, think about it all."

I leaned over to plant a kiss on his rough cheek. "I've got a few more things to do here, and then I'm off tonight. But I'll be home if you need to talk. I promise I'll call as soon as I hear anything else." I jumped down from the truck and watched as he turned around and headed back the way we'd just come.

Once inside in the restaurant, I discovered that all the staff had already heard the news about Letta. Word travels fast in a small town. After listening to everyone's condolences and offers of assistance, I closed my office door behind me and collapsed into the chair.

There was my ham and Swiss, one bite missing. At the sight of it, my mouth began to water. Could I really be hungry after all that had happened today? A loud rumble emanated from my belly. Apparently I could.

Greedily picking it up, I took another large mouthful, allowing myself to momentarily forget the day's trauma. Now that was a good sandwich: soft, chewy bread; salty ham and cheese; crunchy lettuce; sweet pickles . . .

The sound of my cell phone interrupted my reverie—Eric again. Wiping the mayo off my fingers on a handy pad of blank scheduling sheets, I pulled it from my bag.

"Hey."

"Hey back atcha. How you doing?"

"What do you think?"

"You want me to come over tonight? I could bring my accordion." Eric had been forced by his mother at a tender age to learn this much-maligned instrument, and only certain of his closest friends knew of his secret. "A few Beatles tunes on the ol' squeezebox, not to mention my artful rendition of '*O sole mio*,' might be just what the doctor ordered. I'll even let you sing harmony on 'Please Please Me.'" A bass voice in our local community chorus, he usually insists that I take the lead when we sing together.

"That's very sweet," I said with a laugh, "but I think I'll be okay." We hadn't worked out as a couple—four years of living together had ultimately ended in daily power struggles and petty bickering—but I still loved hanging out with Eric. And if I'd wanted any company that night, it would have been him. But what I really wanted was to be alone, to be able to just sit with my own thoughts and have the chance to process this whole thing. "Anyway, I've got a lot of phone calls to make."

"Doesn't sound fun. So how'd Mario take it?"

"Not great. But all right, I guess, given . . ."

"Yeah." Eric paused and then said, "So look, Sal, I'm actually calling because I just got a call from one of the cops over at your aunt's house. Seems there's a dog there."

"Ohmygod! Buster!" I'd forgotten all about Letta's dog. "How is he?"

"I gather he was rather frantic when they arrived, but he's okay now. They let him out to relieve himself and gave him something to eat. But someone needs to go over there and get him."

"And that someone would be me."

"Looks like it. So let me know if you change your mind about me coming over."

"Will do."

I switched off my phone as soon as we hung up. Anyone else who wanted to contact me would have to damn well wait until I finished my sandwich.

Chapter Three

Buster was staring at me intently. Or maybe that was just his normal expression. I don't know. He had that classic Mexican street-dog look: dusty-brown in color and a bit scrawny, with enormous prick ears and a corkscrew tail. And right now, he had an expression of longing in his eyes that would make a beggar surrender his last piece of bread. Must be something he learned as a stray before Letta rescued him from that shelter down in Ensenada.

After finishing up some paperwork at Solari's that couldn't wait, I'd dashed into the grocery store for a pint of half-and-half and some bananas for breakfast the next morning, stopped to check in on Nonna, and then driven over to Letta's bungalow, which isn't too far from my dad's house. The investigators had put Buster out in the garage, where he was being petted and pampered by Santa Cruz's finest. Everyone always loves Buster.

He seemed happy enough to go off with me in a strange car and curled up contentedly on the couch once I got him home. The first thing I did was change out of my work clothes, which smelled of garlic sauce and grease, and into some jeans and a sloppy, yellow crew-neck sweater. I then spent the rest of the afternoon talking on the phone: to the coroner's office, the funeral home, various family members and friends of Letta's, and a reporter from the local paper. Though this last conversation had lasted only long enough for me to say "no comment" and hang up.

I'd tried to get in touch with Letta's boyfriend, Tony, as well as the sous-chef, Javier, but was unsuccessful on both counts. Finally giving up, I left vague messages on their phones asking them to call and then set about making myself some dinner.

A search through the fridge unearthed half a dozen eggs, some green onions and brown mushrooms that had seen better days, and a hunk of Irish cheddar cheese: an omelet, it was. I chopped the veggies, got them sautéing in butter, and then pulled out a grater and turned to the cheese. This was what now had Buster's attention.

"No such luck," I told him, wagging my finger. "You've got a full bowl of delicious kibble. Mmmm!"

But he was not convinced and kept shooting me those bedroom eyes.

As I whisked two eggs with a drizzle of water, I thought about the time Letta had taught me the French technique for preparing an omelet. "The biggest mistake most people make," she'd instructed, "is overcooking the dish. It only takes a few seconds." I'd watched as she poured the eggs into a pool of sizzling butter and then gave the pan a series of quick shakes. A perfectly formed omelet appeared before my eyes, and I clapped my hands in amazement.

Letta had laughed as she tucked an errant strand of raven hair behind her ear. "I know," she said, her blue eyes shining with pleasure. "They're almost magical, eggs, aren't they?"

That simple dish—just eggs, butter, and salt and pepper, topped with a pinch of summer savory—was one of the best meals I've ever had.

Smiling at the memory, I got back to work on my own cheese-and-mushroom omelet and then cut a few slices of *francese* bread to go with it. At the sound of the plate being set on the table, Buster trotted over to sit at my feet.

As I savored my meal—the eggs were soft and almost runny, just the way I like them—I considered what to do about Letta's dog. My apartment complex doesn't allow animals, so it wasn't an option for me to keep him. I'd had to hustle him inside from the car that afternoon as fast as I could, praying no one was around to see and bust me.

My dad couldn't take him either, since he was severely allergic to dogs. I'd always wanted a puppy as a kid and had tried to convince him to let me have a poodle on the grounds that they were hypoallergenic, but this tactic was not successful. I still wanted a dog, but it was going to have to wait until I moved up from apartment living to a real house.

That left Tony, Letta's boyfriend. They hadn't lived together, but I knew she'd been spending several nights a week at his place, so I figured he had to be okay with Buster.

"I'm afraid your momma's not coming back, honey," I said to those big, brown eyes. "But we'll see if your Uncle Tony can take you in." And then I caved and gave him a piece of bread. This is why dogs have succeeded so very well as a species.

Midway through dinner, my landline rang. After all that had happened that day, I was emotionally and physically exhausted, and the last thing I wanted to do was spend more time on the telephone. But I listened as the machine picked up to see if it was Tony or Javier returning my call.

It was neither. "Hello, Ms. Solari, this is Detective Vargas from the Santa Cruz Police Department. I was wondering—"

Jumping up, I grabbed the receiver. Maybe they had some news about Letta's stabbing. But I should have known better; all he wanted was to find out if I'd be willing to talk to him and answer some "routine" questions. After agreeing to stop by the station the next day, I sat down at the kitchen table once more, only to have my cell chime. With a wistful glance at my half-eaten omelet, I retrieved the phone from my bag in the living room.

"Javier—I tried to reach you earlier."

"Yeah, I got your message. I just got back from the police station. They wanted to talk to me about . . . well, you know."

"Oh God, Javier, it's so horrible."

"I know. I can't believe it. Poor Letta . . ." He trailed off, and there was a silence, neither of us knowing exactly what to say. I could hear him take a drink of something and a *clink* as he set the glass or bottle down. After a moment, he went on. "I don't understand who could do such a thing."

"No, me neither."

"So how you doing?"

"Okay, I guess."

"Does Mario know?"

"Yeah. And we went over to my grandmother's house together to tell her." It occurred to me that Javier must have been pretty close to Letta, too. "And how are *you* doing?"

"Not so good, actually. I just can't stop thinking about it . . . her . . ." His voice got soft, and then he stopped speaking entirely. He cleared his throat and went on. "And also, well, they didn't come out and say it or anything, but I can tell. The police think *I'm* the one who did it." He took another quick sip. "It's 'cause they found my knife—you know, the twelve-inch Wusthof—right next to her. And it had blood on it, and . . ." Javier's English was generally free of any accent, but listening to him now, I detected traces of his native Spanish slipping out.

"Hold on, Javier. It's far too early for anyone to have any theories yet about who did it," I lied. I couldn't see any point in telling him what I'd learned from Eric. "They just need to talk to everyone who might know something. They asked me to go down there too; I'm going in tomorrow. And besides, you obviously know about the knife, and the restaurant, and tons of stuff that could be helpful."

"But they kept asking me about the knife cabinet and who had keys to it. They said it had been unlocked with a key, not broken open. Since me and Letta are the only ones with keys, I'm the *obvious* suspect, don't you see?" His accent continued to thicken, and his voice was growing more and more agitated, rising in pitch as he spoke.

"So who's to say it wasn't Letta's key that was used?" I countered, wondering which of the two of us I was trying to convince more. "Did they read you your rights, you know, like on TV? 'You have the right to remain silent' and all that?"

"No. Nuh-uh. They just said they were conducting an investigation, and told me about the knife, and asked if I'd talk to them. I figured it would look really bad if I didn't . . . so I did."

God, it did sound like a TV show. Shaking my head, I sat down and poked with a fork at my rapidly cooling omelet. Classic cop tactics: Scare 'em into talking to you before you have time to think you might want to consult with a lawyer first.

"So," I said, "it looks like, at least for the time being, there isn't anything else for you to do. You've told them all you know, and now they just have to do their job." The melted Irish cheddar cheese, I observed, had hardened and congealed against the plate. "Look, Javier, speaking of jobs, there's something I need to ask you. About the restaurant. Do you think you could take care of things—you know, act as manager—until we figure out what's going to happen with it?" After talking with my dad, I'd realized that I was going to have to be the one to deal with this. I could tell he didn't want to have anything to do with Javier, or Gauguin.

"Uh, I guess so. I kind of do already, at least sometimes. When Letta's gone, which has been a lot, lately, I pretty much do everything." I heard what sounded like a bottle being tossed into the recycling and another being opened and then the clicking of a lighter. "So yeah, I could do it." He took a drink of what I now figured was beer and then a puff off his cigarette. "How long will the restaurant be closed, ya think?"

"Well, when I was down there this morning, I got the impression the cops would be done with their investigation by the end of the day. But that doesn't mean they'd allow us to reopen right away. And even if they did allow it, I'm not sure we'd want to. I mean, maybe it would be best to just close down for a while, give everyone some time to get their bearings?" I realized I had absolutely no idea how stuff like this worked or what happened when the owner of a business died.

No, didn't just die—was brutally murdered, and on the business premises. "I dunno," I went on. "What do you think?"

"I think Letta would want the place reopened right away," Javier answered. "For everyone to—how do you say it?—mount back on the horse as soon as possible. And I know for sure she wouldn't want it to stay closed just 'cause we thought that was the, you know, 'correct' thing to do. She hated stuff like that."

I nodded, staring absently at my cold dinner. Javier was right. Letta despised anything that had the ring of "propriety for propriety's sake" about it.

"So," I said, "you think the best way to honor her memory would be to simply get Gauguin up and running again as soon as possible—do our best to continue on with her work, her dream."

"Uh-huh." Javier's voice cracked, and he cleared his throat. "And besides, I'm not sure what I'd do with a bunch of days off, anyway. At least working will help keep my mind off it all."

After a bit of silence, I asked, "Were there any deliveries that were missed today?"

"No, the restaurant's closed Mondays, so there won't be any till tomorrow. But unless we're gonna reopen right away, I should call and cancel them."

The drumming of my fingers on the table caused Buster to wake up and look my way. I made a decision, since clearly no one else was going to. "Okay. If the cops give the green light, let's plan on reopening the day after tomorrow: Wednesday night."

"Sounds good. I can call the cooks and waitstaff and make sure everyone knows to come in. You think some people might be freaked out by the idea of working where a murder happened?"

"That's entirely possible. Or they may just need a little more time off for other reasons. Everyone deals with grief in different ways, so make sure they know they don't have to come in if they don't feel up to it."

"I wonder if we'll even get any customers. *They* might think it's too weird."

Having seen the crowd trying to get a look into the restaurant that afternoon, I knew better. "Don't worry," I said. "It'll be packed."

Once reheated in the microwave, the omelette was again hot, but that was the best that could be said for it. I have a thing about wasting food, though, so I ate it anyway and then set the plate on the floor for Buster to lick clean.

After washing up and leaving the dishes to dry in the drainer, I poured myself a hefty Jim Beam on the rocks, put on a CD of *Tosca*—the 1953 Callas/di Stefano recording—and plopped down on the sofa.

My dad's a big opera fan, as was his dad before him. In fact, my father and Letta were both named after famous opera characters: Mario from *Tosca* and Violetta from *La Traviata*. One of my earliest memories is of my dad watering the garden on Saturday mornings, listening to the Met broadcast on the radio through the open windows as he adjusted the spray with his fingers, singing along with Puccini and Verdi. I ended up getting the bug too, so I guess it runs in the family. Must be an Italian thing.

I stared out the window and listened to Tito Gobbi's chilling baritone: "*Va' Tosca, nel tuo cuor s'annida Scarpia!*" The afternoon wind had brought with it a storm front from the north, and through the water that was now streaming down the pane, I could see silhouettes of branches bending back and forth as they got caught by gusts.

With a shiver, I pulled the green-and-white afghan Nonna had knitted from the back of the couch and over my legs. My apartment is pretty small—just a one bedroom with a kitchen/dining area, a small living room, and a tiny bathroom—and wouldn't have been prohibitively expensive to heat. But in an attempt to save money, I only turn on the furnace when it's downright frigid. The hot flashes help.

Buster jumped up and joined me on the sofa. Snuggled up with him in my blanket, I reflected on the day's events. It was still hard to believe that Aunt Letta was gone. And who could possibly have wanted her dead—so much so that they would kill her in such a brutal and vicious fashion? I shivered again and got up to pull the curtains shut. Then, walking over to the cabinet between the fridge and kitchen table, I pulled out the bottle and poured myself another bourbon. Maybe the liquor would help me sleep.

Chapter Four

Of course I'd known it was coming, but I was still taken aback by the headline splashed across next morning's newspaper: "Restaurateur Found Stabbed to Death in Gauguin Kitchen." Folding the paper to obscure the headline, I hurried back up the stairway and scurried inside my apartment; I so did not feel like discussing the murder with anyone in the complex.

The story said nothing I didn't already know and thankfully did not name Javier—or anyone—as a suspect. But its publication resulted in a barrage of calls all morning to my landline as well as my cell. I'd finally turned off both ringers so that I could have some peace while I ate a banana and sipped my coffee, skimming over the rest of the paper and trying to keep at bay the image in my mind of my aunt lying dead in a pool of blood.

Buster sat once again at my feet, his hopeful tail percussive on the vinyl floor. Clearly, Letta had not been strict about any no-begging-at-the-table rule. But I was thankful for his company.

Draining the last of my coffee, I set the cup down on the kitchen table with a *smack*. "Okay," I said and shoved back my chair. "No more putting it off; time to get a move on."

Solari's is closed on Tuesdays, but I had a busy day ahead, nevertheless, starting with a nine o'clock appointment at the funeral home. Buster followed me around the apartment, still wagging his tail, while I rinsed my cup, grabbed my jacket and purse, and then, remembering it was raining, searched for an umbrella. When he saw me pick up his leash, Buster ran to the front door and sat patiently while I hooked it to his collar. I was afraid that if I left him home alone, he might bark or cry, thereby alerting the neighbors to his presence, so he'd have to come along with me.

"You're just gonna stay in the car for a little while," I told him as I pulled into the funeral home parking lot. No way would he get overheated in this weather, I figured. But I did leave the windows rolled down halfway.

Waiting in the subdued but elegant reception area, I reviewed the notes I'd jotted down the night before. The coroner had said that Letta's remains would be released to the family within two days, so after some discussion, my dad and I had decided to set the wake—during which the body would be on view—for Thursday and Friday, with the funeral to be held on Saturday.

Presently, a young woman in a natty, mauve suit came out and extended her hand in greeting. "I'm so sorry for your loss," she said and sat down on the striped settee across from me. Though she had no doubt used this exact same line with every single client she'd ever had, I was impressed by her ability to make it sound sincere. I smiled politely and thanked her for her concern.

With that nicety out of the way, she inquired as to the type of arrangements desired. "The family wants a wake with a full open casket," I told her, "a mass at the parish church, and then entombment in a mausoleum." Even though Letta had not been the least bit devout, Nonna, who is, had been adamant about all these things.

Next, the funeral director led me into a large room whose walls were lined with ornate caskets and explained the merits of each. I was aghast at the prices and stared stupidly at the gleaming paint and shiny handles. Reluctantly, I told her what Nonna had specified—bronze with a cream-colored, velvet lining—which I knew was going to be ridiculously expensive.

The details of the viewing and funeral settled, I headed over to the police station, a modern, neo-Spanish-style building at the dodgy end of the downtown area. I announced myself to the woman behind the window, and after a few minutes, Detective Vargas emerged. He was in plain clothes: khaki pants, a dress shirt, and an SCPD badge hanging from his neck. We shook hands, and then he ushered me upstairs into a small interview room furnished with a couch, a comfy chair, and two small tables. I don't know why, but I felt a little like a school kid being escorted into the principal's office.

Motioning me to the sofa, he hiked up his slacks and then settled his burly frame down on the chair opposite me. "I appreciate your coming down here today. I know this must be a difficult time for you and your family. But I'm sure you understand that, as part of our investigation into her homicide, we need to talk to those who were close to Violetta Solari."

It was jarring to hear my aunt referred to that way. No one had ever called her anything but Letta as far as I knew. I told this to Detective Vargas, who nodded and made a note on a pad of lined, white paper. Once finished, he looked up. "So the obvious first question is, do you know of any person who might have had any reason to attack or kill your aunt?"

"No," I said, pulling off my jacket and laying it on the coffee table next to the couch. "I can't imagine why anyone would want to hurt her." In addition to the stack of magazines and box of tissues sitting on the table, I noticed, was a basket of kids' toys.

"What about the chef? Javier Ruiz?"

I turned to give him what I hoped came off as a hard look. "Okay, I know you found his knife next to her, but there's no way he could have—"

"How do you know that, about the knife?" The detective's voice was sharp.

"Uh . . ."

"Never mind. I think I already know. Officer Owens saw you at the scene with one of the DAs." He consulted a previous page of his pad. "Eric Byrne, she said."

When I didn't respond, he just sat back in his chair, his thin lips forming the hint of a smile.

"So go ahead." Detective Vargas leaned even farther back and clasped his hands together behind his shaved head. "Tell me about the chef. Why couldn't he have killed her?"

I explained how Letta had taken Javier under her wing soon after he'd arrived in this country from Mexico, how close they'd become working together, and how she'd promoted him over the years from a lowly busboy to a prep and then line cook and eventually to sous-chef of the restaurant. "Besides," I concluded, "Javier is one of the gentlest souls I know. And he adored Letta. He would never kill her—or anyone. I swear."

"Uh-huh." The detective tapped his pen on his pad several times and then flipped to a new page. "Let's move on."

After confirming that I had not been at Gauguin during the week prior to the murder and asking me briefly about "the boyfriend" (no, I had no reason to believe Tony and Letta were on anything but good terms), Detective Vargas let me go. With the polite request, of course, that I come in again if asked and that I promptly report anything of relevance to the case that I might subsequently learn.

He escorted me back downstairs and into the lobby. Shaking out the cramp in my hands, which I only then realized I'd been holding tightly clenched, I watched the door into the main part of the building close behind the detective with a soft click. The condescending tone in his voice when he'd asked my opinion about Javier had ticked me off. He might as well have just come out and said, "Sure, little lady; whatever you say."

Vargas hadn't blatantly accused anyone of the crime—rather, it seemed to me they were pretty much flailing about at this point—but the interview had left me uneasy. Could the murderer in fact be someone I knew?

I shoved open the heavy glass door and made my way across the parking lot. The rain had passed, and other than some menacing thunderheads to the south, the sky was again clear. But it was still chilly, and once inside my car, I quickly rolled up the windows I'd left down for Buster.

Tony hadn't called yet, so my plan was to swing by his house next and see if he was there. I was worried he might have only just learned of Letta's death from today's paper and be in a bit of shock, but I also wanted to ask him about taking in Buster. Although he worked as an electrician, I figured there was a good chance he hadn't gone in today.

I'd never been to his home, but I knew the place well: it was where my great-uncle Luigi had lived before passing on some years back. Tony's blue truck, with the Nicolini Electric logo painted on its doors, was in the driveway. I parked across the street and admired the front yard as I crossed to his side. I had forgotten what an avid gardener he was. Roses, all just starting to bud out, lined the walkway, and a wisteria dripping in purple climbed up the sunny wall to the right of the front door. The lawn was neatly clipped and edged by beds full of multicolored flowers in various stages of early spring blooming.

A movement caught my eye, and I realized that Tony was on the left side of the house, down on his knees in one of the flowerbeds. As I approached, I saw that he was planting six-packs of red and purple flowers. He looked up as I came down the walkway.

"Hey, Tony. I just stopped by to see how you were."

He dropped his trowel. "Not so great, as you can imagine. I'm trying to take my mind off it all." He nodded toward the freshly dug soil. "Putting in verbena. It attracts butterflies, ya know."

The few times I'd met Tony, he struck me as one of those jokester types, always ribbing you about one thing or another, always ready with the one-liner no matter the subject of discussion. But today his normally laughing eyes were puffy about the edges, his cheeks pallid and taut.

Brushing some of the dirt off the knees of his jeans, he stood up and gave me a stiff hug. "I appreciate your coming by, though." He stepped back and then spotted Buster's head hanging out of the driver's side window of my car. "Buster!" he cried out, his frown becoming a broad smile. "How's my boy?"

Tony trotted across the road, and the dog licked him frantically as he buried his head in its tawny coat. He opened the door, and Buster bounded out and began jumping up onto him.

"Out of the street, boy." Buster followed him back to the front yard, still jumping up and trying to plant wet kisses on Tony.

"I was wondering, actually, if you'd be able to take him in. I can't, and—"

"Of course I can," he said, crouching down to let the dog have its way with his face. "Me and Buster, we need each other now. Don't we, boy?" He rubbed the dog's back for a moment and then stood up. "C'mon inside."

Buster ran up the front steps and pushed ahead of Tony through the front door, and we all went into the kitchen. The dog headed immediately for the bowls sitting in the corner and began lapping up water. He was obviously at home here. "You want some coffee?" Tony asked.

"Sure."

As he found mugs and poured us each a cup, I examined the photos held up by magnets on the fridge: Tony with Letta at the beach; Tony on a boat with a much taller guy, both holding up big fish; two teenage boys sitting with Tony and the same tall guy in stadium bleachers.

"That's my son T. J. with his cousin and my brother," Tony said, noticing my look. "It was taken a few years back."

"Oh. Does your son live here in town?"

"No, he lives over the hill, where his mom is. He's in college now, at San Jose State."

Feigning more interest than I had, I leaned over to take a closer look at the picture. The two boys were wearing sports jerseys with the number ten emblazoned on the front and proudly displaying their foot-long hot dogs and mammoth cups of Pepsi for the camera. I couldn't help noticing that the blue jersey did a much better job of hiding the spilled ketchup than the white one.

"I can sure tell which is T. J.," I said, tapping the stain on the white jersey with my finger. "He looks just like you. Your brother, though, not so much."

Tony smiled wryly and handed me my coffee. "Thanks, I guess." I could hear traces of his New Jersey accent coming out. "Here, let's go sit down." He led me into a wood-paneled den and nodded for me to have a seat on the couch. Buster hopped up next to me and stretched full out, his head nice and comfy on the pillows.

One wall was almost completely covered by an enormous flat-screen TV, and the others were decorated with beer signs and various sports and fishing memorabilia. As I eyed the orange-and-black "San Francisco Giants: 2010 World Series Champs" banner strung up above an enormous stuffed sailfish, I remembered that it was that season that Letta had brought Buster home with her from Mexico. And that, being a big Giants fan, she'd decided to name the puppy after their spunky rookie catcher, Buster Posey.

"The cops were here earlier," Tony said as he lowered himself into a black leather recliner facing the TV. He was several inches shy of six feet but carried himself as if trying to appear larger than he really was. "I was there at the restaurant, you know, Sunday, the afternoon before . . . it happened. I'd brought by some flowers—small branches from my ornamental cherry tree, actually—to use on the tables. Anyway, I guess it's not surprising they wanted to talk to me."

"Yeah, they wanted to talk to me, too."

He nodded and ran a hand through his curly, dark hair. I guessed his age to be around sixty, but although it was thinning at the temples, his hair showed no signs of graying. Tony leaned back in his chair, closed his eyes, and grimaced. "Sweet Jesus," he said, eyes still shut. It looked like he was trying his best not to cry.

I didn't say anything, letting him get control of himself. After a moment, he opened his eyes and smiled weakly. "Sorry about that," he said.

I shook my head and returned the smile, attempting to keep at bay the tears now forming in my own eyes. "No worries."

He took a sip of coffee to cover the awkward moment, and I did the same. "So," I asked after setting my cup down carefully on the glass coffee table. "Do you think you had any helpful information for them? You know, for the police?"

"Hell, I don't know. They asked me a lot about Javier, that guy she has—had—cooking for her. They said it was his knife they found next to her."

"Yeah, I heard."

Tony, who had been staring at his mug of coffee, looked up at me. "We were engaged, you know."

This was news to me, and I told him so.

"Well, it was pretty recent. I'd been asking for a while, and she finally agreed." He stood up and walked over to the window, which looked out onto the backyard. I followed his gaze. A fruit tree—the ornamental cherry, I supposed—was in full bloom, and its paper-like, pink blossoms and black bark reminded me of a Japanese print I'd once seen.

Without warning, I felt desperately hot, claustrophobic almost. For the hundredth or maybe the thousandth time, I marveled at how fast they came on. "Hot flash," I explained to Tony, who had turned back around at the sudden movement as I pulled off my wool blazer. "Don't be alarmed. They've been happening to me a lot lately."

"Really?" He was looking at me funny, and I figured I knew why. "I know. I'm not even forty yet. But lucky me, I seem to be starting early."

"Should I open the window? That's what Letta always wanted. She had them too sometimes, especially at night."

"No, it's okay. I'm fine now. They tend to pass quickly, thank God."

Tony sat back down. "So anyway, I told the police I don't think Javier could have done it. In fact, though I didn't mention this to the cops, Letta said to me a couple weeks ago that she thought he was in love with her." He shook his head. "Poor, ignorant *chalupa*." I detected bragging in his tone, that Letta would of course choose him over Javier. "I mean," he went on after a pause, "why would someone who was in love with her want to kill her?"

"I don't know why *anyone* would want to kill her," I said.

*   *   *

The next item on my agenda was stopping by my old law firm. Parking in the corner space, as far from the partners' gleaming Porsches and Jags as possible, just like I used to do when I'd worked there, I crossed the lot to the entrance and stopped at the front desk.

"Good morning, Sally," said the receptionist, Terri. She had that awkward look that people tend to get when they know something horrible has just happened in your life. "I'm so sorry to hear about your aunt. What brings you here?"

"Monica said she was going to leave a packet for me to pick up."

"Oh, lemme have a look." Terri flipped through a stack of files and envelopes sitting next to the phone. "Here it is," she said, and handed me a manila folder, my name scrawled across the front.

"Thanks." I returned to my car and got in. I knew what was inside: the trust documents that Monica, the firm's probate attorney, had drafted for my aunt. I'd introduced the two of them years ago and had also agreed to be Letta's successor trustee, which status had now been triggered by her death. But I didn't know any of the provisions she had made.

After reading through the papers carefully, I replaced them in the envelope and set it down on the passenger seat. Staring vacantly out the front window at the redwood grove across the street, I found myself unable to move.

She'd given me the restaurant.

Chapter Five

My prediction to Javier proved to be accurate: Gauguin was indeed packed when I showed up there at seven thirty the next evening. So much so that I had to elbow my way through the animated and boisterous crowd to get to the reception desk. Nothing like a murder to stir folks up.

Though, to be fair, there were also all the flowers and other tributes that had been left outside the restaurant over the past two days. Bouquets, cards, stuffed animals, and even a couple baskets of fruit lined Gauguin's low bamboo fence. Not fifty deep, like at Buckingham Palace after Princess Diana died, but there must have been at least a hundred of them there at Gauguin. I'd had no idea so many people even knew Letta; she'd seemed to keep herself so apart from folks in general. But then again, maybe this was simply a show of solidarity— not so much about Letta herself as about the horrific loss of one of our community.

Gloria, the hostess that night, spotted me from afar (my height does have its advantages) and pointed to the far wall, under the large woodblock print of a taro plant. Mouthing a silent "thank you," I made my way to where Eric was already seated, a half-finished Martini and the *New York Times* crossword puzzle on the white tablecloth in front of him.

He'd called me at work that morning and asked to meet for dinner, saying he had more information from the police I should know about. Dad wasn't too happy when I told him I'd be leaving Solari's early that night, but I knew Elena would be able to handle it fine without me. Still reeling from learning the provisions of my aunt's trust, I'd suggested Gauguin for our meal.

He rose to give me a hug and then pulled out my chair, a gesture I had told him countless times I find to be annoying. I didn't say anything on this occasion but did pick up his glass and take a large swallow as a form of private retribution.

"So how you holding up?" he asked once I'd set his drink down and taken my seat.

"I'll be fine once I have my own cocktail." I swiveled in my chair to try to catch the attention of someone to get my bar order.

"No, really." Eric tucked the crossword into the briefcase at his feet and then, leaning forward, looked me in the eyes. "I'm serious, Sal. How *are* you doing?"

I let out a sigh. I honestly didn't know how I was doing and had been doing my best to avoid thinking about the subject. I can get pretty worked up about stuff in my life: my job, relationships, even a baseball game or a meal. And now with my hormones all out of whack, it was even worse. But I'm also a pro at the denial game. So although I can sometimes be over-the-top emotional, I'm not at all crazy about analyzing where those feelings may be coming from.

Eric, on the other hand, is tenacious and is always stubbornly trying to force me to examine my feelings—to look inside, delve into places I don't want to go. I suppose that's one of the reasons we split up. I find it far easier to simply ignore those pesky emotions, hoping they'll just disappear, an attitude that never fails to drive him bonkers.

But best to play the game his way right now. "I guess I'm okay—all things considered." I took a sip of water and set the heavy glass back down. "It's just that I feel like it's only recently that I was really getting to know Letta. That—after what, has it really been nine years since she came back to town?—I'd finally cracked her shell, and we were finally becoming close. Not just the kind of relationship you have because you happen to be related by blood, but real *friends*. But it was just the beginning, and I was so looking forward to getting to know her even better." I sighed again. "Now I'll never have that chance. I dunno . . . I guess I just feel robbed somehow."

I had been studying the intricate napkin-folding job before me, which looked like a sort of white linen bird of paradise, without paying attention to Eric. So I was surprised when he reached across the table and laid his hand on mine. I looked up at him, suddenly self-conscious that my eyes were welling up.

Eric was about to say something when Brandon approached the table to take my drink order. I withdrew my hand and quickly used my fingers to wipe away the tears.

"Brandon," I said, sitting up straight and trying to regain my composure, "I must say I'm a little surprised to see you here tonight."

"Yeah, I didn't know if I'd freak out, coming back again so soon," he said. "You know, after finding her like that. But I really need the money, so I didn't want to give up my shift." He scooted over and allowed Gloria to pass with a threesome being seated at the next table, and then continued. "But I have to admit," Brandon said, leaning closer to us, "it is a little weird being here. After all, they don't know who did it, do they?" He looked quickly about him. "I mean, it could be someone here . . . *tonight*, right?"

I watched Brandon as he headed to the bar with my order. When I turned back, Eric had that look he gets when he's convinced he's been right about something. "What?" I asked, though I was pretty sure I knew what he was thinking.

"He's not the only one," he said. "Nobody's going to come out and say it, of course, but all the staff—you know, they've heard it was Javier's knife. And they're just that little bit worried it might in fact be him that did it."

I fiddled with my table setting: shaking out my napkin and smoothing it out on my lap, readjusting the positions of my flatware and water glass, doing my best to avoid eye contact. I did not want to be having this conversation, did not want to think about the possibility that Javier could be the one. When I finally glanced up, Eric was still staring at me. "Okay," I said, "so what's this new information you have?"

"I got a copy of the crime scene notes and some of the witness interview notes from one of the detectives on Letta's case. It was definitely Javier's knife that was used for the stabbing. And Letta's key chain, with her key to the knife cabinet, was in her purse. Since there's no evidence of any forced entry, either on the restaurant doors or on the cabinet, and since no one else but Javier has a key to the cabinet, it's looking more and more like he's the only one who could have done it."

I didn't say anything, and Eric adjusted his glasses and took a sip of Martini before going on. "Vargas is convinced he's the one. In fact, I wouldn't be surprised if he arrested him pretty soon. Unless, of course, some new evidence emerges," he added.

I had continued to fuss with my silverware while Eric was speaking but withdrew my arms as Brandon returned and set down my bourbon-rocks. "Would you like to hear the specials?" he asked.

"Oh." Eating was the last thing on my mind right at that moment, but we were there for dinner after all. "Sure."

Gauguin is noted for its fresh fish and changes its seafood menu weekly. Seared ahi with papaya chutney, broiled mahi-mahi with a red miso glaze, and panko-encrusted shrimp with house-made wasabi mayonnaise were what Javier had come up with for that week's specials. He certainly had come a long way from his days as a busboy when he first started at Gauguin. Letta had taught him well.

Brandon left us to ponder our choices, and I considered the fact that Letta would never again get to taste her beloved Polynesian-French cuisine. Which immediately put me back into my funk.

"Can I look at the notes you got?" I asked.

"Yeah. I figured you'd want to see them, so I made a copy for you." Eric rummaged through his briefcase and came up with a sheaf of papers stapled together.

"Thanks." I took the papers and flipped through them—at least twenty pages—before shoving them into my bag.

We then set to work examining the menu. After careful thought (I always have a hard time making up my mind about what to order), I decided on the seared tuna. Eric chose the rib-eye steak, rare, with garlic mashed potatoes. Knowing what a wine snob he was, I told him to go ahead and pick one for us, and he ordered a bottle of the Beringer Merlot.

"*Sideways* be damned," he said to Brandon, who laughed politely at this well-worn joke.

After Brandon left, I said, "Well, I have some news, too." Eric raised his brow as I paused for dramatic effect, sipping my Maker's Mark. "I read Letta's trust and pour-over will today. She left her house and that land she has in Hawai'i to my dad." Setting down my glass, I returned Eric's gaze. "And she gave me the restaurant."

He almost spit out his mouthful of gin. "You?" he sputtered after managing to swallow and then wiping his chin with a napkin. "You mean to tell me *you* now own Gauguin?"

"Well, there's the waiting period before the estate can be distributed, of course . . . But yeah. I guess I do." I slowly scanned the walls around me. "And however bizarre you think that is, all I can say is, multiply that by five gajillion and that's how bizarre it is for me."

"So I gather she hadn't told you . . . that you were her beneficiary?"

I shook my head. "I never had a clue."

"But really," Eric said, "when you think about it, it's not all *that* weird that she'd give it to you. I mean, who else would make any sense?"

I'd been obsessing about her bequest for the past twenty-four hours and had eventually come to the same conclusion.

"True. Other than my dad, I am her closest relation. And no matter how much she tried to act like she'd left it all behind her, she was still Italian at her core. You know, *famiglia*," I said with an exaggerated intonation and a wave of the hands, "so I don't imagine she even considered leaving it to anyone outside the family. But I bet she really didn't want Dad taking over Gauguin, given how she felt about Solari's—you know, that it's way too old school, with its veal parmesan and chicken *piccata*. She probably was afraid he'd turn it into something like that if he got hold of it."

Brandon arrived with the wine and poured some for each of us. Since we were still working on our cocktails, there were now six glasses crowding the small table. Eric swirled his Merlot and examined its ruby color.

"Yes," he said, returning to my last comment, "God knows what Mario would have done to Gauguin's wine list."

"Don't even go there," I said with a short laugh. "Besides, Dad already owns a restaurant, so it makes sense that she gave him the house instead of Gauguin. I imagine he'll be pretty relieved about it, actually."

"You haven't told Mario yet?" Eric grinned. "I get it: you're chicken—afraid of how he'll react when he learns you've inherited the place. 'Cause it means now you'll be leaving Solari's. Again."

"It does *not* necessarily mean that," I said with more sharpness than I'd intended. "I have no idea what it means or what I'm going to do. I'm still just trying to get used to the fact that Letta is gone."

I stared at the woodblock print above Eric's head, noting the fluid lines the artist had used to outline the taro leaves.

"But getting back to why she gave it to me, I dunno . . . At least I worked here a few times and got to know some of what the whole 'foodie' thing is all about. And who knows, maybe over the last few years, the closer we got . . . Well, maybe she just started to, you know, trust me in some fundamental way." I finished the bourbon and set the glass down with a shake of the head. "But, man, it sure is weird. All of sudden, I own Gauguin?"

Weird, too, I was thinking, because she'd made the provisions of her will back when I was still working as an attorney, long before I'd returned to the restaurant business. It was as if she'd known, before me, that the law and I were not such a great fit after all.

I was about to mention this to Eric but then noticed that, though listening and nodding, his eyes were tracking a woman in a tight sweater crossing the room. Something in my chest tightened. Jealousy? I shook off the thought. We'd broken up years ago, after all. And a good thing, too: here I was pouring my guts out to the guy, and he couldn't even keep his eyes from bugging out over a pair of breasts?

Once the woman disappeared out the front door, his focus returned to me. "Did Letta ever work at Solari's?" he asked.

"Yeah, when she was a kid, I'm sure, just like I did. Hell, I bussed tables there from the time I was big enough to carry a dish tray, and then my folks had me doing odd jobs at the place all through high school. I bet Nonno Salvatore and Nonna Giovanna did the same thing with Letta and Dad."

"Letta didn't take to it, I gather."

"Not much. As soon as she finished high school she skedaddled up to Berkeley. Mind you, this was the early seventies—you know, those halcyon days of peace, love, and whole wheat bread. So I bet lots of her friends were doing the same thing."

Eric chuckled. "Yeah, right. I'll take my Bombay Sapphire any day over what they were ingesting back then." He drained his Martini and exhaled in satisfaction. "Hey, speaking of whole wheat bread, didn't you tell me she worked for Chez Panisse for a while?"

"Oh God, that's a great story. You should hear Dad talk about how furious their *papà* was when he learned that Letta had started working at 'that hippie place,' as Nonno referred to it." I did my best to imitate Salvatore's lilting Italian cadence, like my father always did: "If she had-a wanted to be a cook, why couldn't she have come back home, where I could-a taught her how to make *real* food: *lasagne col pesto* or *burida* stewed with anchovies that I catch with my own hands. Not that rabbit food they eat up there in Berkeley."

Eric and I laughed—more at my terrible, fake accent than anything else—but when he excused himself to go to the restroom, I found myself feeling a bit down again. Why hadn't I taken the opportunity to spend more time with my aunt when I'd had the chance?

As so often seems be the case, our plates arrived while Eric was still gone. After he returned, we ate without doing much talking. This was unusual for us, but Eric seemed to sense my changed mood.

I couldn't help thinking about Letta. Everywhere I looked, there was something to remind me of her: the frosted-glass banana-leaf sconces she had special ordered from Thailand, the bamboo-motif flatware she had brought back in her luggage from Indonesia, the framed woodblock prints on the walls from the Big Island of Hawai'i. It was so strange being in Gauguin and not having her there like she always was, bouncing from table to table and chatting up the customers.

And now it was mine.

But what on earth was I going to do as the owner of a restaurant? I mean, sure, I had given up the law to work at Solari's, but that was just because of what happened to my mom. Not only had Dad been heartbroken by the loss of his wife, but he'd also been devastated by the hole that was left in Solari's staff. Mom had run the front of the house ever since she and Dad had been married, and he had no clue how to manage the waitstaff; do things like void tickets and cancel credit card charges; or, God forbid, deal with irate customers.

So I'd agreed to come back; it was the obvious solution. But just for a while, until my dad got back on an even keel and we found someone else to take over. I had never intended to spend the rest of my life dealing with linen services and scheduling lunch shifts.

It might have been different if I'd been allowed to cook, but Dad had always refused to teach me the hot line. It was some sexist thing of his: that women should be at the front of the house and men at the back. Which was weird, really, 'cause his father had encouraged Letta to learn to cook at Solari's. Dad and I had argued bitterly about this when I was a teenager, but it just didn't seem like it was worth the fight anymore.

Watching the line cooks in their black chef's caps moving about at the back of Gauguin, I could see Javier darting back and forth on the hot line, tending sauté pans and plating up entrées. I still didn't believe he could have killed Letta, but my belief didn't mean diddly. It certainly wouldn't keep him from being arrested for the crime, not if the police thought there was enough evidence to hold him over for trial. And I had to admit, one of my biggest worries—even though it was out of pure selfishness—was who would run the restaurant if he were arrested.

By the time Eric and I finished our dinner, the place had emptied out some, and it looked like most of the remaining tables had their food. Brandon came to inquire about dessert, which we declined. I would have loved a slice of the creamy macadamia nut pie but knew it would go straight to my hips, so I resisted the urge. But I did order a cappuccino, and Eric an espresso.

"I get the sense you think there's something I could do for Javier," I said once Brandon had set down our coffees and gone back into the kitchen. "You know, when you said earlier that you think Javier's likely to be arrested 'unless some new evidence emerges'?"

Eric unwrapped a sugar cube and dunked half of it into his espresso, letting the black coffee wick up the sides. "Well, the police aren't going to do any investigation on his behalf, that's for sure. If he is in fact arrested, I suppose the public defender might have an investigator do a little snooping around. But let's face it, they don't have the funds to do much." He sucked the coffee from the cube, dropped the remaining sugar into his cup, and looked up at me.

"So . . . what? You're suggesting that I investigate the murder? Jesus, Eric. Do I look like Miss Marple or something? I don't know jack about criminal investigation. Besides, I've already got a job that keeps me pretty damn busy—and a second restaurant to worry about now, too."

"It'll be a lot harder to deal with Gauguin if Javier's in prison," Eric replied. "And you do know, as much as anyone does, about Letta, about her family and friends. And hey, it's perfect: Now that you've inherited Gauguin, you have every reason to be asking lots of questions about her life and about the restaurant. It's the ideal cover." Eric leaned back in his chair and smiled in that self-satisfied way that used to drive me nuts.

And still did, I realized, especially when he was right.

Chapter Six

Eric drained his tiny cup and stood up, pleading an early-morning court call. He insisted on paying the bill—which I let him do; no reason for me to pay myself money, now was there?—pecked me on the cheek, and took his leave.

I pulled out the papers he'd given me and turned to the crime scene notes. Though the Saroyan law firm doesn't handle criminal cases, over the years I'd seen my share of police reports, which these notes reminded me of, as they're often part of the evidentiary record in civil actions. But it was eerie reading the description of a crime scene concerning people in my own life.

The notes started with a detailed, clinical description of the state of Letta's body, which I skipped over, instead moving on to the description of the premises. In the *garde manger* area, other than the body, there were two pieces of evidence that struck me as particularly relevant.

First, the evidence regarding the knife cabinet. As I already knew, it had been unlocked and was left standing open. Letta's key to the cabinet had been found on the key chain in her purse, which was sitting on the counter in the same room. A chef's knife (the twelve-inch Wusthof Trident Classic Wide model, I learned from the notes of Javier's interview) was found on the floor next to the body. It had been wiped clean of fingerprints, but there were traces of blood, which was presumed to be that of the deceased. The knife had been sent off to the lab for testing.

Second, a ceramic, Chinese-style teapot and two small cups were found on the counter next to Letta's purse. They had also been sent to the lab for testing, but it looked like they had been washed and wiped clean of any prints.

Skipping over the rest of the crime scene notes for now, which consisted largely of measurements, sketches, and descriptions of the contents of the room, I turned to the interviews.

The notes of Brandon's interview merely confirmed what I already knew about the knife being Javier's and that it was kept in a locked cabinet to which only he and Letta possessed the keys.

Eric was right, I thought gloomily. This was not good news for the sous-chef. I turned the page and kept reading.

Sunday night's hostess, Tess, reported that the restaurant had been cleaned up for the night and the tables and kitchen set up for Tuesday dinner. The evening's take had been locked in the safe, as usual, before she left for the evening. No cash was missing Monday morning.

Tess also stated that when she left for the night on Sunday, the only two people remaining were Javier and Letta. Javier confirmed this but stated that he had only stayed for a few minutes longer after Tess had gone and that when he left, Letta was in her office going over some papers. He couldn't

recall if she was drinking tea or not. But yes, he did sometimes share a pot of green tea with her after work.

The restaurant staff all confirmed that it was Letta's prac-
tice to drink green tea, often with whomever happened to
be around, after hours. But no one interviewed admitted
to drinking tea with her the night of the murder, nor could
anyone remember seeing anyone who had.

As I was reading, a shadow fell on the report, and I looked
up to see Javier standing before me. His smooth, fine features were drawn and tight, and his dark eyes looked tired. I
couldn't help noticing that his white chef's jacket had a few
yellow-colored spatters next to the Gauguin logo—the restaurant's name with a pink-and-white plumeria blossom—which
was stitched above the pocket. I motioned for him to join me.

"All done for the night?" I asked, slipping the papers back
into my bag.

He pulled out the chair and nodded as he sat down.
"There's a few more desserts, but all the hot-line orders are
finished." As Brandon passed by to serve the three-top next to
us their coffees, Javier asked him to bring out two glasses of
dessert wine. I did not object.

"I saw that guy who was with you here tonight," Javier
said. "He's a cop or something, right?"

"A district attorney. They're the lawyers who prosecute
criminal cases for the government."

"Right. Uh . . ." He glanced at the next table, but they
were laughing at something and clearly paying no attention
to us. "Did he say anything about me?"

"Yeah, he did." I waited while Brandon set down two
dainty glasses of white wine, and then I continued, trying to

keep my voice low. "And you're right, Javier: it looks like you are the prime suspect."

I tried the wine. A little sweet for my taste, but even after a cocktail and half a bottle of wine, I was feeling way too sober to be having this conversation. I drank it down. "And given the facts—the knife, the locked cabinet, you being the last one besides Letta to leave—I guess I can see why they suspect you."

Javier's head was down, and he was swirling his wine around and around in the glass. At this last comment, he looked up.

"But that's *crazy*," he said. "I've been thinking about it, and . . . well, c'mon. If I wanted to stab someone, would I use a *chef's* knife to do it? They're so wide, it would be hard to get one to go very deep. A boning knife would work way better. Don't you see?" he said, leaning forward and slapping his hands on the table. "It's *gotta* be someone who doesn't know about knives."

I didn't care to think about Letta's stabbing in such detail and changed the subject. "Eric, the DA who was here tonight with me, thinks I should get involved," I said, "and do some investigation on your behalf."

"Really? Would you?"

"Maybe. But only if you're completely honest with me."

He leaned back in his chair and frowned, his chin tucked.

"About Letta. And you."

"What do you mean?" he asked. But I could see his grip on the wine glass tighten.

"Look, Javier. It's, um, just that . . . well . . ."

Okay. I know it may seem weird—me having been a lawyer and all—but I was finding it difficult to interrogate Javier about his personal life. What can I say? It's different with strangers than with people you know. And it's not like I had ever been all that crazy about prying into the details of my client's lives, either. But if I was going to find out what happened to Letta, I had to know what Javier's relationship with her had been.

I spat it out. "I heard that you were in love with her."

He didn't say anything right away and just looked at me, lips tight. But from his sad eyes, I could tell—it was true. He *had* been in love with her. *Oh Jesus.* That sure threw a spatula in the works.

"Did you tell the cops?" I asked.

He shook his head and drank down the rest of his wine.

Great. Suppressing information, too. "Well," I said, "they're going to find out, you know."

"How?" he responded. "And I don't see why it's important, anyway."

"Come on, Javier. If I know, they can certainly find out. And don't be so dense. Of course anyone who's in love with the victim is going to be of great interest to the police. Especially if he's hiding it." I tapped my index finger impatiently on the table. "Did you tell her? Letta?"

"Nuh-uh. I never said anything. She was involved with Tony, so what would have been the point?"

"Yeah."

Javier started to get up. "I should really be getting back to the kitchen."

"Wait. Stay for another minute, can you? There's something I've got to tell you."

He sat back down.

"Did Letta ever mention anything about who she wanted the restaurant to go to if she died?"

I could tell the question piqued his interest. There was a look of—what, hope?—in his eyes. "No," he answered.

"I just asked, since I was, well, frankly flabbergasted when I read her will yesterday." He continued to hold my gaze. "Because, uh . . . she gave it to me."

His whole body appeared to deflate slightly, just for a moment. *Could he have been expecting her to give it to him?* I guess that would have made some kind of sense, his being her lieutenant, so to speak. But folks generally tend to will their possessions to family members, not business associates.

Then he seemed to catch himself. "Wow, Sally, that's great. Congratulations." He smiled and raised his glass. "Glad to have you as the new boss. Just don't go changing Gauguin into a singles bar."

"No worries on that front," I said. "In fact, I'm going to be pretty damn dependent on you to keep it going exactly as it has been."

"Well then, you better do your best to keep me out of jail," he said with a grin. But I could see the fear behind the smile.

*   *   *

The next morning I woke early, brain churning. I pulled back the curtains to check on the weather. Not a cloud in the sky. A good, long bike ride was what I needed before my lunch shift at Solari's.

I'm no Mario Cipollini, mind you (my dad's favorite cyclist, and not just because of the shared name). But I do relish the rush of riding hard for an hour or two a few times a week. Plus, by my calculations, for every sixty minutes of cycling, I burn about six hundred calories. That's two buttery croissants, or four bottles of Bass Ale, or a plate of my dad's linguine with clam sauce along with a slice of crusty garlic bread.

And today I could really use some physical exertion. Maybe it would help clear my mind for a while, quiet the continual thoughts of Letta, and still the anxiety that had descended upon learning I was the new owner of her restaurant.

I changed into my cycling shorts and jersey emblazoned with the Tour of California logo, performed a few cursory stretches, clipped into my red-and-white Specialized Roubaix, and wheeled off. I had a hankering for the salt spray and tang of the ocean, so I decided to ride the length of West Cliff Drive and then up to Wilder Ranch, north of town.

But first, I had to stop by my dad's house. I needed to tell him about Letta's will.

Dad also lives on the Westside of town—it seems like all my relatives live within just a few blocks of each other—in a small beach-style bungalow. Since my apartment building is near the yacht harbor on the Eastside, to get across town, I took the walkway over the river at the railroad trestle; rode the length of the Boardwalk, its famous roller coaster silent on this weekday morning; and then pumped up the short hill past the entrance to the wharf.

I cruised down Laguna Street and turned into my dad's driveway. Unlike most of their neighbors, my folks never remodeled their home to add a second story or punch out a master bedroom, so the building is virtually unchanged from when it was built back in the early 1960s: two bedrooms, one-and-a-half baths, a kitchen with avocado-green appliances and a Formica countertop, and a living room decked out with shag carpet, an overstuffed couch, and a Naugahyde recliner.

His truck was there, which meant he was home. *Good.* I unclipped and wheeled my bike through the gate next to the garage. Dad was out back, atop a ladder leaning against the side fence. He was attacking a peach-colored climbing rose with a pair of large shears.

"What are you doing pruning now?" I asked, leaning my bike against the fence and removing my helmet. "Isn't it kinda late in the season for that?" I stepped back out of the way as a huge branch came crashing down, its stems covered in vicious-looking thorns.

"My damn neighbor. *Wanda,*" he added, as if the name produced a sour taste in his mouth. "She's been complaining about this beautiful Westerland rose. Can you imagine anyone not loving it? Just look at the color!"

"What's her beef?"

"She says her grandson plays in the yard and that my plants along the fence line are dangerous."

I gingerly picked up one of the spiky branches. "Well, I guess I can see why she'd think that."

He just snorted and then pointed with the shears at a trumpet vine farther back along the fence. "And the *Brugmansia,* too. She insists I prune it back so none of the flowers hang over onto her property." Shaking his head, Dad climbed down the ladder and gave me a kiss. "So what brings you by, hon? You want some coffee?"

I clomped into the kitchen with him, still wearing my cycling cleats. "I just stopped by to tell you what I learned about Letta's will." Dad handed me a mug, and we went into the living room. He leaned back in the recliner, and I plopped down onto the couch.

"So," I said once we were both settled, "she gave you her house, which still has a bit of a mortgage, I gather, and its contents, as well as her car. Oh, and that property she owns in Hawai'i, too. It's just a vacant lot as far as I can tell."

Dad nodded, but his teeth were clenched. "I gotta say, it gives me the willies thinking about benefitting from what happened."

"Yeah. I hear you." I sipped from my steaming mug. He hadn't asked about Gauguin. Maybe he didn't think of it as being one of Letta's possessions, since she didn't own the actual building.

I cleared my throat. Dad had been staring out the window at a woman and a Yorkie terrier, the latter pulling vigorously on its leash, but now looked back at me. "And here's the weird part," I went on. "She gave me one thing too: her restaurant."

He blinked a couple times, like he had something in his eye, and then swallowed. But he didn't say a word. After a moment, he stood up and walked back into the kitchen. I jumped up to follow and placed my hand on his shoulder.

"*Babbo.*"

"I shoulda known," he said, shrugging off my touch. "You two were always conspiring against me."

"What's that supposed to mean?"

"After Letta came back to town, you were always way more interested in spending time with her than with me and your mom. And it was obvious you were completely infatuated with Gauguin, that you thought it was some kind of, I dunno, French Laundry, come down here to the backwaters of Santa Cruz. I bet you and Letta were talking for years about how you'd take the place over after she was gone."

"But that's just so untrue. I had no idea I was even in her will."

"Go on," he said with a wave of the hand. "Go ahead and run that snooty restaurant with all its gourmet cuisine and leave me to my low-class diner that serves up peasant fare. The same place, mind you, that paid for your food and clothes all those years and helped you through college. I know it's mostly just an embarrassment for you, Solari's." He turned away and busied himself with rinsing out his coffee cup.

"Dad, it's not like that at all. I didn't ask for Gauguin, and I have no idea what I'm going to do with it now that I have it. Why are you being so unfair?" The tears were starting to come, and I just wanted my father to hug me tight and tell me it was all going to be okay.

But instead, he simply wiped the cup dry, replaced it in the cupboard, and then started for the back door. "I gotta finish pruning that rose before work," he said. "I'll see you there in a little while."

Why was everyone in my life so damned stubborn?

Chapter Seven

Eyes still damp, I retrieved my bike from the backyard—Dad studiously avoiding my look—and pedaled off. When I got to the ocean a few blocks away, I headed north on West Cliff Drive, a winding road that hugs the rocky coastline.

I rode for about a mile and then stopped, inhaled deeply, and gazed out across the bay. From the cliffs to the horizon, the sea displayed multiple hues in the bright sunlight: A foamy white where the waves crashed on the rocks, turning gray where the sand was churned about in the shallows. Farther out, a vibrant turquoise as the ocean floor dropped off, then aquamarine to indigo, made darker where patches of kelp floated near the surface. And then, finally, where the water stretched out to meet the sky, a deep steel blue—almost black—broken only by the numerous whitecaps glinting in the sun as they were caught up by the wind.

The tension began to drain from my shoulders and neck. Yes, this had been a very good idea. Precisely what I needed right now.

Looking north toward Natural Bridges, I could see surfers taking advantage of the breeze that was picking up and starting to bring in swells. I squinted to try to see if one of them might be Eric. I knew he liked this spot, but the black, wet-suited figures in the water all looked alike from this distance.

With a smile, I got back on my bike and pedaled off, a sort of exuberance overtaking me. It's almost too much, this panorama. No matter how many times I come out here, it always affects me; the beauty of the coastline is simply astounding.

But then, seeing a fishing boat heading back toward the harbor, my thoughts slipped back to my dad and the conversation we'd just had, and the smile faded as quickly as it had come. I knew his anger came from hurt, but why couldn't he see someone else's point of view for once in his life?

And then I passed the place along the cliffs where Eric and I used to come at sunset to watch as fiery pinks and oranges lit up the sky, bundled up against the chill and armed with cocktails decanted into water bottles. I started thinking about how I missed that: having someone to watch a sunset with.

As I pumped up the coast, I felt the transformation in my body. Where just a moment before I had been in high spirits, euphoric almost, I was now back to where I'd been when I'd left my dad's house, tears once again forming.

Damn these hormones and the violent mood swings they cause.

Not that I didn't have good reason to be down, of course. Letta had also loved this place. Never again would she get to gaze in wonder at the brown pelicans soaring up the coast in bomber formation, or hear the sea lions' hoarse barking as they lazed on the rocks offshore, or watch the packs of dogs chasing each other and romping in the surf down at Mitchell's Cove.

Making a snap decision, I made a U-turn and headed back the way I had just come. The attempt to clear my brain obviously wasn't working, so I figured I might as well do something productive—like checking out Letta's office. Maybe there was something there that could shed light on why the hell she was murdered. And it was a good time to poke around Gauguin. The prep cooks wouldn't show up until midafternoon, so I'd have the place all to myself. Fortunately, I'd gotten a key to the restaurant from Javier the night before and had put it on my key chain.

I wheeled my bicycle around the side of the building and unlocked the door I had been trying to peer through just three mornings before. Leaning the frame against the *garde manger* sink, I closed and locked the door behind me; removed my sunglasses, helmet, gloves, and cycling shoes; and set them down on the floor in a heap.

I looked around. Although it had felt fine being in the crowded dining room the night before, it was unsettling standing alone in this room, where it had happened. There was the counter where her purse and the teapot and cups had been sitting. And *there*, on the floor, was where she had been found, Javier's bloody knife beside her.

Shaking off the wave of nausea that was starting to overtake me—I really should've had some preride breakfast—I padded in my wool socks up the stairs behind the reach-in refrigerator and around the corner into Letta's office.

This had been her sanctuary: her escape from irate customers who'd neglected to make a reservation, from broken hollandaises and shorted meat deliveries, from back-of-the-house squabbles. The wood-paneled room was dominated by a large oak desk. On it sat a lamp made from what looked like a ceramic Chinese vase, a red Bakelite telephone, an old-fashioned adding machine, a small carved-wood tiki, and four neat stacks of papers.

The police must have already been through all this, I figured. No way would Aunt Letta have had the papers so organized, in such precise piles. Tidiness had never been one of her virtues.

I sat down in the chair, a sturdy oak piece to match the desk, and flipped through the pile closest to me: invoices and bills. The next one consisted mostly of files of employee time sheets. Another was tax returns.

Ugh. I was going to have to start dealing with all this pretty damn soon. Or get someone to do it for me. Letta must have had an accountant or bookkeeper who could help me get up to speed and maybe even take over a lot of the paperwork, at least for a while.

But I wasn't going to think about that right now. I picked up the last stack: a few food-related articles and a bunch of trade magazines.

Next I pulled open the desk drawers and rummaged around. Two were empty; the paperwork on top of the desk must have come from those. Another was full of office supplies: pens and pencils, yellow stickies, paper clips, Wite-Out, tape, and a stapler. The last was equally disappointing: Gauguin stationary and envelopes, unused manila folders, and accordion files. *Damn.* I slammed the drawer shut.

What about her computer? That might have something on it.
I knew she had a laptop that she brought from home to the
restaurant when she was here, but it wasn't in the office.

Duh! Of course the cops would have taken anything of
interest away—especially a computer. And her cell phone, too.

I got up from the chair and went to the window. You could
see down into the neighbor's backyard, which was full of fruit
trees with white and pale-pink flowers, a shaggy lawn, and an
unkempt flower garden in full bloom. Aunt Letta must have
enjoyed this view.

I'd been in her office on numerous occasions but had never
paid a lot of attention to its contents. I leaned over to examine a photo that hung next to the window and was surprised
to see that it was of our family, taken at Salvatore's ninetieth
birthday party shortly before he died. There was my grandfather in a silly paper hat, his arm around Giovanna, with my
mom and dad and me on one side and Aunt Letta, in loose
batik pants and a silky blouse, on the other. It was taken in
Nonno and Nonna's backyard; you could see their espaliered
pear tree hugging the brick wall in the background.

Tucked into the corner of the frame was a small snapshot
of Letta and Tony that looked like it had been taken at a park
up in the redwoods. They were sitting at a picnic table spread
with a red-and-white tablecloth and covered with food: a
wedge of cheese, a round loaf of bread, some red grapes, and
a few oranges. Someone else's arm protruded into the picture,
partially obscuring Letta's lower body.

I moved on to the next picture on the wall: a print of
a Gauguin painting of two women in skirts—but nothing
else—one holding a slice of watermelon, the other a sprig of

pink flowers. I'm generally not much of a fan of what I believe is called "primitive" art, but I have to say I quite like that painting: a sort of mix of Polynesian, Impressionist, and old-school "classical" styles.

The only other thing in the room was a floor-to-ceiling bookshelf. I stopped before it and gazed at the titles, a good 90 percent of which appeared to be about cooking. There were food essayists, such as Jean Anthelme Brillat-Savarin and Ruth Reichl, and biographies of people like Julia Child and Auguste Escoffier. And lots of cookbooks. I bent over to read some of the titles: Sam Choy's *Polynesian Kitchen*, Alice Waters's *Chez Panisse Menu Cookbook*, Madhur Jaffrey's *Indian Cookery*, Jacques Pépin's *La Methode*, Ruth Kallenbach's *Cooking at Escarole*.

I pulled this last one out. I'd never been to Escarole, the San Francisco restaurant started by the now-famous Ruth Kallenbach after she left Chez Panisse. But I'd always wanted to try it, especially since I knew she'd taken Letta with her to become sous-chef for the new restaurant. Eric and I had long talked about going up to the City to see an opera and eating at Escarole beforehand, even though Letta had long since left the place, but we had never managed to do so.

As I opened the book to flip through the recipes, two envelopes and a small photograph slipped out and fell to the floor. I stooped to pick them up.

The photo was of a woman with short, blond hair, who looked to be in her thirties. She was standing in front of a two-story wood-shingled house, wearing jeans and a green-and-white button-down shirt, and laughing at whoever held the camera, her eyes squinting into the sun. It was an old photo—from the 1970s or 1980s, I guessed from the faded colors and the pinkish tint. I set it aside and picked up the envelopes.

Both were addressed to Letta, care of Gauguin. Neither had a return address, but the postmarks, which were dated November of last year and March of this one, said San Francisco. Sitting back down, I slid the paper out of the earlier dated of the two, unfolded the sheet, and smoothed it out on the desk. It was a short, printed letter written by someone overly fond of boldface, italics, and exclamation marks:

> *Traitor!*
>
> You *of **ALL** people* should know better! Factory-farmed chicken? CAFO beef? **Veal?!** Not to mention farmed salmon and imported shrimp? Didn't you learn *anything* during all those years in Berkeley and San Francisco? How *could* you?!!
>
> It's time to switch your menu to *humanely* raised meat and *sustainable* seafood! Do the right thing—***NOW***!
>
> *We'll be watching you.*

There was no signature.

Wow. I set the paper down and exhaled. Don't get me wrong: I don't condone either cruelty to animals or the over-fishing of our oceans. I buy free-range eggs when I can, and it's been years since I've ordered Chilean sea bass at a restaurant. But whoever wrote this letter seemed to be pretty, well . . . *fanatical.* And that last sentence sure was disturbing—all the more so given the letter's anonymity.

I read it again. Of course I knew what factory-farmed chicken was: those big sheds with thousands of birds all crammed together. But what the hell did "CAFO" stand for?

I reached for the second envelope and found another letter inside in the same style:

Shame!

It's been over four months and still no change at all to your menu! Serving industrial pork is *odious*! Particularly when done by someone like yourself, who *knows better*! Pigs are sensitive, intelligent creatures. Do you have *any* idea what it would be like to live your *entire* life in a ***farrowing crate***?

Maybe someone needs to teach **YOU** a lesson and give you a taste of just what, by supporting the *heinous* practices of corporate ag, you are guilty (just as guilty as them!) of inflicting on all those poor, helpless, *suffering* animals.

Change **NOW**. *Or we won't just watch anymore.*

Oh my God. Could this be the reason she was murdered? I'd heard that some of those animal rights people could be pretty nuts. But would they really go so far as to actually kill someone?

I set the letter down and pulled my phone out of the back pocket of my cycling jersey. I had to find out if Letta had said anything to Javier about getting these letters.

After four rings, I figured I was going have to leave a message, but then he answered, in a groggy, sleepy voice.

"Mmmm . . . hullo?"

Oh, shit. What time was it, anyway? Eight thirty? Nine? Of course he would still be asleep; I knew enough about chefs' hours to know that.

"Uh, hi, Javier. It's me, Sally. Sorry to call so early . . ."

"It's okay. I had to get up anyway to answer the phone." His laugh turned into a cough—that early morning smoker's hack so common in restaurant workers—and then he cleared his throat. "So what's up?"

"I'm down here at Gauguin, going through some of Letta's things, and . . . well . . . I found something weird. I was wondering, did she ever mention to you anything about receiving anonymous threatening letters?"

"No, she never told me anything about that. Why? Did you find some?"

"Yeah. And they're kinda creepy."

"So, uh, what exactly were they threatening her about?"

"Food."

"Food?" Javier sounded incredulous—and surprised, too, as if he been expecting a different answer.

"Yeah, food. Whoever wrote the letters wanted Letta to stop serving factory-farmed meat, endangered fish, you know, stuff like that."

"Oh, *those* people. Huh." Javier lit a cigarette, inhaled deeply, and then coughed again. "You know," he said, "we did talk about putting some of that—what's the word?—grass-fed meat on the menu a while back after some customers had complained to her about it a couple times. I guess one of them was a real jerk. But when she found out how much it cost, she decided not to do it. Our entrées are already pretty expensive, even with the regular meat, and it woulda pretty much doubled the price."

"You remember when that happened? How long ago?"

He took another puff. "Sometime last fall, maybe? It's been awhile."

Right around the time of that first letter. "Did you get a look at any of the people that complained?"

"Nuh-uh. But Letta told me about it afterward."

"Well, did you ever see anyone strange at the restaurant—you know, visiting Letta or hanging around the back of the house—around that time or between then and now?"

"No, not that I can think of," Javier answered. "So what? You think the people who complained might be the ones who wrote those letters, or even who killed her?"

"I dunno. But it sure seems like something worth checking out."

After we'd hung up, I sat at Letta's desk, staring out the window. Hopefully, this new evidence would help get the cops off Javier's back and prompt them to start investigating other possible suspects. But there was no reason I couldn't do some snooping around as well. How could I find out who'd sent them? And who the hell was that woman in the photo, and why was it with the letters?

My only lead was Escarole. Letta must have had some reason for stashing the letters and picture in that cookbook. And the restaurant was in San Francisco, which was where the envelopes had been postmarked.

It seemed like a good place to start. And maybe I could finally get that dinner I'd wanted for so long.

Chapter Eight

Letta looked fabulous—in a waxy, dead kind of way. Yes, she did have on more makeup than she would have liked had she been around to notice, but then that was what funeral homes always seemed to do with the women.

I'm not being callous or cavalier; it's just that I'm used to being around open caskets. I saw not only my mom's body after her death (she too looked beautiful) but also my grandfather Salvatore (a little shriveled but not bad for ninety), my great-uncle Luigi (pudgy, as always), my second cousin Francesca (simply gorgeous), and Nonna's neighbor Carla just a few months ago (very sweet looking). We Italians just do death better than a lot of other folks.

Nonna had insisted on a two-day wake. In the old days, they called them vigils, but it's still the same thing: where friends of the deceased come to view the body and pay their respects to the family. So at seven o'clock on Thursday evening, I joined my father and Nonna in the viewing room at the funeral home to wait for people to start arriving. Dad hadn't been happy about the two of us being gone at the same time from Solari's—for two nights running—but there was really nothing to be done about that. No way could we not both be present for all of Letta's wake.

I hadn't spoken to my father since our argument that morning. The restaurant had been crazy busy at lunch, and after the rush was over, Dad left the building before I had the chance to track him down to talk.

Well, this was certainly not the time to work out our problems. Any speaking above a muted murmur would be deeply frowned upon during the wake. It would just have to wait.

Letta was laid out in her bronze casket, dressed in a salmon-colored suit I'd never seen before. I have to admit, it did look nice against that cream-colored lining. She was surrounded by a horseshoe of gaudy flower arrangements, heavy on the lilies, carnations, and chrysanthemums. The majority were regular spray types, but there were also several in the shapes of wreaths and crosses with black and gold banners declaring such things as "Beloved Daughter" and "My Loving Sister." Yes, I sent one as well, which stated simply, "Dear Aunt." I would have been hounded out of the family had I neglected this vital detail.

As I gazed down at Letta in her casket, I was taken back to my mother's wake two years earlier. It had been in this same room at about the same time of year, the late-afternoon sun streaming through the leaded glass windows, casting mosaics of yellow and red across the hardwood floor. After enduring months of chemo and radiation, her face had become thin and sallow right before the end. But in death, she'd once again appeared young and vibrant. The irony of cancer. I bit my lip and turned away, pushing the image back into the recesses of my brain.

Tony was the first to arrive after us. He walked over to where the casket rested upon its bier, knelt down, crossed himself and said a quick prayer, and then came over to where we were sitting in the front row of wooden chairs set up in the chapel.

"I'm so sorry," he murmured, taking Nonna's hands and leaning over to kiss her on both cheeks. Jaw set, he gave me a hug and then turned to shake hands with my dad. He took the end chair next to mine, and the four of us sat there silently, no one willing to disturb the reverential atmosphere that hung over the room.

After a few minutes, more people started to drift in: my second cousins, a great-aunt, Dad's golfing buddy and his wife, Letta's elderly next-door neighbors, and various other distant relatives and friends of the family. One by one, they filed by the casket—some kneeling, some just bowing their heads for a private prayer—and then came to pay their respects to our little foursome before taking a seat in one of the rows of chairs.

At first, I wondered at the lack of anyone from Gauguin but then remembered that it was a Thursday night. They'd all be hard at work right now—plating up orders of smoked salmon terrine, serving steaming dishes of *coq au vin*, scrubbing burnt Thai curry sauce off blackened sauté pans. Anyone from Gauguin, or Solari's, who wanted to put in an appearance would have to come tomorrow afternoon.

* * *

Visiting hours on Friday, the second day of Letta's wake, were scheduled from three to five and then again from seven to nine. At two thirty, as soon as the Solari's lunch rush was over and most of the mess had been cleared from the dining room, I cut out, leaving the dinner setup to Elena. I really wanted to get those letters I'd found in Letta's office to Detective Vargas before the wake, since the police station closed at five and wouldn't reopen till Monday morning.

Standing in line in the lobby, I had to wait while a middle-aged couple complained loudly about a homeless camp that had sprung up near their house. The woman at the reception window listened for a few minutes and then picked up her phone. "Okay, an officer will be right out to talk to you," she said after a brief conversation and then nodded for them to take a seat at the bench along the wall.

I stepped forward. "Is Detective Vargas in? Because I have some information relevant to the Violetta Solari murder case."

"Let me check," she said and picked up the phone again.

I glanced at my watch; it was already 2:50.

"He's stepped out for a few minutes," the woman said, replacing the receiver. "Would you like to wait?"

"I actually can't. I've gotta be somewhere in ten minutes. But here, can you make sure he gets these?" I pulled the letters and photo from my bag and, confirming they were the originals and not the copies I'd made, handed them through the window.

"Sure. No problem. And what's your name?" she asked, sliding the papers into a manila envelope and printing "Detective Vargas" on the front.

"Sally Solari."

"Oh." The receptionist stopped writing and looked up. "I'm so sorry."

"Yeah. She was my aunt."

"Well, I'll make sure he gets these as soon as he returns."

I threaded my way through the crowd that had now formed in the lobby and, once outside, raced down the steps to my car. It was only five past three when I got to the funeral home, but I could see Dad's frown as I made my way to the chair he and Nonna had saved for me in the front row.

Javier showed up ten minutes later. I watched as he hesitated at the door, eyes darting about the room. I'd rarely seen him in anything but chef's whites, and from the way he held himself, I'd say he felt a tad self-conscious in his dark suit and shiny black shoes. Catching my eye, he nodded and then walked over to Letta's body.

I looked away, not wanting to intrude on his private moment. But when I saw Tony come through the door a minute later, I couldn't help glancing back at Javier to see if he was still by the casket. He indeed was, head down and hands at his sides. I looked back at Tony just in time to see him take in this scene. I couldn't detect any change in his expression, but he ambled slowly toward the front of the room to stand at Javier's side. Now it's not unusual for, say, family members or a husband and wife to view a deceased's body together. But it is *not* normal for someone to just come up next to another person who's already there. Especially if, as in the case of Tony and Javier, they're not particularly close.

Javier jerked his head at the sudden appearance of another at his side and then went back to gazing at Letta. Tony leaned over and murmured something to him, but from where I sat—able only to see his backside—Javier didn't appear to react to this in any way. He just continued to stand there for another minute and then turned and made his way over to where we were sitting. There were tears in his eyes.

Nonna, who clearly didn't know who Javier was, accepted his condolences with a sad smile and then returned to her subdued conversation with a friend from church. My dad then shook his hand, but from his pinched expression, I could tell he wasn't convinced of Javier's innocence and was making an effort to be polite.

I was dying to ask Javier what Tony had said to him, but this was clearly not the time or place. I simply embraced him and told him how handsome he looked in his spiffy duds. (I had to explain this last phrase for him. Javier's English is so good, I sometimes forget he's not a native speaker.)

Javier sat down next to me, and we continued to make small talk. I started telling him about arrangements for the funeral the next day, but midsentence, he interrupted me and, with a quick look to his left, hastily excused himself. I followed his glance and saw that Tony was headed our way. *What on earth could be going on between those two?* I wondered as Javier slipped away and Tony came up and kissed Nonna's cheeks.

*　*　*

In between the afternoon and evening visiting hours, we went for an early dinner at a steakhouse around the corner from the funeral home. It was just Nonna, Dad, Tony, and me, which made me conscious of how small our family had become over the past few years.

We didn't have a whole lot to say to each other and must have looked pretty morose to the other restaurant patrons—Nonna in her severe black dress and Dad, Tony, and me in our dark suits. And add to that the fact that my dad and I were still barely speaking. I had finally succeeded in cornering him in the Solari's office that afternoon, but even though he'd apologized for his outburst the day before, his curt language and stiff shoulders made it clear he was nowhere near over it yet.

I picked at my pork chop (it was way overdone; I should know better than to order them at restaurants) and tried to look attentive as Nonna recounted in minute detail a story about one of her fellow parishioners who had recently broken her hip while trying to reach for a jar of applesauce at the back of her kitchen cupboard.

After our plates had been removed and our coffees ordered, Dad turned to Tony. "So," he said, "has Sally told you she's now a restaurant owner?"

Nonna's attention at that moment was taken up by a man with long hair and a skull-and-lightning-bolt T-shirt who had just been seated next to us (after forty-some years, she still hasn't gotten used to the idea of hippies), so she didn't react to this question. But Tony sure did. He turned to me, mouth agape.

"Wha—?"

"Oh, you haven't heard?" A faint smile formed on Dad's lips. "Letta gave Gauguin to Sally."

"Though God knows what I'm going to do with a restaurant," I hastened to add, shaking my head. This line of conversation, as well as the resulting sour expression on Tony's face, was making me exceedingly uncomfortable.

Nonna had finally had enough of staring at the Deadhead at the next table and caught my last comment. "What restaurant?" she asked.

"Gauguin, Ma. Letta's place. Sally's going to take it over."

"I'm *not* taking it over," I responded testily. "I have no intention of running her restaurant. I've already got one restaurant job taking up plenty of my time, in case you hadn't noticed." I glared at my father, who just grinned. Sometimes that Italian proclivity for picking fights really gets on my nerves.

I changed the subject and asked who was going to drive Nonna to the funeral the next day. But I could see that Tony was still staring at me.

After dinner, the four of us headed out to the parking lot together. We stopped at my car, and I rummaged through my purse for my keys.

"I think I'm just gonna walk back," Tony said. "I'll see you over there."

We watched him go down the street, and then I turned to my dad. "You can really be a brat sometimes, you know? I mean, I get that you have some sort of macho competition thing going on with Tony, but don't you think that maybe now is not the greatest time to be teasing him like that?"

"It wasn't him I was teasing," Dad replied.

"Oh." I unlocked the car and helped Nonna into the front seat.

My father climbed into the back. "So you like this Accord a lot?" he asked as I walked around to the driver's side.

"It's okay. Why?"

"How would you like something sportier?"

I opened the front door and looked at him, wondering if this was going where I thought it might be.

"I know Letta left me her car," Dad said. He began to search for the receiving end of his seatbelt, which had fallen into the crack between the cushions. "But you know, I've never liked T-Birds. They're a royal pain in the ass. The engine constantly needs tinkering, and I'm way too old and stiff to be climbing in and out of that tiny bucket seat. So I thought maybe you should have it."

He dug into the front pocket of his suit pants and held out a set of keys on a ring emblazoned with a vintage Ford insignia.

*   *   *

I truly didn't feel like going back to the funeral home for the last portion of the vigil, but since I was a close family member, I really had no choice. So once again, I found myself sitting in the chapel, smiling and saying, "Thank you so much for coming," over and over again to people I barely knew.

At about a quarter to eight, Eric showed up, and for once, my smile was authentic. Finally, someone I could have a real conversation with. I tugged him away to the back of the chapel and told him in a hushed voice about the T-Bird. I knew this would make him jealous, since he'd long been an old-car enthusiast, and the 1950s were his favorite era.

"I guess maybe it's Dad's way of making a sort of peace offering. He was pretty upset when I told him yesterday about inheriting Gauguin, and some things that he said were, well . . . not all that nice." I toyed with the car keys, which I'd placed in the front pocket of my black slacks. "He's never been much good at talking about his feelings."

"Kind of a family trait, I'd say."

I swatted Eric on the shoulder. "And there's something else I've been waiting to tell you." I described the letters and photo I'd found at Letta's office.

"You have them with you? I'd love to see them."

"During the wake? I don't think so."

"Yeah, you're right."

Eric and I watched as a tiny, stooped woman with a cane murmured the rosary over Letta's casket, crossed herself, and then tottered over to where Nonna was sitting. I could hear them converse rapidly in Italian.

"I made copies and could bring them by your office on Monday," I said.

"Not such a good idea, actually."

"What do you mean?"

"It's just that . . ." Eric scratched the back of his neck and flashed a halfhearted smile. "It seems our friend Detective Vargas has gotten wind of my discussing the case with you and isn't too happy about it."

"Oh." I'd been afraid something like this might happen. "So does that mean you can't talk about it anymore?"

"Well, as much as it royally pisses me off to let that self-important cop dictate what I do, it does mean I'm gonna have to be a lot more careful from now on. Like, for instance, not having you come to the DA's office to talk to me about the case. But maybe tomorrow I could stop by your place and have a look at the stuff you found."

"Tomorrow's the funeral and repast."

"Oh, right."

"But I guess I could bring them to the repast and you could check 'em out there."

"Sure, that works. Have you shown them to the cops?"

"Yeah. I took the originals down to the station earlier today and left them for Vargas. So who knows? Maybe they'll actually do some of their own investigating. You think?"

"Maybe," Eric said. But he didn't sound too convinced.

Chapter Nine

I swatted at the buzzing alarm clock at seven thirty the next morning and then fell back on the pillow, allowing myself to doze a few minutes more, relishing the realization that I did not, in fact, have to take a test in cellular biology. Slipping in and out of consciousness, I was half aware of the rhythmic pattering on the windowpane.

Hmmmm . . . it's so nice to be snuggled up all warm and cozy while it rains outdoors . . .

Rain? Oh, shit. I jerked myself up and turned to look out the window. It wasn't just drizzling; it was pouring down. And the wind was blowing like crazy, too. I could see the neighbors' trees thrashing about with a vengeance. *Great. What a day to stand around outdoors in a cemetery.*

With a shiver, I turned back the covers and slid my feet onto the cold hardwood floor. *Coffee. Now.* I had to pick up Nonna in an hour and had a tough day ahead.

All the Italian American families I know adhere to a strict regimen for funerals. First thing in the morning, the family and close friends convene in the viewing room at the funeral home for a quick Hail Mary and Our Father with the parish priest. Then it's off to the church, where everyone—extended family, friends, and anybody who wants to get in good with the family—attends a full-blown mass, with the open casket sitting front and center on the altar.

After the mass, there's the funeral procession to the cemetery, which has its own special set of rules. The hearse leads the way, with the priest following in his own car. Next comes the immediate family in a hired limo and then the rest of the mourners pulling up the rear. Everyone drives at a snail's pace with headlights illuminated, which, given the foul weather, would have been necessary in any case for our procession.

Letta's mass and funeral were long and well attended, and we all got a good soaking as we stood around the mausoleum area of the cemetery listening to Father Camillo intone the final commitment service. I examined the faces of the mourners one by one. Could any among them be Letta's murderer? Would it show if they were?

Noticing the priest glance up at something behind me and frown, I swiveled around to see what had caught his attention. Eric, who was by my side, turned to look as well. Detective Vargas walked up and came to a stop at the back of the group of mourners, rain streaming from the shoulders of his black jacket. Our sudden movement attracted his notice, and the detective's gaze rested briefly on Eric and me. Then, with an almost imperceptible nod, he continued to scan the crowd. I wondered if his expert eyes would be able to spot anything mine had missed.

At last, Letta's gold-colored casket was slid into its crypt, and we all bowed our heads. It was an eye-level space, I noted—the most expensive kind. Nonna had really gone all out.

Afterward, there was the repast, a big luncheon, at Solari's. That's when the trouble started.

My father had closed the restaurant to the public for the occasion, and all the mourners were invited. As folks arrived in little groups from the cemetery, they shook out their umbrellas and raincoats, sat down, and started helping themselves to the breadsticks and carafes of wine that sat on each table.

I took a place at one of the big, round tables and lay my trench coat over the chair to my right to save a place for Eric. As I was trying to surreptitiously check my messages, Dad steered Nonna over and sat her down on my other side. I hid my phone away and offered her the basket of breadsticks, but she nodded for me instead to pour her half a glass of white wine. I did the same for myself, except it was a full glass of the red, and we solemnly drank a toast to Letta.

I asked Nonna if she liked Father Camillo's service, but "*Sì, ben fatto*" was all she had to say with a quick bob of the head, and then she looked away. Surmising that she wasn't in the mood for talking, I turned to face the enormous plate-glass window that covered the back wall of the restaurant. This is one of the main draws of Solari's—it's mentioned in all the guide books—as the panorama is truly magnificent.

Sipping my wine, I thought about how, when Eric and I were still together, one of our favorite after-work activities had been hanging out at the Solari's bar, which has the same view. We'd play old Frank and Ella tunes on the jukebox, sip our Martinis, and chat with the suave, old Umberto, who'd been Dad's bartender since before I could remember, gazing out at the fishing boats floating in the shallow inlet and across the water toward the Spanish bungalows and Victorian mansions lining West Cliff Drive.

I shook my head. What was this? Why the hell did I keep dredging up these old memories the last few days? *Get back to the present, girl.* I focused again on the view.

The rain was still pelting down, and the enormous cypress trees across the water on the cliffs where I'd ridden my bike two days earlier were being battered by the wind. The gulls were out in great numbers, wheeling beneath the black clouds and racing across the sky as they got caught by the strong updrafts.

I started as a hand rested on my shoulder. Eric grinned at my reaction and handed me my soggy coat just as my father stood up and clinked his wine glass with a knife to get everyone's attention.

Eric slid into his chair, and the noisy room settled into silence. Dad cleared his throat. I knew he hated public speaking, so I figured this was going to be short.

"Uh, I just wanna say thanks to everyone for being there this wet morning and for all you've done for the family during this sad time. Letta was a one-of-a-kind gal. As they say, they broke the mold after they made her." We chuckled politely, and he glanced at a slip of paper in his hand and went on. "But no matter how . . . uh . . . different she may have been, one thing you could always say about her was she was always genuine, always true to herself, and always fun." This prompted claps and shouts of "Yes!"

Dad cleared his throat again and looked around the room. "So I just want to conclude by saying that she's truly going to be missed. By her friends, by the folks she worked with, by her family." And in a voice so low I could barely hear, he added, "Especially by her big brother."

He sat down quickly and took a drink of wine and the rest of the room raised their glasses in turn and drank to Letta. Almost immediately, as if on a signal, the swinging red door to the kitchen opened, and three waitresses filed into the dining room and started distributing cups of soup to the tables.

My father had preordered the courses for the repast: minestrone soup, green salad with balsamic dressing, garlic bread, linguine with pesto sauce, a platter of breaded calamari steaks, and tiramisu for dessert. Classic Dad, to just assume we'd all like what he picked. I couldn't help wondering if he had taken advantage of the situation to use up some excess squid he had on hand.

The noise level rose again as everyone started talking and digging into their soup, and within a few minutes, the sound of boisterous laughter and clinking spoons filled the room. Yes, we had indeed just been to a mass for the dead and an interment. But now was the time for rejoicing in Letta's memory and enjoying the company of family and friends. A good tradition—very healthy, in my opinion.

I had just speared one of the crispy, golden-brown calamari steaks and was dabbing it with Marinara sauce when a commotion erupted at one of the tables across the room.

"You son of a bitch!" a male voice shouted. This was immediately followed by the sound of a chair crashing to the floor, and I looked over just in time to see two men lunge for each other and start wrestling. They were quickly pulled apart by the other guests, and once untangled, I saw that it was Javier and Tony who were being restrained, panting and glaring at one another.

"What's going on here?" My father had jumped up and now stood before the two men, disbelief and anger in his eyes. "How *dare* you! At a funeral—"

"He started it," Tony interrupted, pointing at Javier. "He grabbed me first."

"I don't give a damn who started it. Out! Out, the both of you! You're both a disgrace." He turned his back before either could respond and walked slowly to his table, shaking his head in disgust. Several large men escorted Tony and Javier to the door, and I heard them warn that any continuation of the altercation out in the street would not be tolerated.

That sure put a damper on what had, up till then, been an almost festive occasion. It put my dad in a foul mood, and the guests, not wanting to further upset him, kept their conversations quiet throughout the rest of the meal. Nonna wanted to know what had happened, and I responded with a shrug. But I did have an idea.

*   *   *

Eric walked me outside after the repast was over. I pulled out the copies I'd made of the letters and photo I'd found in Letta's office and showed them to him as we took shelter from the rain under the restaurant awning.

"Looks like an old photo," he said. "I'd say from, what, the 1970s, '80s?"

"That's about what I thought, yeah. Back when Letta was living up in the Bay Area."

He read through the two letters, a scowl on his face, and then handed them back to me. "Freaks—that's what those people are. They love their animals more than their fellow human beings."

"Well, maybe the animals deserve love more than we do. At least they haven't started wars or poisoned the planet with DDT and car emissions."

Eric snorted. "Animals can be plenty vicious, Miss Pollyanna. I watched a pair of coyotes rip a house cat to shreds last year not too far from this very spot. Anyway, are you really going to stand there and defend those radicals when one of them may have been who stabbed your aunt to death?"

I returned the copies to my purse. No point responding to a purely rhetorical question.

"Sorry." Eric used his sleeve to wipe a raindrop off his glasses. "Those PETA types just sometimes really piss me off is all."

"No worries." I started across the road to where I was parked, and Eric followed.

"So," he said. "About that altercation between Javier and Tony . . ."

"Yeah. What the hell?"

"Javier was the one who started it—he shoved Tony pretty hard. You have any idea what's going on between them?"

"Well . . . I did find out that Javier was in love with Letta."

"That's certainly something."

"But not enough to make them *this* weird toward each other, it doesn't seem. After all, she was involved with Tony. Engaged to him, it turns out."

"Really?"

"Yeah. Tony told me that the other day. I guess it was pretty recent. And both Javier and Tony knew she wasn't interested in Javier. Javier says he hadn't even told her how he felt, though it turns out she did know and told Tony about it."

We stopped behind the T-Bird, and a brown pelican perched atop the wood railing nearby flapped clumsily off, disturbed by our intrusion. "Nice ride," Eric said.

I smiled and searched for the car keys in my bag. "Yep, real nice. But I've gotta say, I'm having a hard time getting used to the idea of it. It's still very much Aunt Letta's car to me."

"She'd be glad you were using it, I'm sure." Eric ran his fingers along the ridge of the left fin. "Very Jetsons. I hope the ragtop keeps the rain out."

The showers had now slowed to a drizzle, but I quickly unlocked my door and slid behind the wheel. "So far, it seems to work pretty well," I said, pulling the door shut and cranking down the window.

Eric buttoned his coat and turned up the collar. "Getting back to Javier and Tony," he said, "it does sound like there's reason for jealousy on both sides—even if it's not rational. Jealousy often isn't. And it's a nasty emotion. Especially when mixed with your dad's cheap Chianti."

I reached through the window and poked him in the ribs, even though I agreed that the wine had been pretty bad. "Look, I am going to ask Javier about him and Tony; don't worry. I just need to find the right time."

Eric nodded. "So does it surprise you? Javier being in love with her?"

It had, actually. And when I'd first heard it from Tony, I thought Letta must have been mistaken about Javier's feelings. But after talking to Javier the other night at the restaurant and seeing his face when I brought up the subject, I realized that it made a lot of sense.

"Well," I said, "she was really kind to him when he first started at the restaurant. I think he'd only recently arrived from Mexico, and she sort of took him under her wing. And it's been, what, almost seven years they've known each other? They must have become pretty close, working together like that for so long. And even though she was a lot older than him, she was still quite the looker."

An image of my aunt flashed through my brain—cruising down the road in her yellow convertible, red sunglasses on, ebony hair shot through with silver streaming back in the wind. "I bet he's been smitten with her for some time."

Chapter Ten

The next afternoon, I called my father. We'd decided it would be best to skip Nonna's Sunday dinner this week; after the wake, funeral, and repast, it just would have been too much for her. So I figured he'd probably be at home zoning out, watching golf or baseball on TV. I'd be seeing him that night at Solari's but still wanted to check in beforehand.

He picked up after the fourth ring, slightly out of breath. "Hi, hon. I was out back trying to prop up that rotted part of the fence down by the tool shed. With all this rain, it's starting to really sag."

"Oh, sorry to make you have to rush in. I just wanted to see how you're doing, since we didn't talk after the repast."

"Okay, I guess. It seems like it all went pretty smoothly yesterday, especially given the rain an' all." He seemed to be acting completely normal with me, as if nothing had happened between us. Well, if he was going to just let it slide, I guessed I'd do the same.

"Up till the end," he added. "What the hell is up with those two—Tony and Javier? Fighting like that? *At Letta's repast?*"

"Yeah, that was pretty bad. I'm not exactly sure what that was all about, but I think there may have been a jealousy thing going on between them. Over Letta. Which doesn't excuse it, of course."

"Sure doesn't. And Jesus, with her killer still out there somewhere? Makes ya wonder if maybe one of them . . ."

I let this unfinished sentence hang there in space, having nothing reassuring to say in response.

After we hung up, I spent the afternoon vegged out on my couch watching the Giants beat the Padres one to zip. Nothing like a good pitching duel and a cold bottle of Heineken to take your mind off the stresses of work, family discord, and murder.

I had to be at Solari's at five, but before heading over there, I pulled the Escarole website up on my laptop. I wanted to see if it had any information on how long the folks working there had been at the place—whether they might have known Letta, in other words. There was of course no list of employees; I hadn't expected such a thing. But there was a link titled "Our Chefs," which I clicked on.

Voilà: descriptions of all their work histories. Ruth Kallenbach was listed as "Chef de Cuisine," Tom Nakamoto and Laurie Evert simply as "Chefs," and Martine Dufour as "Pastry Chef." Besides Ruth, the only one of the four who'd been at Escarole since Letta's time was the pastry chef.

I checked the "Contact Us" page, but the only phone number listed was one for reservations. I dialed this number, and a man with a smooth voice answered the phone: "Escarole. May I help you?"

I asked when Ruth Kallenbach would next be working, and he consulted a schedule. "Not till this coming weekend," he informed me. "She'll be in both Friday and Saturday nights."

"And Martine, the pastry chef?"

"Oh, she only works mornings—early, from about five AM to eleven or so. And let's see . . . she's scheduled for Saturday morning but is off Sunday."

"Great," I said. "I'd like to make a reservation for three for this Friday night at, say, seven?" Nichole, a law-school pal of Eric's and mine, lived up in the City with her partner, Mei, and I was hoping they'd be up for joining me.

* * *

Solari's closes at nine PM on Sundays, so after cleaning up, balancing the register, and setting up the dining room for the following day, I was able to make it home before eleven. Less than twelve hours later, however, I was back there again.

Monday lunches can be hectic at the restaurant, since lots of other establishments are closed that day, and the business crowd always needs a place to eat. But this one thankfully didn't seem to be too bad.

As soon as I had a free moment, I phoned Javier, figuring he should be up by now. He was, and I told him I wanted to get together to talk about a plan for Gauguin. But although this was true, what I really wanted was to find out what the hell was going on between him and Tony. He agreed to meet me that evening at Dixon's, a burger-and-beer joint across from the Boardwalk that I knew he frequented.

At three fifteen, I was getting ready to leave for the day, when Dad found me in the wait station. Giulia was at a small table, prepping a stack of Solari's red cloth napkins for the dinner shift in a simple pyramid fold—Nothing like the exotic fans and flowers at Gauguin.

"Can I talk to you a sec?" Dad asked and motioned toward our office. I followed him inside, and he closed the door. So maybe he did want to iron out our differences after all.

"Look, if this is about Gauguin," I started, but he cut me off.

"No. It's something else. It's about my neighbor."

"Wanda," I said, and he nodded and frowned.

"It seems she's gotten herself a lawyer. At least, so she says. I saw her this morning on my way out to my truck, and she told me she had a surveyor come out. Don't they need my permission for that?"

"Not if they don't go on your property, they wouldn't."

Dad grunted. "Well, anyway, Wanda's now saying that it turns out the fence is on *her* property, which means she can cut the rose and the *Brugmansia* back herself if she wants. In fact, she's threatening to take the plants out altogether. So I thought I'd ask you about it. She can't do that, can she?"

"Well, she certainly can't just start whacking stuff back without some kind of proof or court order. Did she give you the results of the survey?"

He shook his head.

"Then you should get that from her, first off. But even if it turns out the fence is on her property, it still doesn't mean she necessarily has the right to cut down the plants. I'm not real up to date on property law anymore. It's been two years since I quit the firm, after all, and that kind of stuff doesn't tend to stay in your brain. Not in mine, anyway. But I did do a fair number of property dispute cases when I worked there, and it seems to me you might have a good prescriptive easement argument . . ."

I stared at the dog-eared poster tacked to the wall—it depicted all the various kinds of pasta, from *anelli* to *ziti*—and mentally transported myself back to my previous life. "In order to create a prescriptive easement," I murmured, as if reciting some religious incantation, "a party must show a use that was open and notorious and hostile to the true owner for a period of at least five years." And then I smiled, remembering how all of us first-year students got a real kick out of that "open and notorious" language and how Eric had once shouted the phrase at Nichole when he saw her smoking a joint at a party. You gotta take your humor wherever you can find it when you're in law school.

"Uh, okay," Dad responded, but when I turned to look at him, I could see his eyes had completely glazed over.

"Sorry," I said. "All that means is that if you use someone else's land for a long enough time, you get 'grandfathered in' and can continue to use that property for the same purpose. Are you the one who planted the trumpet vine and the climbing rose?" He nodded. "How long ago?"

"I dunno . . . ten, fifteen years back?"

"And I take it you're the one who's maintained them all this time?"

"Yeah, sure."

"Good. Get me a copy of that survey if there really is one. I can't officially act as your lawyer, since I've gone inactive with the State Bar, but I can probably at least figure out if you need to hire one."

He smiled. "Thanks, hon. I really appreciate it."

I wanted to come back with something like "So aren't you glad, after all, that I went to law school?" But I managed to restrain myself.

*　*　*

When I walked into Dixon's at six o'clock, Javier was already at the bar laughing at something the bartender had just said, a newly pulled pint of amber ale in front of him.

"Hey, Sally. This is Eli," he said as I took the stool to his left.

"Howdy." I nodded a greeting to the barkeep and ordered a Stella Artois.

"Any news about Letta?" Javier asked as soon as my bottle had been set down and Eli had left to ring up another patron's tab.

"No, not yet. But I'm gonna go up to the City this weekend to talk to some folks at Escarole, where she used to work. Maybe they'll know something."

"About those animal rights crazies?"

"Right. I'm hoping they'll have some idea who wrote Letta those creepy letters."

Javier nodded and took a slug of beer. I followed suit and neither of us spoke for a minute, both watching the Giants game on the bar TV. The score was tied, but the Padres had runners on the corners with only one out. As a run scored on a base hit up the middle, Javier shook his head and took another swallow of beer.

"So I've been meaning to ask you," I said after the inning finally ended with a double play. "What *was* that with you and Tony at the repast on Saturday?"

"Yeah," Javier mumbled. "Tell your dad I'm really sorry, okay?"

But he didn't answer the question. I pressed on. "I mean, c'mon, Javier. First there was that weird thing at the wake. And then that scuffle at Dad's restaurant? What the hell's going on between you two?"

Javier still didn't respond and instead just stared at the oversize truck splashing through a river of mud on the TV screen. Finally, he sighed and turned to face me. "I dunno, Sal. He's acted strange with me ever since I met him. I think he must just be jealous of how close me and Letta were—you know, pretty much running the restaurant together and all. And also . . . well . . ." He paused and lifted his glass.

"And what?" I prompted.

"Oh, nothing." He finished his beer and motioned Eli to bring another. "I was just gonna say that ever since Letta died, he's started making these nasty comments whenever he sees me."

I didn't buy that that was really what he had been about to say, but I let it slide. "Like what?" I asked.

"Like, for instance, Tony said, 'Letta told me she thought you were a real pussy.'" Javier's voice lowered to a macho *basso profundo* as he imitated Tony. "An' he said—and this is what got me so mad at Solari's the other day—he said Letta told him she didn't think I was all that great a cook and that she only kept me on at Gauguin 'cause she felt sorry for me." Javier took a long drink from his fresh glass of beer and set it down with a *smack* on the polished wood bar top. "She woulda never said that. I know she wouldn't." But the pain in his eyes told me he was hurt by the possibility that it could in fact be true.

"You know she didn't think that, Javier. She thought the world of you." I reached over and touched his wrist. "I remember one night when I was filling in for one of the cooks at Gauguin, and I was nervous as hell about screwing up—"

"I remember that night," Javier said with a chuckle. "I told you I was going to put you in charge of the hollandaise, and you panicked, not realizing I was just joking."

"Oh God, that's right." I took my hand off his wrist and then slapped it. "There. Now you're finally punished for being so mean. Anyway, Letta told me that night that all I needed to do was watch you and listen to what you told me—that you were a natural in the kitchen. And I remember she said she trusted you like she would family. That's saying a lot, you know, coming from an Italian."

Javier nodded, but his mouth was still tight.

"And she was right," I went on. "You're a fabulous chef. That meal I had the other night when I was there, the seared ahi with papaya chutney? It was amazing! And so was Eric's steak. The food's *always* great when I eat at Gauguin. You know Tony's just trying to yank your chain. Try not to let it get to you."

"Yeah, I know." Javier nodded again and drank some more beer.

I then led the discussion away from Tony's comments and toward the coming week at the restaurant. "Do you have the specials planned yet?" I asked, and we chatted about mackerel, skate, asparagus, and snap peas.

"I'm meeting with the bookkeeper tomorrow," I said after we'd finished discussing the menu. "I've really got to start figuring out what running a restaurant's all about."

Javier turned to face me. "So you've decided you're gonna do it? Take over Gauguin?"

I shook my head. "I haven't decided anything yet. I've barely had time to even think since Letta's death. But if I'm going to make any kind of intelligent decision one way or another, I better learn what it would entail if I did take it over. Like, for instance, I don't even know if Gauguin's making a profit or not."

"I'd say so, though Letta didn't talk a whole lot to me about that kind of stuff. But Shanti, the bookkeeper, will be able to tell you all about that. You'll like her, by the way. She's really organized and efficient. Good thing, too, since Letta was, well . . ."

"Not those things," I filled in for Javier. "She excelled at the creative side of the business. I know."

He flashed a quick smile, and we lapsed into silence. The Giants were now down by two runs. "I'm going to order a burger," he said after a minute. "You want anything?"

"No thanks. I really should be going. I'm pretty beat. And I have some leftover enchiladas that need eating." I drained my beer and pulled a five out of my wallet. "This enough, you think?"

"Yeah. It's happy hour, so that should be plenty."

I slid off my stool and pecked him on both cheeks. "Okay, then. *Ciao, bello.*"

"See you." He waved good-bye and then turned back around to watch the game.

Chapter Eleven

The name Shanti is not an unusual one in Northern California. But this being Santa Cruz, a "new-age crystal town," as my dad is fond of saying, I must admit I was expecting someone called Shanti Das to be clad in orange-colored clothing with sandalwood beads draped about her neck and wrists. So I was a bit surprised, not to mention relieved, when the woman who answered the door on Tuesday evening had on tight, black jeans, topped by a teal turtle-neck jersey. Turns out her parents are Bengali, so she came by the name honestly.

She greeted me with a firm handshake and a polite how-do-you-do and showed me into her dining room. A laptop was sitting on the table next to a glass of white wine. "Would you care for some Chardonnay?" she asked in a smooth voice carrying hints of her Indian roots. "I have red, too, if you prefer."

"Whatever you're having is fine. Thanks."

As Shanti went to the kitchen to fetch the bottle from the fridge, I glanced around me, observing that she appeared to be a fan of Scandinavian-style decor. The condo was neat and sparsely furnished, with lots of blond-wood furniture and a few tasteful prints on the walls. But the whole effect, bright and clean-looking though it was, seemed a bit too cold and sterile for my taste. I prefer a little clutter in my life—books and magazines strewn about and the odd knick-knack here and there. Not to mention comfy, overstuffed chairs and sofas.

Shanti returned with my glass of wine and motioned for me to sit down at the table. "I was so shocked to hear about Letta's death," she said as she took the seat by the laptop. "Do they have any idea who did it?"

"I know. The whole thing is really horrible. And no, I don't think the cops have a clue who's responsible."

I tried the wine. It was good—one of those dry, flinty, French-style Chardonnays—and not cheap, I imagined. "Actually, I should rephrase that," I said, setting my glass down. "They found Javier's knife by her body, and since they don't have anything else to go by at this point, I guess he's what you'd call the prime suspect as of right now." Seeing Shanti's eyes widen, I hurried to add, "But there's no way he did it. They just need someone to focus on."

"No, I can't imagine him doing such a terrible thing." Shanti frowned with distaste. "He's always seemed to me to be such a sweet man."

"I'm actually doing a little snooping around for him, since it doesn't look like the cops are going to be much help. You know, to try to see if I can uncover anything that might shed some light on who the real murderer is."

"Oh?"

"But I've come up empty-handed so far." I shrugged. "The problem is I don't really know much about conducting a criminal investigation. It's not something they teach you in law school. So I've been kind of flailing about."

Shanti nodded sympathetically. "I'd be awful at that," she said. "I'm not very good at getting people to open up, since I'm fairly shy myself."

"And also," I went on after another quick sip of wine, "I've been so busy, it's been hard to find the time to do much investigating, what with my job at Solari's and all the organization and planning for the wake and funeral and then dealing with this whole Gauguin thing. Speaking of which, I don't want to take up too much of your time, so maybe we should get started?"

By way of response, Shanti opened her laptop and brought a page up on the screen. I pulled my chair closer to get a better view. "So how much do you know about bookkeeping?" she asked.

"Not much. I learned a little bit when I took a basic business law class in law school, but that was ages ago. And I've picked up some working at Solari's, but my dad has his own bookkeeper there who does it all. I'm just in charge of the cash register and dealing with credit card charges and stuff like that."

"Okay," Shanti said. "Well, all software programs use what's called the double-entry system of bookkeeping. In essence, what that means is that every financial transaction is recorded twice: as a credit and also as a debit. It's a way of keeping errors to a minimum, because the debit and credit columns have to match up. If they don't, you know you've made a mistake somewhere."

I nodded as she paused to take a drink. "Got it."

The first thing she showed me was the current balance sheet for Gauguin, which, she explained, was a snapshot of the assets and liabilities of the restaurant. "Here at the top, you can see the current assets." Shanti tapped a red-painted fingernail on the screen. "In other words, what's presently in the checking and savings accounts as well as the current inventory and accounts receivable. Right below are the fixed assets—you know, furniture, office equipment, appliances, and the like. Next are the liabilities. That's what's owed by the business: accounts payable, outstanding loans, credit cards, salaries and rent owed, taxes."

She moved her finger down the screen. "Finally, here at the bottom, you can see the net worth of Gauguin is listed: $21,875."

"Net worth," I repeated. "That's the value of the business, right?"

"Not exactly. The rule—it's actually one of the primary principles of bookkeeping—is that assets plus liabilities equals the net worth."

"So net worth is kind of like the net assets, and what's listed here as 'total assets' is equivalent to gross assets?" I was trying to wrap my mind around these new concepts. Too bad I hadn't taken that accounting class that had been offered as an elective during law school.

"Well, I *guess* you could look at it that way," Shanti answered slowly, "but they're not called that in accounting."

"But the bottom line is that we're in the black, right?" And then I laughed. "Ohmygod—I just realized where that metaphor must have originated. Since that amount is, in fact, *the bottom line* of the balance sheet. Ha!"

Shanti chuckled. "Right," she said, "on both counts. You can see here, on the bottom line, that your net worth right now is at almost twenty-two thousand dollars. That's a lot for a restaurant when you don't own the building it's in."

"Well, that's good to know." I reached over to pet a large ginger cat that had just jumped up onto the table.

"Shoo, Bhaji! You know you're not supposed to be up here." Shanti swatted her hand in the air, and the cat jumped back onto the floor and proceeded to give itself a good cleaning, making a show of ignoring its two human observers.

"Bhaji?" I repeated.

Shanti smiled. "It's a kind of *pakora*—you know, Indian-style fritter. My mom makes them all the time. They're usually an orange-brown color and quite high in fat content, so I thought it would be a good name for this big guy."

"Cute. I like it." We both lifted our wine glasses while I studied the balance sheet. "So how does stuff get entered into the system?" I asked. "I mean, for example, when I get a bill from a vendor and pay it, should I give you the invoice?"

"That would be great." Shanti set her wine down again and clicked a button to bring up a new page. "Letta always saved the invoices and deposit slips and things like that, and I'd come by and pick them up once a week to record them. Here." She pointed to the spreadsheet that had appeared on the screen. "What I just did was run an accounts payable report for the week of March nineteenth. You can see all the invoices that I entered, along with the names of the vendors, the check numbers, and the amounts."

She indicated one of the rows. "See here, for example, is one for $272.33 from Quality Meats, which was paid on March twenty-fourth." Scrolling down the list, she showed me how all the invoices from that week had been recorded. "And what's great about this software is that once you've entered an invoice or a deposit or tax payment or anything, it's in the system. You don't have to enter it again in order to generate a general ledger or profit and loss statement." She leaned forward. "Here, let me show you—"

"Wait," I said, interrupting her. My eye had been caught by one of the entries on the screen. "What's that?"

Shanti looked where I was pointing. "Bolinas Farms? Why, I imagine it's an invoice for produce. Why?"

"Scroll back up, would you? Look, there's another one from the beginning of the same week. I thought I'd seen it."

"So?" Shanti was looking at me like I was a crazy woman. "What's so odd about produce invoices for a restaurant?"

"Well, don't you think it's a little weird that Letta would order produce from Bolinas, all the way up in Marin County? It's over a hundred miles from here. And when there are so many great farms right here in Santa Cruz and Watsonville?"

"Maybe they grow something special that you can't get around here." Shanti peered at the screen. "Let's see, $84.23 for this one . . ." She scrolled back down to the second entry six days later. "And $115.77 for the other. That seems like a fair amount of produce."

"Do you recognize the name?" I asked. "I mean, have you been entering invoices from Bolinas Farms on a regular basis?"

"Well, the name is familiar to me, so I may have. But that's easy enough to check." She clicked a couple more buttons and then typed in the name "Bolinas Farms," bringing up a new page showing all the entries for the calendar year for that vendor. There seemed to be about one invoice per week, and they all ran between about $70 and $130.

"Can you show me the list for Bolinas Farms for last year?"

"Sure." Shanti brought up a new screen, and we both leaned forward to examine it. "It looks like Letta first started buying from them last August," Shanti observed. "There don't appear to be any entries before that date."

"Huh. Well, I think it's odd." I settled back in my chair. "I guess I'll just have to ask Javier about it."

Chapter Twelve

"English peas are just coming into season. What do you think about a creamy risotto with morels—I saw some great ones yesterday at the farmers' market—and shelling peas?" Javier chewed on the end of his pen and contemplated the list he held in his hand. "I could do it with a little grated Romano cheese."

I had dropped by Gauguin the next afternoon to ask about those purchases from Bolinas Produce and found Javier up in Letta's office working on the next week's specials. He encouraged me to hang out and help him with the menu, more out of politeness, no doubt, than any need for my opinion. But I was happy to assist. Although I'm certainly no expert when it comes to the cooking side of the restaurant business, I do consider myself a pretty good judge of what makes for an innovative and tasty dish. And besides, learning the ropes of menu planning would have to be an important part of my education—*if* I did decide to take on Gauguin.

"And maybe a dash of mint," I responded.

"Yeah, I like that." Javier made a note and then tapped his pen on the pad of paper. "It could be a side, but maybe it would be better as a vegetarian entrée. That would be more cost-effective."

I nodded. "Good idea."

"And I thought maybe a broiled salmon with habanero-lime butter. I've done that before, and it was a big seller. You marinate the fish in orange and lime juice, tequila, and crushed habanero peppers before you cook it, and then you finish it with a scoop of the butter right before service."

"I shoulda eaten a bigger lunch," I said. "I'm already getting hungry again."

"Now for the veg." Javier grabbed a clipboard that was sitting on top of the desk. "It's sort of a slow time of year for new produce, but the asparagus is still good. And there's always Asian greens. I think I can get some mizuna and baby bok choy from Day Valley Produce." He flipped to the second page on his clipboard. "Yeah, I thought so. They'd be good as a wilted salad, maybe with a sweet shallot vinaigrette."

I'd been waiting for the right opportunity to jump in with my question. "Speaking of produce," I said, "I wanted to ask you something."

Javier stopped shuffling through the papers and looked up. "Yeah?"

"I met with Shanti last night, and as she was showing me the books, I got curious about one of our vendors, Bolinas Farms. You know it?"

"Sure. We get lettuces and greens, fresh herbs, stuff like that from them. And also sometimes things like fennel, or beans and peas when they're in season."

"Well, I mean, I just thought it was kind of odd that y'all would get produce from all the way up there. When, you know, there's so much similar stuff around here."

He refused to meet my eye and was slow in responding. "Uh, well . . ."

"It's just that I'm wondering . . . I mean, I know it's a long shot, but I was wondering if maybe it could have any connection with those letters and the photo I found here in her office."

"What photo? I remember the letters, but I don't remember you talking about any photo."

"I didn't? Oh. Sorry." I grabbed my bag and pulled out a copy I'd made and handed it to him. "Here. This was stuck into the Escarole cookbook along with those two letters."

Javier's eyes got big as he looked at the snapshot.

"What?"

He just kept staring at the picture and didn't answer.

"Come on, Javier—I'm doing this for *you*. What is it?"

"That's her," he said finally. "The woman from Bolinas Farms. Though she's a lot younger here." He handed the photograph back to me. "She's got gray hair now and is a little heavier."

"Really? How do you know?"

"I've seen her. Here at the restaurant. I think she's the owner of the farm, but she makes the deliveries herself."

"Huh." I looked at the picture again. If she was Letta's age, she'd be in her early sixties now. Javier had gone back to his clipboard and was making a pretense of studying one of the pages, but I got the feeling there was something he was leaving out.

"Okay, Javier. What is it? What else aren't you telling me?"

He looked up from reading. "What?" he asked, all innocent-like.

"Come on, fess up." I crossed my arms and gave him a stern look.

His shoulders slumped, and he set down the clipboard. "Okay. It's that, well . . ." He was tapping his pen like crazy on the pad, and I reached over and stopped it.

"Out with it."

"I think she and Letta may have been . . . involved."

At my gaping look, he went on. "I walked into Letta's office a couple months ago without knocking. I didn't realize anyone was in there with her. And there she was, that woman." He nodded toward the photo in my hand. "Kate is her name, I think. And she and Letta were . . . kissing. And I mean really going at it, you know? I shut the door as soon as I opened it, but Letta came running out and followed me down the stairs and into the *garde manger*. She told me it didn't mean anything, that they'd known each other for a long time, and this was just a weird one-time thing. And then she swore me for secrecy—is that how you say it?"

"*To* secrecy," I answered automatically. But the correct usage of prepositions was the last thing on my mind at that moment.

"So you see, I had promised her I wouldn't ever say anything about what I'd seen that day. I know she's dead now, and it can't hurt her for anyone to know, but I *promised*." Javier looked close to tears. "Just 'cause she's gone—I mean, it would still be disrespectful to talk about the dead like that."

I just let him run on. Letta with a woman? It had never occurred to me; she didn't seem the type. She was so . . . well, *straight*-seeming. Not only did she dress in frilly clothes, but she flirted with guys constantly in that typical way that so many Italian American women acted around men. And she was engaged to Tony.

And then it hit me: no matter how much she may have tried to deny it or leave it all behind her, Letta couldn't help but be a product of our culture. And to be gay or lesbian in that culture, where macho men and femmie women were the imperative? That would have seemed like the ultimate disgrace to her *famiglia*. I couldn't even imagine telling my dad—or, God forbid, *Nonna*—if I were gay.

No wonder she'd sworn Javier "for secrecy."

I shook myself out of my reverie. Javier was still talking. "Sally . . . Sal! You listening?"

"Sorry. I was thinking about Letta. But I hear what you're saying. And I get it: why she wanted to keep it a secret and also why you didn't tell anyone, even after she died. You're a good friend."

He gave me a sad smile.

"But I swear to God, Javier," I said, returning his smile but with my hands on my hips, "if you keep anything *else* from me . . ."

*　*　*

The first thing I did when I got home from Gauguin was pour myself two fingers of Jim Beam over ice and then kneel down in front of my CD rack and peruse the titles. I had almost two hours before I needed to be back at Solari's for the dinner shift, and a little opera seemed just the ticket. Nothing beats it when you need to emote. I pulled out *La Bohème* and slipped the first disc into the slot.

Next, I got a pot of water heating for some tortellini (store bought and dried—Nonna would not approve), grated some Parmesan cheese, and took a jar of pesto (this was my dad's, homemade) out of the fridge and set it on the counter. That done, I dropped onto the couch to sip my drink and think.

What a heavy burden it must have been for Letta to conceal her affair with Kate from the world. And how alone she must have believed herself to be, to have no one to confide in.

But she could have confided in *me*; I would never have been judgmental about such a thing. Why had she kept it a secret? The realization washed over me that my aunt must not have felt the same way about me as I had about her. How close could she have felt if she didn't feel safe enough to tell me about Kate? Had I completely misread the depth of our friendship?

I closed my eyes and listened to the music. Mimi had brought her candle stub upstairs to Rodolfo in search of a light—and a love—and was now singing to him about her lonely existence in a cold Parisian garret waiting for the spring, when the first rays of sun, the first kiss of April, would be hers:

> . . . *ma quando vien lo sgelo,*
> *il primo sole è mio,*
> *il primo bacio dell'aprile è mio*!

The orchestra swelled up along with the ascending soprano line, and as Mimi held onto her high note, the intensity of the moment caused my eyes to fill with tears.

I invariably cry at this point in the opera. And it's not just the hormones: I had this reaction even before "the change" began. I guess I just find the concept deeply moving—that after a cold and bitter winter, something as basic as a warming ray of sunshine could bring such profound joy. Add to the mix Puccini's drop-dead-gorgeous melody, and the passage is a guaranteed tearjerker.

And right now, there was the additional factor of learning that my aunt had not trusted me with the details of her life, with the things that truly mattered to her.

Wiping my eyes, I stood up and switched off the stereo before Rodolfo's boisterous friends could destroy the mood by shouting up at him from the street.

I had to talk to Kate, obviously. But the idea of simply calling her up on the phone to ask about Letta made me uneasy. It would feel as if I were prying into a part of their lives that was way too private for the likes of me to be poking my nose into.

But I suppose that's the way it has to be when somebody ends up murdered.

Before I could think better of it, I reached for my phone and punched in the number Javier had given me for Bolinas Farms.

"Hello?"

"Oh, hi," I responded, flustered that someone had actually picked up. I'd assumed that it was a business number and I'd just be leaving a message. "Could I please speak to Kate?"

"You got her."

"Oh," I said again. "Um, you don't know me, but I'm the niece of Letta Solari."

It was her turn to say, "Oh."

"Yeah. I know. This is weird." I cleared my throat. "So I imagine you've heard about Letta?"

Please, please don't make it be me who has to tell her . . .

There was a slight pause, and then I heard "Yes" in a voice so soft it was almost a whisper. "I read about it in the papers." Another pause. "Do they know yet what happened? Who . . . did it?"

"I'm afraid not. But it's only been a little over a week, after all."

The conversation was becoming increasingly awkward because neither of us was expressing any of the traditional "I'm so sorry for your loss" language. The problem was that I did, of course, want to tell her how sorry I was, but since she didn't know that *I* knew of her relationship with Letta, it didn't seem appropriate. And Kate no doubt also felt that she should tell me she was sorry for *my* loss, but given how sad *she* must have been feeling about Letta's death, I could imagine this wouldn't have been easy.

I decided to just let it go. "Anyway, so it turns out that I've inherited Gauguin."

"Really?"

"Yeah. Another thing that's weird, 'cause I had no idea I was even in her will."

"Oh."

"So anyway, I've been going over the restaurant books and stuff, and I saw that you're one of the produce suppliers."

"Uh-huh."

"And I also gather that you and Letta have known each other a long time. And that you were pretty close."

"Yeah," she admitted, almost as a sigh.

In for a dime, in for a dollar. I plunged on. "So I was thinking it might be good for us to meet—partly because I'd like to get to know all the restaurant vendors but also because you were a friend of Letta's. And also," I added, deciding the forthright approach would probably be best, "I've been doing some poking around, trying to figure out what exactly happened with Letta. I thought maybe you might be able to help with some information I don't have."

"Okay . . ." It sounded like she was thinking about it and then came to a decision. "Yeah, sure. I'd actually like to meet you, too. Did you have any particular time in mind?"

"Um, I know it's kind of short notice, but I'm actually going to be up in the Bay Area this weekend, and I was wondering, is there any chance I could come by to see you on Saturday?"

"Sure, that would work. I'm pretty much always at the farm."

"Oh, and I'm thinking of coming up there with a friend. Would that be all right?"

"Yeah, okay. Whatever." I could tell she wasn't thrilled at the idea of another person tagging along, but my thought was that having along Nichole—who's about as "out" as one can be—might be a good thing, that it might make it easier for Kate to talk about her relationship with Letta. And I figured that once I dropped my bombshell about Letta, Nichole would jump at the chance to meet her mysterious, secret lover.

Chapter Thirteen

Santa Cruz can sometimes seem like an island, isolated as it is by the mountains on one side and the vast Pacific Ocean on the other. There are only two major roads in and out of town: Highway 1 along the coast and the twisty, redwood-lined Highway 17 over the Santa Cruz Mountains into Silicon Valley. Seeking to avoid the hazards of the rain-soaked mountain route—which locals tend to treat as their own miniature Indianapolis 500—I decided to take the coast highway up to San Francisco on Friday afternoon for my dinner that night at Escarole. Not only was I driving an unfamiliar car, but I was also having to get used to driving a stick shift, something I hadn't done in years.

When my dad had asked why I wouldn't be at work that night, I'd told him I needed to deal with "something to do with Letta's death." He merely shrugged and said, "Fine," without asking for any details. Part of me felt bad for keeping the entire truth from him, but the other part knew damn well my father would not be at all happy to hear I was snooping around, trying to find her murderer.

But I wasn't going to worry about that now, I told myself as I cruised north out of town in the T-Bird.

It's a glorious drive up Highway 1, along fields of brussels sprouts and artichokes, past driftwood-strewn beaches, and through rolling hills dotted this time of year with splashes of wild mustard and purple lupine.

The sun came out around the time I got to Pescadero, and I had to fumble for my sunglasses and pull down the visor. The late-afternoon light was making the whitecaps sparkle, and for the first time since learning of Letta's death, I felt able to let it go—for right now, at least.

Time for something more raucous: I ejected the Puccini arias I'd been listening to, popped in a new disc, and joined in David Byrne's frenzied vocals as he sang of discos, brownstones, and peanut butter.

* * *

I got to Nichole's place at a quarter to five. It was after five, however, by the time I found a place to park and actually made it to her doorstep. She and her partner Mei live on Eighteenth Street, just west of Dolores Park, and parking can be a real bitch in that neighborhood.

"Dude!" she shrieked upon opening the door and then crushed me in a bear-hug embrace. Skate punk is Nichole's native tongue, and she tends to pepper her speech with words like "awesome" and "sick." Except, that is, when she's in "professional mode" (her term), at which time she can act as proper and lawyerly as the best of 'em. As long as I've known Nichole, she's had this ability to walk both lines. During law school, she sported a Mohawk and fire-engine-red Converse high-tops, and I swear that half the time she smoked a bowl before class. Yet she was always the professors' favorite and ended up graduating third in our class with her pick of plum jobs. Go figure.

"Ohmygod, Sally! That is so *freakin' weird* about your aunt!" Nichole had bleached her hair blond, and it was cut short and spiked with some sort of gel. Last time I'd seen her, about three months back, it had been a flaming red. I liked the blond look better; it went with her blue eyes and baby face. "C'mon in and put your stuff down. You want a drink? It is five o'clock, after all. Cocktail hour!"

Following Nichole down the hall, I dumped my bags on the sofa bed in the study and then followed her back out again and into the small kitchen, her talking a mile a minute all the while. She pulled two stemmed Martini glasses out of a cupboard and set them on the counter.

I sat down at the kitchen table. On the wall behind me was a cork board with a map of the Noe Valley attached to it. Several pushpins in various colors were stuck in and around the map.

"What's this?" I asked.

"Oh, that's new. We got sick of always having to remember where the hell we parked. One day last month when I woke up, for the life of me, I had no memory at all of where I'd parked the night before. It took me almost a half hour to find my car."

"Funny."

"Not. I almost missed a client's asylum hearing." Nichole is an immigration attorney at one of the big nonprofits in town. "Which would have *big-time* sucked. After that, we put up the map and started marking where our cars are with one of the pins as soon as we get home. I'm yellow, and Mei is red."

"Okay, I'll be blue then." I found where I'd parked and marked the spot with one of the pins stuck to the side of the map.

"Mei'll be here in a little while. She went hiking at Mount Tamalpais with a friend. I bet they got soaked. So what'd ya want?" Nichole opened the liquor cabinet to display the wares. "I'm having a gimlet." Without waiting for an answer, Nichole filled a stainless-steel cocktail shaker with ice, dropped three cubes into each Martini glass, and then filled them with water from the faucet. I smiled, remembering how she'd taught me one of the first times we hung out that this was the best way to chill a cocktail glass quickly.

"Yeah, a gimlet sounds good to me. I could use a drink after today."

"Oh Jesus, I haven't even asked you about the funeral. How did it go? And how are *you* doing, girl?" She paused and held the Beefeaters bottle over the shaker, giving me a hard look. It seemed like I'd been getting a lot of those of late.

"I'm fine. Really," I added when she continued to eyeball me. "But it has been weird, to say the least. Go on. Finish the drinks, and then I'll tell you all about it."

This seemed to satisfy her, and she continued pouring the gin and then added a few glugs of Rose's lime juice. Next she inserted an inverted pint beer glass into the shaker and deftly shook the concoction until it turned a foamy white. She dumped the ice water out of the now-frosted glasses, dropped a slice of lime into each, and then carefully strained in the pale-green liquid.

"Limeade for grown-ups!" Nichole proclaimed, holding up her glass to clink with mine.

We sat in the living room, and I told her everything I could remember that had happened since I'd learned of Letta's death. When I got to the part about the papers falling out of the Escarole cookbook, I put on my best poker face as I handed her the copy I'd made of the photograph.

"Here, check this out."

Nichole snorted. "Dyke," she said.

"Really?" Since she was staring down at the picture, she failed to notice the grin I now allowed to appear. "How can you tell?"

"Oh, c'mon." Nichole tapped the photo with her index finger. "Just check out that flannel shirt and the jeans and that short hair: classic lesbian look circa the late 1970s," she recited as if reading from a textbook. "You have any idea who she is?" She finally looked up and saw my cat-who-ate-the-canary expression. "What the hell?"

"I think she was Letta's lover," I said. "Javier told me he walked in on the two of them making out in her office a while back."

"No shit." Nichole examined the photo more closely and frowned. "That is so weird. I mean, I met Letta a bunch of times, and I woulda never guessed. So much for my powers of gaydar." Setting the picture on the coffee table, she picked up her glass and sipped her gimlet.

"Well, since she's also been involved with men, I guess technically this makes her bi," I said. "Maybe gaydar doesn't work so well in that case. Kate's the woman's name, by the way. She's one of the produce vendors for Gauguin. She owns a farm up in Bolinas, and I'm driving up there tomorrow to meet her. Any chance you'd care to come along?"

"Really?" Nichole leaned forward, lips parted in anticipation. "I'll have to check with Mei first to make sure we don't have anything else planned, but if not, yeah, for sure. That would be really interesting." She picked up the photo again. "So where'd you say you found this?"

"In an Escarole cookbook in Letta's office. That's why I wanted to go there tonight: to see if anyone knows anything about her. Or these. They were stuck in the book with that photo." I handed Nichole the two letters, and she read them over, eyebrows arched.

"Jesus." She dropped the photocopies onto her lap and reached for her gimlet again. "Those are creepy."

"Exactly my thought."

"You think whoever wrote them might have killed your aunt?"

"Who knows? But I figure I should at least check it out. Wasn't it one of those PETA types who fire-bombed that professor's house at UC Berkeley a couple years back? You know, the one who was using lab goats to produce antibodies or something like that?"

"I think they finally decided it was a more radical group, like the Animal Liberation Front, actually," Nichole said. "But yeah, those animal rights folks have been known to do some pretty violent stuff." She read through the first letter again. "But as far as I know, most of their violence has been limited to things like bombings. And toward big corporations and universities or chain restaurants—not privately owned places like your aunt's. And I've certainly never heard of any of them doing anything like *stabbing* someone." She set the letter back down and turned to me. "You don't think this Kate woman wrote them, do you?"

"Well, Letta did put them with that photo of her . . ."

Nichole shook her head. "I dunno. Whoever wrote these seems like he or she has some kind of personal animus against Letta, or Gauguin, not someone who's romantically involved with her."

I just shrugged by way of an answer, and we sipped our drinks and stared out the window at the Muni trolley bus rattling up the street. "So you think someone at Escarole will know who wrote the letters?" Nichole asked after a minute.

"Maybe. Maybe not. But it's as good a place to start as any. And I have always wanted to eat there. Which reminds me: what time will Mei be home? 'Cause we have a seven o'clock reservation."

"Soon, I imagine. But I say we have another drink while we wait for her, and you can finish telling me your story."

* * *

We took a cab to Escarole. After two gimlets each (Mei quickly caught up once she got home), not to mention the wine to come, we all agreed that would be the most judicious course of action. Plus, parking down in the Civic Center on a Friday night is even worse than in Noe Valley.

"Looks like there's both an opera and a symphony performance tonight," I observed as the taxi headed up Van Ness. "I wonder what the opera is."

"It's actually the ballet," Mei said. "Opera season doesn't start up again until June." She turned to look at the people streaming into the Opera House, many in fancy evening wear. "My parents had season tickets to the ballet when I was a kid, and I never could figure out what the hell they saw in it."

The cab turned left and pulled over to the curb about a half block down. "Here, I got this." Mei handed the driver a few bills, and we all climbed out. "But now that I'm all grow'd up," she continued once we were standing on the sidewalk, "I finally get it. It's all those guys with those amazing bodies in those tight leotards. Hell, even *I* love to watch them leap around and strut their stuff." She laughed, and Nichole and I waited while she put her wallet back in her purse and zipped it shut.

Nichole and Mei looked quite the odd couple—one, short, blond, and boyish; the other, tall and athletic with long, black hair and elegant Chinese features. Mei is a Pilates instructor, and the two met when Nichole enrolled in a weight-training class at Mei's gym. They'd been involved for two years now, and I thought they worked well as a couple. Mei's calm demeanor was a good foil to Nichole's tendency toward the manic.

Nichole held the door open, and we made our way through the Escarole bar to the reception area. The restaurant was smaller than I had expected but also way more glitzy. I'd always assumed it would be homey in a classy sort of way—kind of like the downstairs room at Chez Panisse, where Escarole's chef had started. But Ruth Kallenbach had clearly wanted to make a different kind of statement with her own place.

The first thing I noticed was all the gleaming metal. An enormous chandelier with spiky protrusions made of polished steel dominated the ceiling, and the periphery of the dining area was divided into numerous visually discrete alcoves by screens made from the same material. The walls were painted a pale green and were lined with black-and-white photographs of curvaceous vegetables.

We were seated right away in the main center room next to a large modernist sculpture in green glass. I remarked that it reminded me of some sort of sea creature, like coral or maybe an anemone.

"It's a head of an escarole, you dork," Nichole said, shaking her head with an exaggerated roll of the eyes.

"Oh, yeah. Duh." I opened my menu, pretending to ignore Nichole and Mei's chuckling at my expense.

"So what exactly is escarole, anyway?" Mei asked. "A kind of lettuce, right?"

"It's more bitter, like endive," I said. "But yeah, it is a leafy green and is often used in salads."

Nichole laughed. "Well, aren't you just the culinary expert. It appears Letta was right to give you Gauguin."

"Check it out." Mei held up her menu. "It explains about escarole here." I looked where she was pointing and saw that there was an entire section on the first page dedicated to salad greens with a description of what they all were.

"Yeah. It says that escarole is a kind of chicory. Isn't that what they put in the coffee in New Orleans?" I read on, fascinated. "Did you know that endive, escarole, radicchio, and frisée are all members of the chicory genus?"

"Yeah, Sal, we do, since we're reading the same thing you are."

I punched Nichole lightly in the arm and continued reading, but this time to myself. There were all sorts of enticing appetizers and salads listed: an endive and leek gratin topped with Gruyère cheese and panko; a *salade Lyonnaise* made with frisée, *lardons*, croutons, and a poached egg; sautéed rainbow chard with pine nuts and a balsamic vinaigrette; and, of course, an escarole salad with slices of blood orange and avocado.

As I scanned over the rest of the menu, my eye was caught by a box at the bottom of the page with the following statement:

Escarole is committed to promoting responsible agriculture and food practices. We therefore serve only organically grown produce, free-range/pastured meat and poultry, and sustainable seafood. We also strive to obtain our ingredients from local sources wherever possible.

I set down the menu. Ah yes, the reason I was here. I'd momentarily forgotten, what with the gimlets, the taxi ride, and the excitement of being in the City with Nichole and Mei. But I'd have to start asking questions about Letta at some point during the dinner.

Chapter Fourteen

"Okay, I think I'm going to start with the roasted red pepper soup," Mei said, reading from her menu, "and then have the grilled halibut with porcini and sorrel risotto."

"Well, since I'm here, I'm going to try the escarole salad," Nichole said in turn, "and then I think the pork with apple coulis. Though why they don't just call it apple sauce, which would be *so* much clearer, is beyond me."

They were both looking at me expectantly. From experience, they knew of my difficulties with making up my mind in restaurants. "You guys go ahead and pick a wine," I said. "I promise I'll decide by the time the waitress comes to take our order."

Nichole and Mei conferred over the wine choice, concluding that a Côtes du Rhône would go best with both red meat and fish. Meanwhile, after much agonizing and prompted by the sight of our approaching waitress, I finally settled on the lamb chops with cracked pepper sauce and potato croquettes and the endive and leek gratin for my first course. I'm a sucker for anything with cream in it.

When the waitress returned with our bottle of wine, I decided the time was right to begin my sleuthing. "So um . . . I have a question." *Lame! Miss Marple would have had a much better opening line*, I berated myself, remembering what I'd said to Eric that night at Gauguin. *You can do better than that.* "My aunt was the sous-chef here back in the early eighties, and I was wondering if Ruth Kallenbach might be available to come out and talk to me?"

"Absolutely," the server answered, working the cork off. "She often comes out to chat with patrons." She pulled the cork out with a satisfying *pop* and poured a small portion into Nichole's glass for her to sample. At Nichole's nod of approval, she poured us all a glass, then set the bottle down on the table and turned to go.

"Oh, and you can tell Ruth I'm Letta Solari's niece."

"Will do."

After just a few minutes, Escarole's owner approached our table. I recognized her from the picture on the cookbook in Letta's office: short and slightly plump with dark eyes; an elegant, aquiline nose; and shoulder-length gray hair pulled back into a single braid. I stood up and started to reach out to shake her hand, but she grabbed me in a hug instead.

"I was so sorry to hear about Letta," Ruth said, giving me a final squeeze before releasing her grip. She stepped back and looked me in the face. "You have her eyes."

Blushing—I don't know why—I mumbled, "Uh, thanks. I'm Sally. And these are my friends, Nichole and Mei."

Ruth nodded toward the empty place. "May I?"

"Please."

"It's a good time for me now," she said as she got herself settled, "before the rush really gets going. But I can only stay for a few minutes."

"That's fine. I totally understand. I just had a couple things I wanted to ask you. About Letta. Her death, that is."

Ruth sighed and squeezed my hand again. "How you holding up, dear?"

"Okay, I guess. It's just so freaky, having someone you know—your aunt—be *murdered*." It was still hard to even say that word out loud, and I shuddered a little as I did so. "Look, I don't want to keep you too long, so I'll get to the point." I fumbled for my bag under the chair and pulled out the copies of the letters and the photo. "I wanted to show these to you. I found them in the Escarole cookbook in Letta's office, and so I thought maybe they were there for a reason?"

I handed the letters to her, and she pulled a pair of reading glasses from the pocket of her chef's jacket. A frown grew on her face as she read through them. "So this is what she was talking about," she said when she'd finished.

"Who? Letta?" I asked.

Ruth nodded. "She was here last month and told me about getting some nasty letters." She handed the pages back to me with a shake of the head. "Ugh. Makes me almost embarrassed to be a part of the sustainable food movement. Though whoever wrote these, of course, is way out on the fringe. It's one thing to have those beliefs, and I'll be honest with you, I do share most of them. That's why we're so careful about where we source our food here. But to make threats of violence like that?" She pursed her lips. "I cannot condone such behavior."

"Do you have any idea who might have written them? I mean, it's not like I think you would hang out with people like that," I quickly added. "It's just 'cause of where I found them, in your book, you know. I figure Letta must have had a reason for putting them there."

Ruth shook her head. "I'm afraid I don't. Letta asked me the same thing and even showed me a photo of someone she suspected, but—"

"She did? Really?" Nichole and I exchanged glances. "Can you tell me anything about the photo? 'Cause it might be important. For all we know, the person who wrote these letters is the one who killed her."

"I can do better than that. I can show it to you. Wait a sec." Ruth stood up and headed for the kitchen.

"Ohmygod," I said and reached across the table to grab Nichole's forearm. "This could be the breakthrough I've been hoping for!"

Ruth returned, smartphone in hand, and sat back down. "It's a shot Letta took with her phone of this man who'd been coming into Gauguin and harassing her about her meat sourcing. When I said I didn't recognize him, she asked if I'd be willing to ask around about the guy and sent me the picture. Here, lemme find it." Scrolling through a series of photographs, she finally stopped on one and handed me the phone.

The photo was dark and out of focus, but you could tell it was of the Gauguin dining room, taken through the pickup window in the kitchen, it looked like. The man pictured had shoulder-length, but neatly styled, dark hair—not what my dad would call a "hippie cut." He was wearing a gray, button-down shirt that hung loosely on his slight frame. Another man sat across from him with his back to the camera.

"Javier—that's Letta's sous-chef—told me about a guy that had come to the restaurant a couple times and given her grief for not serving free-range beef or whatever. This must be the guy." I handed the phone to Nichole, who studied the photograph. "He looks to be in his thirties or maybe forties," I said. "Younger than Letta, anyway."

"Probably," said Nichole, passing the phone on to Mei. "But it's hard to tell for sure from this picture."

I turned to Ruth. "But what I'm wondering is, if he was a customer, why wouldn't Letta have had a name and number from the reservation?"

"I asked that same thing, but she said he was apparently a walk-in both times he came." Ruth took the phone back and set it on the table. "She thought maybe that was on purpose, that he intentionally didn't make a reservation so she wouldn't have his information."

The chef had been staring down at the image on the screen, but when she looked up, I saw there were tears in her eyes. "I told Letta she should go to the police if she was frightened, but she didn't want to get them involved, she said. And now I can't stop thinking that if only I'd been a little more persuasive . . ."

"I doubt it would have made any difference," Nichole said. "All the cops would have done is take down her report. There's no way they would have actually opened an investigation based only on a couple kooky letters and an obnoxious customer."

"But it would probably be good if you sent them that photo now." I nodded at the phone.

"Oh, I already did—as soon as I heard about the murder. And I talked to a detective down there—"

"Vargas?" I asked.

"Yes, that's his name. I e-mailed him the photo and told him what Letta had told me." Ruth started to get up. "Look, I should probably be getting back."

"Before you go, there's one other thing I wanted to show you real quick if you don't mind." I handed her the photograph, and she put her glasses back on. "You recognize her by any chance?"

She shook her head. "No. Sorry. Was she a friend of Letta's? It looks like an old picture."

"She owns a farm up in Bolinas, and Letta was buying produce for Gauguin from her. And I think they may have been more than friends."

Ruth raised her eyebrows and took another look at the photo. "Huh. Interesting. Perhaps you should talk to Martine, my pastry chef. She was closer to Letta than I was, and she's been around the Bay Area food scene for decades. She'll be here tomorrow morning if you want to stop by. I'm sure she'd be happy to talk to you."

"Yeah, maybe I will. Thanks." I folded the letters up and put them and the photo back in my bag. "Oh, and any chance you could you send me that photo, too?"

"Sure." As Ruth was typing in my e-mail address, our appetizers arrived. "There, sent." She stood and, giving me another quick hug, headed back to the kitchen.

"Well, that was something, anyway," Nichole observed, digging into her salad. "A real-live clue. So you gonna try to

talk to that pastry chef woman tomorrow? Who knows—
maybe she'll break the case wide open."

"Right, that'll happen." I picked up my fork with a shake
of my head, but one taste of the leek and endive gratin I'd
ordered chased off all thoughts of photographs and clues.
Oozing cheese and cream, it had been topped with *panko* and
placed under the salamander until crispy and golden brown.
Pure, unadulterated joy.

*   *   *

I woke up Saturday morning with a parched mouth and a rag-
ing headache. After our dinner, Mei had suggested a nightcap
at Absinthe just a few blocks away. Standing at the bar, which
was packed four deep with the thirsty postballet and symphony crowd, I had been talked into trying a Sazerac, a sort
of old-fashioned with the addition of a shot of fluorescent-
green Absinthe. Deadly, in other words. Especially after our
predinner gimlets and my share of the two bottles of Côtes du
Rhône we ended up ordering.

The luminous clock face on the side table read six fifteen,
and all was silent except for the occasional car motor rattling
the wood-frame window above my head. I rolled out of the
saggy sofa bed and crept down the hallway, tracing the walls
with my fingers as I made my way through the dark and unfamiliar house to the bathroom. Locating a bottle of Advil in
the medicine cabinet, I downed three pills along with a large
glass of water. I then returned to bed and slept for another
three hours.

I'd arranged to show up at Bolinas Farms the next day
around one, which gave me plenty of time to stop back by

Escarole in the morning. Since Nichole was coming with me up to the farm, she tagged along as well.

As soon as we got out of the car, we could tell that Martine had already been at work for some time. Wafting across the parking lot came the heavenly aroma of freshly baked . . . bread? Pies? Napoleons? It was impossible to say exactly what we were smelling. Probably a combination of all of the above.

I opened the screen door into the kitchen and poked my head inside. A tall, slender woman in chef's whites and a pink baseball cap stood in the corner of the room with her back to us, working with some dough at a long countertop. The stereo was on, blasting out vintage Fleetwood Mac, and she didn't hear when I called her name. I waited for the end of the song and then called out again. "Martine?"

She started and turned around.

"Sorry to scare you."

"That's okay. I just wasn't expecting anybody." I thought I detected a slight foreign accent, but it could have just been a product of my imagination on account of her name. "Can I help you with something?"

I told her who I was and that Ruth had suggested I speak to her concerning my questions about Letta.

"Oh." She shoved a loose lock of blond hair back under her cap, leaving a streak of flour on her forehead. "Sure. Come on in." Nichole followed me into the kitchen, and I introduced her. "I've got to get these rolls formed right away; they won't wait," Martine said, turning back to the counter. "But I can talk to you while I do it."

She started tearing pieces of dough from the large mound before her, deftly rolling them into small, evenly sized balls and setting them on an enormous baking pan lined with parchment paper. "So do they know who did it yet?" she asked, finishing one row and starting another.

I had come to expect this question by now whenever I talked to anybody new about Letta's death and had my stock answer ready.

"It's been ages since I've seen her, you know." Martine hefted the now-full pan, and Nichole and I backed out of her way. Sliding it onto the top shelf of a bakery rack, she pulled out an empty one and started lining it once more with balls of dough. "When she left Escarole to go gallivanting about the Pacific, she pretty much cut off all her old friends. So I don't know how much help I'll be."

"Well, here. Check out this picture, and see if you recognize the woman in it."

Martine ceased her rolling and leaned over to take a look at the photo I was holding before her. "Yeah, as a matter of fact, I do. That's Kate. She used to bartend at some women's bar in the Castro that was popular back in the early 1980s. I don't think it exists anymore." She set the ball of dough down on the pan and scratched her nose. "Wow. I haven't thought about her in *years*. You know, I do believe she and Letta actually hooked up together at some point . . ."

Martine turned to face me, her expression saying, "Oops, maybe I've said too much."

"It's okay. I know about her and Letta. And as a matter of fact, I think they'd recently gotten back together again."

"Whad'ya know." Martine resumed forming her rolls, a pensive look on her face. "I must say I'm a little surprised, because Kate had quite the temper back in the day. A real

Dr. Jekyll and Mr. Hyde, if you know what I mean. I think it might have been one of the reasons they originally broke up. But then again, maybe she's mellowed with age." Martine started to set a ball onto the sheet pan, but then her shoulders tensed, and she turned toward me again. "You don't think . . . Kate?"

"I don't think, or know, anything much at this point. That's why I'm asking everyone all these questions. But I am going up to Marin to see her this afternoon. She's got a farm there now."

"That's a change from bartending. But then I guess all of us have changed a lot from the way we were back in the eighties."

Next I showed her the letters and the photo Ruth had forwarded to my phone. But no luck on either front; Martine couldn't think of anyone in particular who might have sent the letters to Letta or complained about the meat on her menu.

"But then again," she said, "I've never hung out with the hardcore foodie types. And being a baker, I don't get too much flak from animal rights folks. Maybe I would if I used lard—which makes for *such* a better pastry crust—but since we've never been able to find a reliable source of lard from pastured pork, Ruth thinks it best that I stick with butter." She shrugged. "And I guess after seeing those letters, maybe she's right."

Chapter Fifteen

"You got cash for the toll? How much is it these days, anyway?" We were just entering the Presidio and the Golden Gate Bridge—the tips of its rust-red towers lost in the low-hanging clouds—had jumped into view.

"It's like seven bucks now, if you can believe that. Unless you've got FasTrak, and then it's cheaper." Nichole swiveled her body to follow the flight of several ducks that had taken off from the Palace of Fine Arts pond. "But it's only for the other direction," she said, turning back around. "And they don't take cash anymore, in any case. They'll just send you a bill in the mail."

"You're kidding."

"You must not cross the bridge much, 'cause they changed it ages ago. If you don't have FasTrak, they scan your license plate or something and mail you the bill. It's to speed up traffic."

"Well, it doesn't seem to be working that great right now," I observed as we slowed to a crawl. It was a rain-free Saturday morning and sightseers, as well as folks like us fleeing the City for the wilds of Marin County, were out in droves. I braked behind a stopped pickup truck, and as I shifted into first and let out the clutch to creep forward again, the T-Bird stalled.

"Shut up," I said.

"What? I didn't say anything."

"But you were thinking it, I know." I restarted the engine. "I'm still getting used to the stick shift. It's been a while."

"Want me to drive?" Nichole asked, hope in her eyes.

"No way, José."

We picked up pace again once past the vista point on the other side of the bay and cruised along until we hit Sausalito. Luckily, we were turning off the freeway right after the yacht harbor, as I could tell it would have been mighty slow going continuing on up to San Rafael.

Taking the exit for Highway 1, we twisted and turned our way west back toward the coast. In my old Accord, I would have thought this an unpleasant experience, but in the T-Bird, it felt like being a kid on the old Disneyland Autopia ride, whizzing around the corners in our nifty little sports car.

"So that was interesting about Kate having been a bartender," I shouted over the wind.

"Yeah, and in the Castro," Nichole yelled back. "Man, I wish I coulda seen it back then in the eighties before the area got so yuppified."

"Ah yes, those romantic days of AIDS and the ghettoization of gays," I said, prompting Nichole to hit me in the arm. "Ow! No fair accosting the driver."

Once at Muir Beach, since we still had two hours to kill and were only about thirty minutes south of Bolinas, we decided to stop for a bite to eat at the Pelican Inn. This half-timbered Tudor knockoff, Nichole informed me, had been constructed near the site of the landing of Sir Francis Drake's galleon of the same name—a ship he later rechristened the Golden Hind—some four hundred years earlier. "They do nice lunches," she said, "and more important, they have a great selection of British beer."

Still feeling the effects of all the liquor from the night before, I wasn't sure how well a large meal was going to sit. But once I stepped inside and smelled that glorious pub food, my stomach and salivary glands informed me that this was indeed the perfect remedy. I was trying to decide between the shepherd's pie and fish 'n chips when Nichole came to my rescue and suggested we get one of each and share.

"Oh, and *do* let's have pints of Fuller's London Pride," she added with a terrible British accent.

"Bloody brilliant!" I responded in kind.

* * *

Our plates wiped clean with the last remaining soggy chips, we made a quick trip to the ladies' loo, as the waitress called it, and then climbed back in the T-Bird. I noticed that, like me, Nichole undid the top button of her jeans as she settled into her seat.

Searching for the end of her safety belt, which had slipped between the bucket seats, Nichole reached down and came up with a wad of papers and a smashed to-go cup. "Gross. Don't you ever clean your car?"

"Those are not mine," I said, relieving her of the trash, "but Letta could be a bit of a slob." I climbed back out and, as I crossed the parking lot to the dumpster in the corner, unfolded the slick piece of paper on top of the stack. It was a receipt from a Santa Cruz sporting goods store, and I was about to toss it out with the cup and dirty paper napkins when my eye was caught by the name of the item bought.

I returned to the car and handed the paper to Nichole. "Check this out."

"Pepper spray," she read.

"And take a look at the date of purchase: March twenty-ninth, right after Letta got that second threatening letter."

"Whoa."

"Yeah. I guess she really was scared." Settling back down into the bucket seat, I turned to face Nichole. "But you know what's odd? I don't remember reading about them finding any pepper spray in her bag in the crime scene notes Eric gave me. Wouldn't you keep it in your purse if you went to the trouble to buy some?"

"I don't use a purse," Nichole said. "But yeah, if I did, that's where I'd put it."

"But then again, this is Letta we're talking about. She no doubt bought the stuff and then immediately spaced out about it."

We both just sat there for a moment, staring out the windshield at a pair of matronly women holding hands and giggling as they negotiated the steps from the pub down to the parking lot.

"I wonder if it would have made a difference if she'd had it with her," Nichole said after a bit.

"That we'll never know." Shoving the sales receipt into my jeans pocket, I started the engine.

Twenty minutes later, we passed through the driftwood-toned vacation homes of Stinson Beach and then saw the beginning of the Bolinas Lagoon stretching out before us. The tide was well out, and flocks of white egrets were pecking about in the glistening mud flats.

Once past the lagoon, we took a hard left and came back down its other side into the picturesque little community of Bolinas. A surprising number of roads didn't have street signs, and Nichole squinted at the directions I had scribbled the other day. "Does this say turn right *at* the white picket fence or turn *right after* the fence? You have the worst handwriting, girl."

I pulled over and snatched the paper from her. "Lemme look. *At* the fence." Handing the directions back, I put the car in reverse. We followed the single-lane road for about a half mile and then turned right again at the hand-painted wooden sign for Bolinas Farms, bumping our way up a dirt driveway until we came to a row of large greenhouses.

"This is where she said to meet." I switched off the engine as a huge, white dog bounded up, barking ferociously. Unsure whether it was safe to emerge, we remained in the car.

Almost immediately, however, a woman in a blue long-sleeve T-shirt and brown pants stuffed into black rubber boots emerged from the first greenhouse and called to the dog. "Xena! Come!"

I recognized her as an older version of the woman in the photo but with gray hair. The dog immediately ceased its barking, ran to Kate's side, and sat down, panting happily. *What a good dog*, I thought.

She took in the car. Of course she would know it as Letta's, I realized. But she didn't say anything about it.

"You must be Sally." Kate strode forward as I opened the door and stepped gingerly onto the muddy road. Nichole and I shook hands with her, and I told her I was impressed with the dog's obedience and its prowess as a watchdog.

"That's her job. She's a Great Pyrenees, and they've been bred to do that for centuries. I have her mostly to guard a small flock of sheep I keep, but she's also useful for keeping out intruders of the human variety." She leaned over to scratch Xena behind the ears and got a slobbery kiss in return. "In reality, though, she's a big sweetie."

We all stood there looking at the dog, and I tried to think of what to say. Nichole sensibly started with the obvious: "So how big is your spread?"

"It's small: only seventeen acres. But I grow all my crops pretty intensively, so I manage to get a fair amount of yield. And these new greenhouses help a lot. They extend the growing season to pretty much all year round. I'm certainly not getting rich, but I do okay." She turned and started up a gravel path. "C'mon, let's go sit where we can talk."

We followed her over to the other side of the greenhouse, where a picnic table sat under a large live oak tree. Xena ran on ahead and lay down in the shade, and we three humans got comfortable around the table, which had a pitcher and three glasses set on it. Kate picked up the pitcher. "You want some sun tea?"

Nichole and I both accepted the offer, and I immediately drank down half my glass. "How'd you end up in the farming business, anyway?" I asked, wiping away an errant dribble with the back of my hand. "Martine, the pastry chef at Escarole, said you used to be a bartender back in the eighties."

"Yeah. That was a bit of a change, eh?" Kate chuckled. "But it isn't really all that strange. I actually grew up on this farm, right up there." She pointed to a white Victorian house in the distance that had been hidden by the greenhouses when we drove up. "I didn't appreciate it at the time, though. I mean, I liked it fine when I was a little kid, but as a teenager, I thought it was really boring living on a farm. And then, when I came out my senior year of high school . . . Well, you can't imagine, but being a lesbian in Bolinas back in the mid-sixties, before the poets and hippies moved up here—it wasn't much fun, I can assure you."

Nichole nodded sagely, though I knew damn well she hadn't even been born till the end of the following decade.

"So I hightailed it down to San Francisco as soon as I finished high school." Kate lifted her glass, contemplated its contents for a moment, and then absently took a sip.

"Is that when you met Letta?" I prompted her.

"That wasn't till much later. I spent about twenty-five years in the City—first as a student at the city college and then working a bunch of different jobs. I eventually ended up as a bartender. Turns out, that wasn't such a great idea." She laughed. "I liked the bar scene a lot. Too much. Anyway, that's when I met Letta." Kate set her glass down and turned it slowly in a circle. "I wanted to come to the funeral, you know. But I felt like I couldn't . . . or shouldn't . . ." She trailed off, staring at her glass of tea.

As if on cue, Xena stood up abruptly and shook, the jangle of her chain collar ringing out in the silence that followed this last sentence. The big dog slowly stretched—front legs first, then the back—and trotted over to where Kate was sitting, shoving her great muzzle into the hand dangling over the edge of the table. Kate smiled sadly and obligingly stroked her head.

"Look," I said after a minute, "I know I can't possibly understand all you must be going through right now, but I want you to know that I do get it to some extent 'cause I was close to Letta, too. Or at least I thought I was," I added, trying to keep my voice steady. "I gotta say it kinda hurts that she kept from me this whole part of her life"—I motioned with my hands to indicate the greenhouses and surrounding hills—"something so very important to her, yet she didn't trust me with it, and I didn't find out until too late, until after she was gone."

Kate shook her head. "I don't think she ever told anyone about us. The thought of people knowing terrified her." She reached over and took my hand. "But she should have told you. She used to talk about you a lot, and I know it would have made her supremely happy to have your blessing."

She gave my hand a squeeze and then let go. "I guess you'd like to hear the whole story. That's why you drove all the way up here, after all. And I've got to admit it feels good to finally be able to talk about it." Kate laid her hands on the table, fingers extended, and studied them. "Okay," she said and exhaled in a long stream, like a gymnast preparing to mount the parallel bars. "So Letta used to come into the bar where I worked. A women's bar," she added with a quick glance at Nichole.

"Which one?" Nichole asked in return.

"It was called Diana's Moon. I know—pretty heavy-handed." Kate shrugged. "But this was the early eighties, after all. It's long gone; there's probably a sushi shop there now."

"More likely a Starbucks," Nichole countered.

Kate slapped her knee with a chuckle. "No doubt."

I smiled too but for a different reason. I *knew* it had been a good idea to bring along Nichole.

"Anyway . . ." Kate cleared her throat. "Letta and I eventually got together. It must have been around 1981. Or maybe '82? And it was a lot of fun—while it lasted. Which wasn't all that long."

"Why? What happened?" Nichole asked.

Kate didn't answer right away. Instead, she frowned and took another sip of her tea. Nichole and I waited while she carefully set the glass down on the table and licked her lips.

"I came home from work unexpectedly one day. I think I must have been sick or something. And . . . oh jeez, this sounds like something from a daytime soap." She ran a hand through her gray forelock. "And so I find Letta in the bedroom . . . with some *guy*."

Nichole's eyes got wide. "No shit!"

Kate nodded. "I didn't stick around to hear her excuses. I just walked right out of the apartment and came back to get my stuff the next day, when I knew she'd be at work. And that was that. I barely saw her again. She stopped coming into the bar, and I certainly wasn't going to go and seek her out. Then the next thing I hear about her—this must have been about five years later—she's split for the South Pacific."

"Wow." I couldn't believe what I was hearing about my aunt. Just how much *was* there she hadn't told me? "But then, uh, you two got back together again recently . . ."

"Yeah, that's right. Which brings us back to the question you asked earlier—about my being a farmer—'cause the two things are actually related.

"About fifteen years ago, my dad died, and my mom decided to sell the farm. She was too old to run it anymore and didn't think me or my brother would be interested in keeping it going. But I'd had enough of the city life by then and told her I'd like to come back up here and run the operation. That worked out fine until my mom passed on six years ago, and my brother and I inherited the farm jointly. He's down in LA and has no interest whatsoever in farming. Since I couldn't afford to buy out his half, he was insisting that we sell the place."

"Common story," I said. "I think that's one reason there are so few family farms left around."

"Yep." Kate's mouth tightened. "It really pissed me off, 'cause I knew he didn't need all the money up front, and I was willing to pay him over time." She shook her head. "Anyway, so I did some investigation, and it turns out there's this land trust organization here in Marin—MALT is its name—and they agreed to purchase what's called an agricultural conservation easement on the property. In other words, they pay me a lump sum to ensure that I keep the land as farmland rather than, say, sell it to a subdivider."

"Yeah," Nichole chimed in, "I've heard about those land trusts. They're awesome."

"So I was able to use that money to buy out my brother and keep the farm after all."

"What all do you grow?" I asked.

"Oh, the usual for this region: broccoli, green beans, brussels sprouts, leafy greens, beets, leeks and onions, herbs. That field over there was just planted with mesclun and arugula." Kate gestured toward the freshly plowed hillside beyond the greenhouses, where I could make out tiny green shoots poking up from the reddish-brown dirt. "And I've got a few fruit trees—cherry and plum—up by the house.

"Anyway, getting back to why you're here, so last summer, I was helping some friends put on a farm-to-table dinner up in Tomales Bay, and who shows up but—"

"Let me guess: Letta," I filled in.

"You got it. And I just couldn't help it. There I was, loaded down with a case of heirloom tomatoes and Little Gem lettuces, gaping at her from afar as she chatted up one of the gals who was hosting the event, and I realized, after all those years—and after what she had done to me . . ." Kate shook her head impatiently. "I still carried the goddamn torch."

Chapter Sixteen

Kate fell silent, and Nichole and I said nothing, letting her take her time. An oak leaf fluttered down into my glass, and I picked it out and tossed it aside. In the quiet, I became aware of the background sounds: birds chattering in the tree above us, the faraway buzz of machinery, Xena's sigh as she rolled over onto her side.

After a minute, Kate sat up, stretching her back, and then leaned forward again, elbows on the table. "It was funny," she finally said, continuing her account of the farm-to-table dinner, "because the woman Letta was talking to brought her over to me to introduce us. When Letta saw that it was me, she shrieked and gave me a big hug, acting as if everything was all fine between us. And I guess it was. The passage of time will do that, sometimes.

"She told me all about her restaurant, and when I told her that I was now running my parents' farm, she insisted that she start buying produce from me. I didn't object, even though it did seem a little crazy for me to sell to a place all the way down in Santa Cruz. I liked the idea that I'd have an excuse to see her again on a regular basis. And I think she had the same thought."

The picnic table was now in full sunlight, and Kate pulled off her long-sleeve T-shirt to reveal a red knit tank top underneath. At the sudden movement, Xena awoke and moved back into the shade.

"It wasn't very long before we started . . . I guess 'seeing each other' is the appropriate euphemism. But Letta made me promise to keep it a secret, especially from her family."

And from Tony, I was thinking. But then I wondered if there was any chance Letta might have told him. And whether she'd told Kate about Tony, for that matter.

Kate glanced over at me. "I guess that didn't work very well—her keeping it a secret."

"No. I mean, yes, it did. I only just learned about it the day I called you."

"How'd you find out?"

"Javier, Letta's sous-chef. He's the guy who walked in on you in Letta's office."

"Yeah, I remember. She was pretty freaked out about that."

"Well, I gather he did keep it a secret, like she asked him to. He only told me because I was curious about Letta buying produce from you, and so I was giving him the third degree."

"That's good, I guess." Kate removed a pack of Camel lights from her pants pocket. "You mind?"

Nichole and I both shook our heads, and she lit one up. "I don't smoke all that much, actually. Letta hated it when I did—said it made me and my clothes stink. But it's an old habit I picked up back when I tended bar." She tilted her head back and exhaled a thin stream of smoke straight up, toward the live oak branch overhanging the picnic table.

"So"—I cleared my throat—"I know this sounds kind of hokey and melodramatic, but do you have any idea who might have wanted to hurt Letta or why anyone would have done . . . what they did?"

Kate didn't answer immediately, and I wondered if she'd even heard my question. But after a moment, she gave a quick shake of the head, still staring up at the sunlight filtering through the foliage above. "No, I don't. I really don't."

I took a deep breath and hoped my next question wouldn't completely destroy any trust I had gained so far. "Well, any chance you were down there—at Gauguin or in Santa Cruz— around the time when she was killed?"

She dropped her gaze to rest on me and raised the cigarette to her lips.

"Because," I stuttered, "you know, you might have seen something while you were there."

"Or maybe noticed if Letta's mood was weird or something?" Nichole added, doing her best to help me out.

"Look, if you want to know where I was 'at the time of the murder,' as they say, just come out and ask it, for chrissake." She took another quick drag from her cigarette and puffed out a plume of smoke.

"Okay," I said. "So where were you?"

"Here, at the farm. And several of my guys can confirm it if you need proof. The last time I saw Letta was the end of the week before she was killed, when I brought down my produce delivery. I'm sure you can find it in the books." She tapped her forefinger impatiently on the picnic table. "Any other questions?"

"Uh, actually, I do have another." Rummaging through my bag, I extracted the two letters. "Here. Take a look at these. I found them in an Escarole cookbook in Letta's office at the restaurant."

Kate read them through. "Huh" was all she said.

"They don't surprise you?" I asked.

"Well, they are rather vitriolic, but then again, feelings do run pretty hot for some people on this subject."

"You sympathize with them," I said. It was a statement rather than a question.

"On some issues I do, yes. And I told Letta I did."

"You knew about these letters?"

"Yeah. And I told her that although I didn't agree with their tone or their threatening manner, I did think they had a point."

I picked up the first letter. "What's CAFO mean?"

"Concentrated animal feeding operation. That's where about 99.9 percent of the beef cattle in this country spend the last six months of their lives." Kate reached for a coffee can that was sitting at her feet, set it on the table, and tapped the ash from her cigarette into it. "Did you know that down in Kern County, the *average* number of steers in the feedlots is over ten thousand? And not only are they jam-packed into pens where they have to stand knee deep in manure, but they're fed a steady diet of corn, which they can't even digest." Her tone had become pedantic and slightly testy, like a teacher lecturing a not-so-bright student. "Cattle are ruminants, grass eaters, so the corn ends up giving them gas and makes them bloated and sick. So what do the feedlots do? They just pump 'em up with antibiotics as a short-term fix-all." Kate took one last puff from her Camel and then crushed it out with a vengeance. "And that's what Letta was serving her customers."

After this diatribe, I was hesitant to ask my next question, but I wanted to know: "And what's a farrowing crate?"

Kate gave me a hard look. "You own Gauguin now you said, right?"

"Uh-huh."

"Well, you should do your homework and learn about all this 'cause it's important."

Nichole again jumped in to my rescue: "It's like a stall where pigs give birth and nurse their babies, isn't it?"

"That's right. Except the word 'stall' is way too generous. In most commercial pig farms, sows used for breeding are kept for their entire lives in cages that are just two feet wide. You know how big a full-grown pig is, right?" She looked at me as she said this. "About two feet wide. They have just barely enough room to stand up and lie down. No room to turn around or scratch or do anything except be a baby-making machine. When you think how smart pigs are . . ." Kate shook her head. "It makes me sick."

"I had no idea," I mumbled. "Why would they need to do that?"

"Because the sows would fight otherwise. Not if they were pastured, they wouldn't. But when they're crammed into warehouses under artificial lighting and can't act like, well, pigs—you know, nesting and having their own natural hierarchy among themselves?—then they'll fight. Chickens are the same way. But it's our unnatural way of raising them that causes the problems."

I digested this information. I knew pigs were supposed to be smart—smarter than dogs, even. What horrible lives they must have. But would I be willing to give up baby-back ribs and Mortadella sausage? And bacon?

"I try to buy free-range meat," Nichole said. "But it's not always that easy to find, even in San Francisco—especially pork and chicken."

"So go without if you can't find it. That's what I do. I told Letta I thought she should switch to grass-fed and pastured meat, but she wouldn't go for it. She was afraid the higher prices would drive off her customers."

"Well, you're apparently not the only one who was pressuring her to change her menu. This guy was, too." I pulled out my phone and found the photo Letta had taken from the pickup window at Gauguin. "Here. You recognize him?"

Kate shaded the screen with her hand and peered down at the picture. "No," she said with a shake of the head. "He doesn't look familiar."

I dropped the phone back in my bag. "'Cause I think Letta was pretty freaked out by the two events—getting those letters and then that guy coming in and harassing her."

"She never mentioned him to me. Did he actually threaten her, you think?"

"I dunno. But I was at Escarole last night, and Ruth—you know, the chef Letta used to work for—she told me Letta seemed shaken up by it all. And I know she went out and bought some pepper spray right after she got that second letter."

Kate frowned. "I wonder why she never told me about the guy."

Maybe because of how unsympathetic you were about the anonymous letters, I thought. But I left this unsaid. Instead, I nodded toward the two letters sitting on the table. "You have any idea who might have sent those?"

"Nope," Kate responded, picking one up. But the narrowing of her eyes as she examined it made me wonder if maybe she did have an idea.

She set the paper back down. "These look like copies. Can you leave them with me? I know some folks who might know, and I can ask around."

"Yeah, sure. I've got another set. Thanks."

Kate folded the letters and shoved them into her back pants pocket. "You know," she said, "there's something else I should tell you about Letta and me. You haven't heard the whole story yet." She fiddled with the pinkie ring on her right hand, and Nichole and I waited for her to go on.

"So early last month this guy shows up at the farm—a real dick, all posturing and macho and stuff. He pulls up in front of the cold storage shed as I'm loading boxes of broccoli raab and cauliflower into my truck for a delivery, rolls down the window, and asks if I'm Kate. I say, 'Who wants to know?' and he answers, 'I just wanted to get a good look at you.' And then he gives me the once-over in this really disgusting way."

"Yuck," Nichole offered.

But I was thinking, *Tony*?

"Yeah. Agreed," said Kate. "But I figured he wouldn't get out of the car, since Xena was with me, and as you've seen, she can be pretty intimidating. It was weird, though. I mean, I'm used to occasionally getting shit from guys who have a problem with me being a lesbian, an' all but having one actually go to the trouble of seeking me out at the farm—that was a new one. I found out later he'd been asking about me down at the lower gate, and one of my field hands had told him where to find me." Kate shook her head. I imagined the worker would think twice before directing strange men her way again.

"Anyway, when I told Letta about it a few days later, I just expected her to be annoyed and disgusted like I was, but she reacted in this odd way, asking me to describe the guy and his car. Kind of heavyset, I said, with dark hair and a big ol' Giants tattoo on his forearm. Probably in his fifties? He had one of those really loud muscle cars with big wheels. And then I told her I thought it was funny 'cause he almost got stuck in the mud as he left."

I exhaled in relief, as Letta no doubt must have done, at this point in Kate's story: Tony drove a pickup, not a muscle car.

"But she didn't laugh like I expected her to. Instead, she just stared out the window after hearing my description and wouldn't meet my eye. I said I thought she was acting really weird, and she got all silent and didn't want to talk about it. And so then I just said, 'Fine,' and left the room to go do something else. But after a few minutes, she came and found me and said we had to talk. She'd been feeling guilty, she told me, and the episode about the guy had made her realize that she was starting to get paranoid about it all. 'About all what?' I asked. And then she told me about being involved with this guy named Tony."

Kate lit another cigarette, shaking the match out impatiently. "I was dumbfounded. I'd had no idea she'd been seeing anyone else. Stupid, *stupid*!" She smacked her hand on the table at the repeat of the word, startling Nichole and me, as well as the sleeping dog.

"Letta insisted it wasn't that serious, that she had been planning on breaking it off with him and would do it the next time she saw him. But at that point, I realized I didn't care whether she did or not, that I couldn't take it anymore. She'd already done this once before. And to have it be a *man—again.*"

Her eyes, staring down at the wooden table top, had a steely, hard look to them—kinda scary, actually. But what was even more scary was that, from the set of her jaw and the white knuckles on the hand holding her Camel, I could tell she was actually trying to minimize how enraged she felt about what Letta had done. I decided to play a card.

"You know, Letta was actually engaged to Tony. I just found out."

Kate turned her gaze to me. I could see a solitary vein on her temple that I hadn't noticed before. And then she just exploded.

"I *knew* it!" With one swift movement, she stood up and swept her hand across the table, taking precise aim at her glass of iced tea. I gaped as it flew through the air and smashed against the trunk of the oak tree, sending liquid and shards scattering at the feet of the surprised Xena.

Kate moved slowly to pick up the pieces as Nichole and I sat there stunned.

Chapter Seventeen

Nichole and I left the farm in a bit of a daze. Although Kate apologized for her outburst, she also clammed up afterward, making it clear she just wanted us to get the hell out of there. So we did, after a few perfunctory thanks-for-your-helps and let-me-know-if-you-find-out-anythings.

"Well, that was certainly not how I envisioned our conversation would end," Nichole remarked as we made our way back down the coast to San Francisco. "Why the hell did you drop that bombshell about Letta's engagement, anyway? At least you could have done it a with a little more tact."

"But that would have defeated the purpose. I couldn't stop thinking, the whole time Kate was talking, about what Martine had said about her having 'quite the temper.' And I just figured if I surprised her with the news, we might see, you know, the 'real' Kate. It just came to me as an idea."

"An idea that could have landed me in the emergency room with glass splinters in my eyeballs."

"Yeah. Sorry about that. But I wanted to see how she'd react, especially given how belligerent she'd been about the

159

whole free-range meat thing. It got me wondering whether she's just one of those vocal types or if she has an actual violent streak as well."

"I think you got the answer to your question." Nichole turned to look out the window. The ocean had a golden tint to it in the afternoon light, but the sun was about to disappear behind a thick layer of clouds sitting just above the water. "You think she might have done it?"

I just shrugged. "Hell if I know." But I had been wondering the same thing.

*　*　*

My dad does a spaghetti Bolognese at Solari's that's a pretty hot seller, but it's nothing compared to Nonna's Sunday gravy. When I say "gravy," I don't mean the kind you'd serve over fried chicken and mashed potatoes. This is Italian gravy, and Nonna's is the very best there is.

For as long as I can remember, the family has gathered at her house for dinner every Sunday at two o'clock, and the menu has never varied: an antipasto course of prosciutto and salami, marinated vegetables, and provolone and mozzarella cheese; a first course of spaghetti with Nonna's gravy and chewy Italian bread to wipe the plate clean; then the meat that had been braised to make the gravy, served along with sautéed broccoli and a green salad; and for dessert, an enormous bowl of tiramisu doused with coffee and Marsala wine and dusted with powdered cocoa.

A proper gravy takes hours to make, and Nonna gets going as soon as she wakes up on Sunday. She starts by heating olive oil in the hefty enameled Dutch oven that belonged to her mother and then browns the meat—a combination of beef chuck roast, pork chops, and sweet Italian sausages—to ensure a good color and rich flavor. Next she adds garlic and onion to the pot and cooks this with some tomato paste until aromatic and then dumps in several cans of Italian plum tomatoes, a half bottle of Chianti, some chopped herbs, and a large spoonful of sugar. She lets this all simmer for several hours while she attends Sunday mass. When the meat is so tender it's falling apart at the touch of a fork, the gravy is done.

Although she allows me to watch her prepare it, Nonna won't let me lift a finger to help with the Sunday gravy. But now that she's in her eighties, she does grudgingly suffer my assistance with such menial tasks as boiling the pasta and frying the broccoli.

At a quarter past one on the day following my trip up to Bolinas, I therefore found myself at Nonna's house, shredding iceberg lettuce for the Sunday dinner salad.

I was replaying in my mind the meeting with Kate— and the startling end to the conversation—when the kitchen door opened and Eric breezed in and planted a pair of *baci* on Nonna's cheeks. Nonna adores Eric, and she just can't understand why we haven't yet gotten married.

"He's a lawyer and so handsome, too!" she's told me countless times. "Why you two no settle down and give your *nonna* some *bambini*?" Since we still hang out together (and she can't fathom a couple breaking up and remaining friends), she doesn't get that this is simply not going to happen.

"My God, it's hot in here," Eric exclaimed, fanning himself melodramatically. "Why don't you open a window?" He stuck two fingers under his collar, pulling it away from his neck. I'd assumed it was hot flashes making me feel so warm, but as he said this, I noticed the steam from the simmering gravy coursing down the windows. The rain had returned last night, and the contrast between the brisk, blustery outdoors and the hot, humid kitchen when he came in must have been intense.

Eric ripped a hunk of bread from the loaf sitting on the kitchen table and dunked it in the gravy pot, prompting Nonna to swat at him affectionately with a dish towel. "You gon' spoil your appetite."

"I brought some wine for dinner," he said by way of an answer, holding out a bottle of Dolcetto d'Alba.

"No, no, no." Nonna wagged a forefinger at him. "This a special occasion—the first Sunday dinner since Letta's gone. We'll drink Salvatore's wine. You go down and bring us up a bottle, okay?"

Eric looked at me and mouthed a silent groan. "Maybe we can pour my wine into an old bottle of his, and she won't notice?" he suggested as we descended the stairs into the dank cellar. Although my namesake grandfather had been fiercely proud of his winemaking ability, the products of his labors were, at best, what Eric would describe as "plonk."

"C'mon, his Zin isn't all *that* bad."

Eric just made a face. "Why's she waxing so sentimental about Sunday dinner without Letta, anyway? I don't remember her ever even being at one."

"True, she didn't come that often. But now that she's no longer here, well, let's just say memories often get readjusted to suit the needs of the ones still living."

I fumbled for the light switch at the bottom of the stairs, and we looked around the room. As a kid, I'd had a love-hate relationship with my grandparents' cellar. I was fascinated by all the jars of colorful fruit and vegetables stored in the cupboards, by the bunches of rosemary and basil, and by the strands of garlic and onions strung from the rafters. But I was simultaneously frightened of the place—the dark, cobweb-filled corners; the strange, musty smells; the menacing-looking scythes and other ancient gardening tools hanging from rusty nails on the walls.

Now that Nonno was gone and Nonna was too old to do a lot of canning, the cellar wasn't used much anymore, and the stockpile of foodstuffs was rapidly diminishing. But the redwood shelves were still lined with jars of beans and tomatoes, preserved lemons, Olallieberry jam, pickled sweet peppers, and, of course, Nonno's wine.

"What's that doohickey?" Eric asked, pointing toward an odd-shaped tool hanging next to a pair of shears. It had a long handle like a shovel, but its business end consisted of five curved prongs of varying lengths with small spade-like tips. From the number of dust-encrusted cobwebs blanketing it, the tool had clearly not been moved in years.

"I dunno. Some thingamajig for crushing grapes?" I answered.

"No way. It's more like a rake gone all satanic. I know, it's a . . . you know, a . . . a whatchamacallit."

"A thingamabob?" I jumped into the game with glee, relishing the reprieve from obsessing about Letta's murder.

"Yeah, a gizmo."

"No, more like a doodad."

"A whassis."

"A gadget."

"Sal, I've got it. It's a dumaflochie for—"

"*Dumaflochie?*" I interrupted. "No fair! You can't just make them up."

"I didn't. My cousin says that all the time."

"Yeah, sure." I was not convinced. "Okay, here's my final answer. It is most definitely . . . a widget!"

"Ha!" Eric slapped his knee. This had been another favorite legalism—after "open and notorious," that is—we'd learned as first-year students. I remember being surprised by the number of companies our professor discussed in contracts class that manufactured "widgets" and wondering what exactly this popular item could be, only to be abashed when Nichole finally clued me in as to the meaning of the word.

Eric admitted defeat. "Okay, you win."

We turned our attention to the rack of wine bottles. Eric pulled one out at random and brushed off the dust and cobwebs in an attempt to decipher the faded, handwritten label.

"Zin '92. Gotta be vinegar by now." He replaced the bottle and tried another that looked a little cleaner. "Nineteen ninety-nine—also a Zin."

"He didn't make much wine after then," I said. "That's probably about as recent as we're going to get."

"Okay, we'll go with this one."

I turned to head back up the stairs, but he stopped me with a hand on my arm.

"Sal, wait. I wanted to ask how it went yesterday, but I didn't think I should in front of your *nonna*."

"Oh, man," I said and sighed. It had been a short-lived reprieve.

We sat down at the bottom of the stairway, and I filled Eric in on what had happened with Kate: about the farm, her lecture to Nichole and me about meat, the mystery man who came to harass her, her history with Letta, and most important, her reaction when I'd told her about Letta being engaged to Tony.

"Did she know who the guy was in that photo Letta took?" he asked when I'd finished. "Or who wrote the letters?"

"She said no, but I'm not sure she was being completely honest."

His eyebrows raised. "So ze plot thickens."

"Playing Hercule Poirot to my Miss Marple, are we?" I reached out and broke a sprig of rosemary off the faded bunch tied to the beam next to the stairs, rolled it between my fingers, and raised it to my nose—virtually no scent. "She did ask to keep the letters, though, and said she'd ask around."

"Nevertheless, I think we need to add her to the list of possibilities. Who all is there at this point, anyway?"

I tossed the crushed rosemary on the floor and started ticking people off with my fingers. "Well, number one has got to be Javier, I guess. Though I still can't believe he could have done it. And what would have been his motive, anyway? You know: means, opportunity, and motive?"

Eric shook his head. "You've been watching too many cop shows, Sal. Don't you remember Roberts's crim law class? The three elements of murder are, one, a killing; two, with malice aforethought; and three, without legal justification."

"Yeah, but evidence of means, opportunity, and motive is admissible to prove those elements, right?"

"True," Eric conceded. "And Javier clearly had the means and opportunity: access to the knife cabinet and knife, and he was the last one seen at the restaurant that night. But juries are often most swayed by the existence of a motive. So okay, what would have been his motive?"

"Well, we know he was in love with Letta. How 'bout jealousy? Of Tony . . . and of Kate too?"

"Maybe. It's a common enough motive, God knows."

"Though I can see his killing Tony for jealousy way before Letta," I added. The image of Javier raising his chef's knife against the woman he loved, his mentor and savior, simply did not compute in my brain.

Eric drummed his fingers on his knee and mused. "Any chance he thought he might get the restaurant if she died? Money is the number-two motive after love, I'd say."

I remembered back to when I'd talked to Javier about the fate of Gauguin after Letta's death—the interest in his eyes when I'd raised the subject and how his shoulders had slumped when he'd learned she'd given it to me.

"He did seem a little, shall we say, deflated when I told him I'd inherited it," I admitted. "But I can't believe he'd murder her based on a mere possibility that she'd give it to him."

"Maybe she said something to him at some time that suggested she'd put him in her will."

"Perhaps." The subject was starting to annoy me. "Let's move on. Tony seems like the next most obvious suspect. They always say that murders of passion are most often committed by boyfriends and husbands."

"Or girlfriends . . ."

"Yeah, but we'll get to her in a minute. The only motive I can think of for Tony would be jealousy—"

"You don't think he might have hoped to inherit Gauguin?" Eric broke in.

This hadn't occurred to me, but they had been engaged, after all. Could that be why he had asked her to marry him? To get her to change her will? I thought back to his reaction when my dad had told him I was getting the restaurant. "I suppose that's possible."

"And as to jealousy," Eric went on, "didn't you say he's the one who told you Javier was in love with Letta?"

"Uh-huh. But he seemed to just think it was funny."

Eric raised his eyebrows again. "She did spend most of her waking hours with Javier. And they shared a passion for cooking and the restaurant and all. I could see a guy becoming jealous in that situation. I wonder . . ." He went back to his finger drumming. "Any chance he knew about Kate? You say he didn't fit the description of the guy who came up to her farm?"

"It didn't seem like it. I'm pretty sure he doesn't have a muscle car. And from what Kate said, Letta didn't seem to think it was Tony. But I guess I should probably check if he has a Giants tattoo on his arm. I know he's a big baseball fan, and he did have a Giants World Series pennant on the wall. And I suppose he could have borrowed the car, or maybe he has one hidden away in his garage."

"Okay." Eric tapped a finger on his front tooth. "Now for the farm woman, Kate. She sounds like a loose cannon to me."

"Yeah. She certainly exhibited violent tendencies yesterday. And as for motive, there's the fact that Letta's cheated on her—twice, now—and both times with a guy, which seemed to really piss her off."

"And hurt her too, no doubt, which may be the stronger of the two emotions. At least in my experience as a prosecutor, I've noticed that often to be the case."

"I've also got to wonder about the whole animal rights thing, too," I said. "I mean, you could tell she's pretty fanatical about it all. I can't help wondering if maybe she's the one who wrote those letters."

"That would be a pretty weird thing to do, don't you think? Sending threatening letters to your lover?"

"Stranger things have happened," I said. "Just look at what Alfredo did to Letta's namesake in *La Traviata*." We'd seen this opera together several years earlier—a local, somewhat amateurish performance.

"Sure, in Opera Land people will do all sorts of crazy things. And anyway, he was wildly jealous of Violetta. Wait!" Eric sat up straight. "Did the letters come before or after Kate found out about Tony?"

"The first came months before; the second, I'm not sure—around the same time, I think."

"Oh. Dang."

"Yeah." I chewed my lip and thought for a minute. "Okay, assuming Kate didn't write the letters, then whoever did is suspect number . . ."

"That would make four. And if the man in the photo Letta took at Gauguin is a different person, then we have five. And there's also that guy who visited Kate. Could he be the man in Letta's photo, I wonder?"

"No. Not unless Kate is lying, that is. She said she didn't recognize him. So the guy in the muscle car would be number six. Though I'm not sure exactly how his visiting Kate makes him a suspect for Letta's murder. It was Kate he was harassing. Plus, you gotta ask, what was that all about, anyway? I mean, why would some mystery man suddenly show up at her farm? It makes me wonder if maybe she simply made the whole thing up. Though again, I'm not sure why she would."

I stared across the basement at the tools hanging on the wall and then started to giggle.

"What?" Eric asked.

I nodded toward the thingamabob/whassis/widget. "I think we'd better add Nonna to the list."

Eric followed my gaze. "Oh man, you are so right," he said with a laugh. "Just check out the blades on that thing. Hmmm . . . Now what would be her motive?"

"She did always like Dad best. And then there's the fact that Letta hardly ever came to Sunday dinner—"

I stopped speaking when the door at the top of the stairway opened, throwing a bright shaft of light down upon us.

"Ohhh . . . jus' look at these two!" We turned around to see Nonna's short frame silhouetted by the light with my dad standing behind her. "So sad to stop your lovey-dovey," Nonna said with a broad smile, "but your *papà* is now here, and is time for *mangiare*."

"Just don't let her handle any knives," Eric whispered to me. "You can cut the bread, okay?" Grinning, he grabbed the bottle of Salvatore's wine, and we stood and climbed back up the stairs into the bright, aroma-filled kitchen.

Chapter Eighteen

I don't think it's an exaggeration to say that I'm an excellent waitress. I can remember every order for a table of eight without having to write anything down, juggle five plates of chicken cacciatore without spilling a single drop, and muster a winning and charming smile with even the most truculent customers. After all, I've been waiting tables since I was a teenager.

But that doesn't mean I have to like it.

For Monday's lunch shift, however, that's what I was doing at Solari's. As manager of the front of the house, I was usually able to schedule staff in such a way that I wasn't one of the servers, but Elena had covered for me over the last weekend, and now it was payback time.

Setting down two orders of pasta primavera at table twelve, I asked if they needed anything else and then headed back to the steam tables to ladle out a bowl of minestrone for the woman at table five.

But my mind was not on the job. As Sean and I cleared away the mess of bread crumbs and spattered Bolognese sauce that a table with three small children had created, I couldn't help thinking about the list of suspects Eric and I had come up with the previous afternoon. The three mystery people, in particular, were driving me bonkers. Who the hell had visited Kate at the farm? And who had sent those horrible letters? And what about that guy who came to Gauguin? Letta had obviously been concerned about him, enough to take his picture and show it to Ruth. And then she had gone out and bought a can of pepper spray. Could any of these three be connected with the murder?

On Tuesday morning, after spending much of the previous night staring at the ceiling unable to sleep, I finally decided I couldn't stand it anymore. I had to take some kind of decisive action. Grabbing my phone, I punched in Kate's number.

"Hullo!" she said. It was almost a shout, and I could hear the loud whine of machinery in the background.

"Hi, Kate. It's Sally."

"Who? Sorry, but it's hard to hear!"

"I said, it's Sally! But I guess maybe now's not a good time to talk?"

"Yeah, I'm right in the middle of something here. Can I call you back later?"

"Sure, no problem."

"Okay, great. Bye." There was a click, and the line went quiet. I replaced the receiver with a dejected sigh.

* * *

It was almost six and I had settled down at home with a drink after doing some grocery shopping when Kate called back. I'd sent her an e-mail earlier in the afternoon explaining why I'd called and saying that I'd be free to talk that evening.

"Sorry to bother you earlier while you were working," I said, walking over to the CD player to turn down the volume on R.E.M.'s "Losing My Religion." (If that had been a vinyl record, the grooves would have been well worn by now, given the hundreds of times I played it during college.)

"No problem. It's just that I was in the middle of spraying the beets in the greenhouse, and it's pretty loud with the air compressor on."

"You spray your vegetables? I thought all your stuff was organic."

"I do, and it is. We were just applying sulfur, which I can assure you is totally kosher, organically. It's for the goddamn powdery mildew that's trying its best to make my life miserable."

"Ah. Right." I went back into the kitchen to refresh— gotta love that euphemism—my glass of Jim Beam. "So the reason I called earlier, as I said in my e-mail, was 'cause I was wondering if maybe you'd had any luck finding out who sent those letters to Letta?"

Kate chuckled softly. "As a matter of fact, I did have some luck in that regard."

"Yeah?" I set down my glass and grabbed the pen and pad of paper sitting by my landline.

"Yeah. It was apparently this guy who calls himself 'Noah.' No last name."

"Let me guess: he's an animal rights activist. Clever."

"Yep." She didn't appear to notice the sarcasm in my voice. "He's the friend of some political types I used to hang around with, and they put me in touch with him."

"So how do I get hold of him?"

"You don't. He won't talk to you."

"What do you mean? I *have* to talk to him."

"And he only talked to me on the condition that I not tell you how to find him."

Great. So I had to take Kate's word on what he said. "So what did you find out from him?"

"Well, first of all, it's obvious that the whole murder thing has got him really spooked. That's why he wants to remain anonymous. He knows those letters, coming when they did, implicate him."

No shit, Sherlock.

"And also," Kate went on, "I gather he's been involved in a variety of, shall we say, legally questionable activities? Hence the alias."

"Did he say anything about the letters he sent Letta? Like, why her? I mean, there must be thousands of restaurants in the Bay Area whose menus don't meet his standards."

"I guess he had some sort of connection to her, though he didn't specify exactly what. And I didn't need to ask him why he wrote the letters. I think that's pretty obvious, don't you?"

I didn't respond to this question.

"Noah did say he was sorry that Letta had been killed." Kate lit a cigarette—I could hear the click of the lighter—took a puff, and exhaled. "But he also said that he had to admit he was glad someone else was taking over the restaurant. When I told him about you, he asked me to tell you to check out the Eat Wild and Seafood Watch websites."

Yeah, right. The last thing I needed was this jerk telling me how to run Gauguin.

"For what it's worth," Kate added, "I don't think he had anything to do with Letta's murder in case you were wondering. He really did seem truly sad about her death."

Too bad I just didn't trust her.

After we hung up, I set about making dinner. I opened the packet of chicken, mango, and jalapeño sausages I'd just bought, removed two from their wrapping, and dropped them into the cast-iron skillet I had heating on the stovetop. Listening to the plump sausages sizzle in the pan, I was once more taken back to an evening I'd spent with my Aunt Letta. So much of what we'd done together had revolved around food. Would I forever more be reminded of her each time I cooked myself a meal?

We had come back to her place after a frenzied buying spree at the farmers' market, arms loaded with sacks of produce: rainbow chard, leeks, eggplant, red peppers, French beans, and tiny zucchini squashes with their bright-orange flowers still attached. Letta had fired up the barbeque, and we'd feasted on grilled veggies and spicy Merguez sausages, made with lamb from a friend's ranch, and then stayed up talking until almost midnight.

That was the night I'd told her that Eric and I were breaking up. When she asked why, the reasons I gave were pretty superficial. "It just seems like all we do anymore is fight about stuff," I remember saying. I explained how I was still a new associate and obsessed with my billable hours and how Eric would pout when I didn't take a Saturday off to hang out together. And I'd be equally upset when he'd work late without calling, leaving me waiting at home with an overcooked pork roast.

But Letta had seen through me. "There has to be more to it than that," she'd said. "I've seen you two together enough times to know that can't be the real reason you're splitting up." And so we'd talked it through, and she'd helped me articulate a more fundamental issue: my tendency toward unbridled enthusiasm was simply at odds with Eric's need to control the things around him. I couldn't stomach his attempt to dictate how I lived my life, and my over-the-top zeal about something like a dinner party, or working nonstop on an appellate brief at the law firm, would drive him nuts.

"It seems to me," Letta had remarked, "that, in some ways, the problem is that you two are actually too much alike—the obsessive and the control freak."

A wise observation. But it had also made me reflect on her life and how she had yet to hook up with anyone (as far as I knew at the time, that is; this was before Tony). And now that I was privy to more about her personal life, it was obvious that she had never done relationships well. Just goes to show that being able to give sage advice to others about their love life doesn't mean you'll be any good at your own.

My sausages were now crispy and brown, and I set them aside on a paper towel to drain. Slicing up half an onion and a red bell pepper, I tossed them into the hot pan. While these were frying, I toasted a split *francese* roll under the broiler. The resulting sandwich—slathered with hot mustard—looked dangerously messy, so I grabbed a stack of paper napkins before sitting down at my laptop.

Time for some research, to see if I could find out anything regarding the "Noah" guy Kate had told me about. I thought for a moment and then typed "noah animal rights activist" into the Google search box.

This produced about a zillion entries. Apparently, there was some Norwegian animal rights organization called NOAH, and they were almost all related to it.

I took a bite of my sandwich, wiped the sausage grease off my fingers, and then added the words "san francisco" to narrow my search.

Now we were on to something. Near the top of the list was an article from the *San Francisco Chronicle* with the headline "Rash of Threatening Letters Alarms Bay Area Restaurateurs." Scanning through it, I saw that someone calling himself Noah had taken credit for sending letters similar to those Letta had received to a variety of restaurants in San Francisco and Berkeley. Some had been signed, some had not. I scrolled back up to the top to see the date of the article: July of last year.

There were several similar articles in the Google list, all from the previous summer and fall and all concerning letters to restaurant owners from a character called Noah, threatening violence if the restaurant didn't stop serving factory-farmed meat and unsustainable seafood.

Then I noticed an entry mentioning "food contaminants." I clicked on this link. "Police Believe Food Contaminant Incident Connected to Letter-Writing Noah," the piece was titled. According to the article, dated January of this year, an inordinate amount of rat droppings had been found in a produce delivery to a high-end bistro in the East Bay. "Authorities are working on the assumption that the contaminant was intentionally added and that whoever did this was attempting to induce a bout of food poisoning among the restaurant patrons, as rodent feces can transmit a variety of diseases to humans," the article reported. "A source from the Berkeley Police, who requested not to be identified as the investigation is ongoing, stated that the prime suspect is 'Noah,' the author of a series of threatening letters received by various restaurants last summer." Apparently this bistro had been the recipient of one of those letters.

Interesting. But scary, too. If he was still out there, he could well try the same tactic with Gauguin. I'd have to talk to Javier about being sure to check out the produce deliveries carefully when they came in.

Taking off my Monterey College of Law sweatshirt—another annoying hot flash—I used its sleeve to dab the sweat that had formed on my brow and continued my search, trying to find out if they'd ever caught this Noah or at least figured out his identity.

Nothing. *Damn.* How the hell could I find the guy? Kate was my only link, but it didn't look like I was going to get anything else out of her.

I was about to log off when I noticed a new e-mail message from Kate—a reply to the one I'd sent her that afternoon. Maybe she'd had a change of heart and was going to tell me more?

I opened the e-mail and was momentarily confused. It didn't look like a message to me. And then I realized that it wasn't, in fact, meant for me:

Ted—

I'm forwarding you Sally Solari's message to me, as you asked.

I just talked to her and told her you were the one who wrote the letters to Letta and gave her your message like we discussed. And don't worry, I didn't give her any info that could help her figure out who you are or how to find you—just that you're called Noah.

But don't think this means any kind of truce between us. No matter how much we may agree about some things, I'll never forget your betrayal from before. And I'd prefer that you don't talk to me at the Slow Food dinner this weekend. No offense (or maybe a little), but I can't afford to be associated with you and your crowd.

Holy crap! How could Kate have made such a huge blunder? And then I realized what had obviously happened. It was originally my e-mail to Kate—I could see my message to her at the bottom, and the thread had the subject line I'd given it. She'd clearly meant to forward my message to this Ted guy but had hit the "reply" button instead by accident. Amazing how easy it is to do dumb stuff like that with e-mail.

I read the message again. So "Noah" was really someone named Ted. And Kate knew him after all—how readily she'd lied to me! What else was she lying about? She hadn't reacted when I'd shown her the photo of the man who'd come into Gauguin, but maybe it was this Ted guy, and she'd lied about that, too. Maybe that's how she'd known to contact him.

But what the hell had he done to "betray" her?

Well, at least now I had a lead to try to track him down. A Google search for Slow Food told me they had several chapters in the San Francisco Bay Area. I checked out the websites of the most likely ones: San Francisco, East Bay, Marin-Petaluma, and Alameda. There seemed to be only one dinner event going on this coming weekend: in Berkeley on Sunday at five. It was a brown-bag wine-tasting dinner (i.e., bring your own bottle to share) to raise funds for kitchen gardens in local schools. That had to be the one.

I clicked on the button to buy tickets.

Chapter Nineteen

The next afternoon before my dinner shift at Solari's, I stopped by Gauguin to organize the bills and invoices for Shanti, who would be coming by to get them the next morning. I still hadn't arrived at any decision regarding Letta's restaurant. Truth be told, I was doing my best to avoid thinking about it.

I suppose my reluctance to address the issue came down to pure, simple fear—fear of change or perhaps fear of *not* changing. Because I knew damn well that no matter what decision I eventually arrived at—continuing at Solari's, leaving it to become restauranteur for Gauguin, or even something completely different, such as finding a nonprofit where I could use my lawyer skills—there was a good chance I'd spend the rest of my days wondering if I had made the wrong choice, if maybe I should have taken one of the *other* paths.

It's never been easy for me to make choices. I mean, I can agonize for ten minutes over what burger toppings I want. So how could I be expected to decide quickly on something as momentous as a new career?

Unfortunately, however, the Gauguin bills weren't going to wait for me to make up my mind. It was a little after four when I got to the restaurant, and Javier was at the Wolf range stirring a saucepot as I came through the side door. Reuben, the line cook, was at the other end of the kitchen slicing steaks from a long hunk of meat—a strip loin, by the looks of it. New York steak wasn't a regular menu item, so it had to be one of the specials tonight.

I stopped to watch Javier as he dropped chunks of butter into the pot and whisked them into the concoction. "What'cha making?" I asked.

"Beurre blanc. I'm gonna drizzle it over the asparagus I've got roasting in the ov—*mierda*!" He dropped the whisk and yanked open the oven door. I could see a couple of large roasting pans inside, lined with spears of asparagus just beginning to brown. "Thank God," he said, grabbing two oven mitts and lifting the pans out to set them on the rangetop. "I didn't want to cook them all the way right now. I'll finish them up as they're ordered."

"Good thing I happened by," I said.

Reuben chuckled as he continued to slice his steaks, and Javier graced the two of us with a sheepish grin. "Yeah. Thanks."

"Well, I'll be up in the office if you need any more help with tonight's specials." Snitching one of the stalks from the pan—don't try this at home; you develop asbestos fingers when you work in restaurants as I long as I have—I slipped past Javier's attempt to swat me on the behind, dunked it in the pot, and crunched the dripping asparagus as I headed for the stairs.

"By the way," asked Reuben as I passed by him, "how's Letta's dog doing?"

"Oh, Buster's fine. He's with Tony and seems pretty happy there." Javier stopped stirring to look at the two of us, a strange expression on his face. Anger? Hurt? And then I noticed that Reuben was chuckling again. I gave him a questioning look, but he just shrugged and turned back to his strip loin. *Now what was that about?* I wondered as I climbed the steps to the office.

A few minutes later, Reuben came upstairs to look for something in the storage closet across from the office door.

"Hey, Reuben, can you come in here for a sec?" I asked him what was up with Javier.

"Oh, it's just a joke is all—about the dog."

"What do you mean, a joke?"

He looked a little abashed. "It's, well . . . When Letta brought the puppy back from her trip to Baja, she started talking about how she'd adopted it just like she'd done with Javier. And then eventually, it became a sort of joke with her. You know—that Javier and Buster were her two adopted Mexicans."

"Let me guess. Javier didn't think it was all that funny."

"No. It always annoyed him when she said it." Reuben grinned.

I could well imagine this would not be amusing to a working-class Mexican like Javier, whose culture is less prone to pampering dogs and considering them a part of the family than ours is. So, though Letta likely had thought of the joke as affectionate teasing, he no doubt found it humiliating.

"And you've decided to continue this charming tradition now that Letta's gone?" I pursed my lips in an attempt to show my disapproval.

Reuben looked down at his sauce-spattered shoes. "Yeah. Sorry."

I waved him impatiently out of the office and continued with my work. I'd just finished going through the invoices and was about to start on the checkbook when Javier popped his head in. "All ready for the big dinner rush?" I asked.

"Not much of a rush tonight. We've only got twelve reservations. But Wednesdays are usually pretty slow."

"Hey, since you're here, I wanted to ask you something. I was just going over the invoices from Quality Meats, and I was wondering if you knew if they ever carried grass-fed beef."

"I doubt it. Why? You thinking of switching over? You know, me and Letta talked about it, and she decided it would be way too expensive."

"Yeah, so you said. But I was thinking: what if we just offered it as an option and still kept the other meat on the menu? You know, like, for an extra five or ten bucks you get the same dish but with free-range meat? It might prove to be pretty popular in a place like Santa Cruz."

"I dunno." Javier's frown suggested he was not convinced. "But I can find out how much it would cost if you want."

"Sure, go ahead." He continued to hover in the doorway. "Did you have something to ask me?"

"I just wanted to tell you—I didn't wanna say anything in front of Reuben—that the police came by a couple hours ago to talk to me again."

"Oh yeah?" I motioned for him to sit. Checking the seat of his chef's pants first to make sure they didn't have any stray gobs of food stuck to them, Javier sat down on the pale-green wing chair across from the desk. "Did they have new questions for you?" I asked.

"It seemed like pretty much the same stuff as before." He shrugged. "I dunno; maybe they think I was lying last time and hoped I'd say something different if they asked me again."

"But they didn't arrest you, so that means they still don't think they have enough evidence for a charge to stick. That's good." *But it's not good that they came back a second time*, I was thinking.

"Yeah." Javier had slumped in his chair and was staring at the Gauguin print on the wall. "They did tell me not to leave the area, though."

I snorted. "The police have no authority to prevent you from going wherever you want, Javier. I may not be a criminal defense attorney, but I do know that. They can only keep you from leaving if you've been charged and then release you on your own recognizance." At his blank look, I added, "You know, let you out until trial without having to post bail."

"Well, it's not like I'd go anywhere, anyway. I've got my job here, and besides, where would I go?"

Mexico, was the obvious answer. *And that's certainly where the cops are afraid you'll go*. But I kept such thoughts to myself.

Javier shifted in his chair. "Also, I was wondering if you had any news about . . . you know . . ."

"As a matter of fact, I do. You got a minute right now?"

"Yeah. Reuben's got it under control for the moment."

I told him about meeting Kate and then what I'd found out about the letter-writing Ted. "So I think it might also be wise to start checking the produce deliveries and stuff like that, just in case he decides to strike again."

"Great. That's all I need: something else to worry about. As if I didn't have enough problems already." Javier picked up the small, wooden tiki that was sitting on the corner of the desk and rubbed its smooth surface absently with his thumb.

"But the good news is I think I might get the chance to meet this Noah guy in person this weekend. Who knows? Maybe I can get some important information from him."

"Won't that be kind of dangerous? If he knows you're on to him—I mean, you think he might be the murderer, right?"

"Don't worry, Javier. It's gonna be in a room full of other people at some fancy-shmancy restaurant in Berkeley. And I'm betting he won't know that I know about his secret identity. If Kate realized she sent that e-mail to me instead of him, I'm thinking she wouldn't tell him. What good would it do? It sure doesn't sound like there's any love lost between them." I was trying to convince myself as much as I was Javier. The prospect of meeting an ecoterrorist who had me on his hit list was more than a tad daunting. "Anyway, it's more likely that she doesn't even know about her e-mail goof-up. Besides, I'm thinking of taking the big, bad Eric with me. He can fend off any thugs who come my way."

Javier set the tiki back on the desk with a laugh. The idea of the slender, five-foot-six Eric taking on anyone in a fight was pretty amusing.

"Oh, and another thing I forgot to mention about what I found out from Kate: so she's at her farm working last month—fertilizing her carrots or some such thing—and out of the blue, this guy she doesn't know drives up and starts harassing her—"

"Was it Tony?" Javier blurted out.

"No. At least, I don't think so." I looked at him hard. "Why do you ask that?"

"Uh . . . I guess it just sounded like him."

"How could it 'sound like him'? I didn't even say anything about the guy."

"I dunno; for some reason, it just reminded me of him." Javier picked the tiki back up and fiddled with it, not meeting my eyes.

I stood up, leaned over the desk, and grabbed the tiki out of his hands. "Dammit, Javier! What the *hell* is wrong with you? Are you really keeping something *else* from me?"

He sighed. "Look, Sally, there is something I haven't told you . . ."

I was incredulous. "How *could* you? This is your *life* we're talking about. Do you really want to go to prison for murder?"

"No! It's just that, well . . ."

I sat back down and shot him the gravest look I could muster. "*Dígame*, Javier."

Another sigh, even bigger. "*Bueno*. So the truth is, about a month ago, I was at Dixon's on my night off, when Tony comes in with this other guy. I'd been there awhile and had already had a few beers. The two of them sat at the other end of the bar from me, but Tony kept giving me these looks. I tried to ignore him and had a couple more beers, and well . . . I guess I was kind of drunk, you know?"

I nodded. "Got it."

"So on my way to the bathroom, as I'm passing by where he's sitting, I lean over and say something like, 'You know, you may think you're so special for Letta . . .'"

To Letta, I corrected him silently in my head.

"'But I happen to know she's got a girl on the side.' Or something like that."

At my open-mouthed look, Javier added, "I just wanted to piss him off, okay?"

"I can imagine that did the job."

"Yeah, it did. He turned around in his chair and hit me. Hard. Right in the face. Gave me a bloody nose." Javier's right hand went to his nose, and he touched it gingerly. "It still kinda hurts sometimes."

Realization hit me, like one of those light bulbs that appears over a character's head in a comic book. "That's why you had that pushing match at Letta's repast. I get it now. And why you two were acting so weird at the wake. I *knew* that lame excuse you gave me before couldn't be right. Why the hell didn't you tell me this the first time I asked about you and Tony?"

"I was too ashamed." Javier hung his head like a scolded spaniel. "I still can't believe I betrayed Letta that way, by saying that to Tony."

That word "betrayal" again. This was the second time in two days it had come up. I couldn't think of a time when I'd heard it used before—in real life, that is, as opposed to a TV drama or a lurid romance novel. But then again, this case seemed to be turning into something like that, what with the love triangle between Letta, Tony, and Kate. No, make that a rectangle, because you had to add Javier to the equation as well. It was obvious that his jealousy was a major reason for his decision to taunt Tony that night at the bar, even if he wasn't willing to admit it. And then there was that creepy Ted character, not to mention the mystery men in the photo and in the muscle car. Quite the collection.

"An' so I was just worried that the guy you talked about," Javier continued, "the one who came to Kate's farm, that he mighta been Tony."

"I don't think so—not from the way she described him."

"Good." Javier's face relaxed. "I'd feel even worse if I'd caused that kind of thing to happen. So you have any idea who it was? You think it might be someone related to Letta's murder?"

I shrugged. "All I know about the guy, other than he drove some kind of macho car and acted like a total jerk, is that he's got a Giants tattoo on his arm. You know of anyone with a tattoo like that?"

Javier looked pensive for a moment and then shook his head. "I don't, actually. Which is kinda weird when you think about it. I mean, the Giants are so popular around here, you'd think lots of people would have that as a tattoo." He stood up. "Look, I gotta get back downstairs. But you'll let me know if you find out anything else, right?"

"I will if you will," I answered, giving him a stern look. "There aren't any more secrets you're keeping from me, are there?"

"No, no more." He made the sign of the cross over his chest. "I swear."

Javier went out the door, and I could hear his quick, light steps descending the staircase. Turning to look out the window, I gazed down at the petals scattered over the grass next door like pink-and-white confetti and contemplated what I'd just learned. It didn't *seem* from what Kate had said that it could have been Tony who had driven up to her farm that day, but Javier's bombshell was making me rethink that assumption. The timing was what made me nervous: the mystery man's visit had apparently occurred just a week or so after Javier's drunken blabbering to Tony.

I needed a definitive answer to the question, or I could tell it was going to drive me crazy. If nothing else, I needed confirmation that it *wasn't* Tony so that I could move on to the other people on my list.

Standing up to stretch, my eyes strayed to the wall next to the window. There, tucked into the corner of the family photo, was the snapshot of Letta and Tony at the picnic table. *Ah ha!* It wasn't the best likeness of him on earth, but it would certainly do. Since I knew Kate was going to be at the Slow Food dinner on Sunday, I could show it to her and find out once and for all if Tony was the mystery man. I took the snapshot from the frame and tucked it into my wallet.

Chapter Twenty

Saturday morning, I had a few errands to do before work. First on my list was stopping by Aunt Letta's house. I was hoping to find the pink slip for the T-Bird, since I needed to change the insurance and registration to my name, but I also thought it couldn't hurt to do a little snooping around while I was there. The key was in its usual place, on a nail at the back of the garage, and I let myself in through the side door into the kitchen.

The house smelled stale—not unusual when a place has been closed up for a while in this beach town. But it still gave me the heebie-jeebies. Even though Letta hadn't actually died in the house, the dank air brought to mind the inside of a crypt or some other ghoulish place. Forcing open the stubborn wooden window above the sink, I took a few deep breaths and tried to get a grip on myself.

After a couple minutes, I felt relatively normal again and headed for the study. A filing cabinet stood against one wall. *Let's hope she was organized enough to have a file for the T-Bird.* I was in luck. Removing the manila folder labeled "Car," I checked to make sure the pink slip was inside and then set it on the desk. I then turned back to flip through the remaining files: "Maps," "House Insurance," "Water/Sewage," "Instruction Manuals," "Gardening." No letters, photos, phone records, credit card bills; all the potentially helpful stuff had obviously been carted off by the police. Being second in line searching for clues was clearly a disadvantage.

I shut the cabinet and wandered through the house, trying not to think too much about how its former occupant met her death. Maybe something would pop out at me, something that the cops had missed but I would recognize as important, because of my superior analytical skills. Right.

After making an uneventful sweep of the house, I returned to the kitchen. Opening the drawers one by one, I poked idly through the myriad cooking utensils, flatware, aluminum foil, plastic bags, potholders, and cloth napkins that Letta had accumulated over the years. I was about to close a drawer overflowing with pens, scratch pads, scissors, a phone book, and a pile of to-go menus when my eye was caught by a small piece of card stock with a picture of a fish on it.

As I withdrew it from the drawer, it opened up accordion style. "Monterey Bay Aquarium Seafood Watch: West Coast Consumer Guide," I read. Unfolding the card, I saw that it contained three columns: "Best Choices," "Good Choices," and "Avoid." But more interesting to me was that there was writing in red ink on the card.

I sat down and studied the list. Some of the entries under "Best Choices" had been circled: Alaskan salmon, farmed scallops, yellowfin tuna (US troll- or pole-caught varieties), and US Pacific halibut. I recognized these as kinds of seafood currently on the Gauguin menu, but I wasn't sure if they were from the sources listed in that column.

Other items, ones in the "Avoid" category, had lines drawn through them: Atlantic farmed salmon, imported farmed shrimp, imported swordfish, and yellowfin tuna (except troll, pole, and US longline). I also recognized these as Gauguin menu items.

Had Letta been the one who made these markings? I wondered. Had she been considering switching the fish choices at Gauguin? Or had someone who wanted her to do so marked the list and then given it to her? Too bad there was no handwriting on it that could be identified. I slid the card into my back pocket. Javier could tell me if Letta had talked to him about Gauguin's seafood sourcing.

Next I tried the kitchen cupboards. Several had glass fronts through which I could see plates and dishes stacked high. Letta's china was a hodgepodge of all completely different patterns—her "mad tea party" set, she'd called it. I wondered if my dad would let me have the dishes; he certainly would never use them.

Behind the wooden doors were Letta's staples. One cupboard contained dry goods—flour, sugar, dried beans, rice, pasta—and the other, condiments. I rummaged through this second one. Maybe there were some things I could snitch for my own kitchen.

Dad probably wouldn't want that unopened jar of fermented black beans, nor the harissa or mango chutney. Shoving aside a bottle of white wine vinegar (which he would definitely use), I reached for a small, red can and extracted it from near the back of the cupboard.

And then I laughed—a sort of ironic, sad chuckle. It was Letta's pepper spray, in one of the least useful locations possible. I could totally see my aunt, in one of her distracted moods, seeing the word "pepper" on the can and absentmindedly placing it on the shelf along with the hot chili oil and sriracha sauce.

I took the can and dropped it into my bag.

*　*　*

After stopping by the ATM for some cash and buying a new watch battery, I decided to stroll down Pacific Avenue before heading to Solari's for work.

For several years after the big Loma Prieta earthquake of 1989, which destroyed some of its buildings and caused others to be red-tagged and torn down, this shopping area appeared to have gone the way of many city centers across the country and had become almost a ghost town. But then, after a nine-plex movie theater moved in, downtown Santa Cruz underwent a renaissance, and folks flooded back. It's been a happening place ever since.

It felt good to take a break from my regular life—which, of late, seemed to consist solely of work and obsessing about Letta's murder and what to do about Gauguin—and spend a couple hours on completely unrelated activities: window-shopping, checking out the racks at the Gap, and browsing the new arrivals in the cooking section at Bookshop Santa Cruz.

The day after my talk with Javier, I'd made a color copy of the snapshot of Tony and Letta, being sure to crop out the half with Letta in it. No need to further provoke Kate, I figured. I also called Eric to see if he wanted to accompany me to the Slow Food dinner on Sunday. He'd readily agreed upon learning he'd have the chance to meet the enigmatic Ted, not to mention get a meal on me at a swank Berkeley restaurant. Other than satisfying those two logistical details, however, I hadn't made any progress in the last two days toward figuring out who might have killed Aunt Letta. And now the search of her house had pretty much been a washout as well.

For the moment, though, I was enjoying the warm sun on my face as I sprawled on a bench, sipping a latte, admiring the cherry blossoms as they fluttered in the breeze, and watching the world go by. Setting down my cup, I rolled up my shirt-sleeves and pulled my sunglasses from my purse. After several weeks of cold and blustery weather, we finally had a truly warm day—bliss!

I closed my eyes and leaned my head back, listening to the sounds of the passing parade. A pack of teenage girls were chattering about a boy named Ryan. A cyclist pedaled by with the rhythmic scraping of a misaligned chain. Several dogs barked in the distance, and a car horn beeped. A gruff, male voice started shouting.

The proximity of this last noise prompted me to open my eyes. An old man with gray stubble and a tattered, gray jacket to match was standing in front of the *taquería* across from my bench, shaking his fist and shouting at the patrons as they entered and exited.

As I watched his ranting, I noticed someone inside the restaurant at the table nearest the window staring out at me. It was Tony.

When he saw me returning his gaze, he smiled and waved. On an impulse, I stood up and walked into the shop and over to where he was sitting. He appeared to be alone, a partially eaten burrito and can of 7-Up on the table in front of him.

"Hey, Tony."

"I thought that was you, Sally. How ya doing? You wanna eat?" He motioned to the chair across from him. "You're welcome to join me."

"No, I had a late breakfast, and I gotta be at work in a little while. I just came in to say hi. But I will sit for a minute if you don't mind. I actually had something I wanted to ask you. Go ahead, though." I nodded toward his plate and sat down.

Tony picked up his burrito and bit into it, wiping a dribble of guacamole off his chin with a paper napkin. He had on brown canvas work pants and, I noted with regret, a long-sleeve, white T-shirt. I wouldn't get a chance today to see if he had a Giants tattoo on his arm.

"How's Buster doing?"

"He seems to be doing pretty good. I'm sure he misses Letta—I sure do—and wonders what the hell's going on, but he seems to like living with me just fine. Of course, it's not that huge a change for him, since he's used to hanging out at my house a lot."

I nodded and watched as he took another bite and chewed, washing it down with 7-Up. "Nice day," I observed. "Finally."

Tony grunted. "Yeah, but the salmon sure aren't biting."

"Oh, right. I read that the season just opened. You go out this morning?"

"Yep. But I had to make do with a dozen sanddabs and a couple black cod. No one's catching any salmon yet."

"Overfishing?"

"Not by me, that's for sure." Setting his can down on the Formica table, he looked at me. "You wanna know what I think, though? Seriously? It's 'cause we're destroying their spawning grounds. Polluting the rivers and taking all the water for golf courses. And then there's that farmed salmon. It's even worse. They get covered in these sea lice, and then when they escape from their pens, they infect the wild salmon with 'em. It's a disaster." He shook his head in disgust and took another bite.

"I never pegged you for an environmentalist, Tony," I said with a smile. But I was thinking, *Ohmygod, could Tony be the one who wrote those letters?* They did mention farmed salmon, after all. *No way,* I decided. *He wouldn't even have a clue what a farrowing crate was. Or would he?*

Remembering the Seafood Watch card in my pocket, I took it out and showed it to him. "I found this at Letta's house this morning. Did you give it to her, by any chance?"

He shook his head. "Not me. I know about those people, though. I used to think they were all a bunch of left-wing reactionaries, but now I'm starting to think maybe they have a point. I mean, when me and my brother used to go out fishing as teenagers, there was *always* salmon in the bay, every year—boatloads of 'em. And now they're talking about closing the fishing *again* next season because the numbers are so low? Something has gone the hell wrong. If that makes me a goddamn environmentalist, then so be it."

His expression softened. "It's funny," he added. "Letta used to tease me about the same thing. Must be in your family's genes or something."

"You know, I wanted to ask you something about Letta . . ."

Tony finished off the burrito and said, mouth full, "So you're still trying to help that Mexican, eh?"

"As a matter of fact, what I want to ask does have to do with Javier."

"Ask away. I'm happy to help however I can. You thinking he might be the one who did it? Stabbed Letta?"

"Well, you yourself said before that you didn't think him capable of it."

Wiping his hands, he crumpled up his napkin and dropped it onto his plate. "Yeah, he does strike me as pretty much a wuss. But I gotta say, after the way he went at me at the repast at your dad's restaurant . . ." Tony shook his head. "I dunno; maybe he's not such a wimp after all."

"So what? You think now it could have been Javier?"

The question seemed to take him by surprise. Leaning back in his chair, he folded his arms, frowned, and thought for a moment, staring out at a young man with frizzy hair who had taken up the ranter's former position in front of our window and was strumming a guitar. A plush-lined case sat open at his feet, a couple of dollars tossed in as seed money. "I don't know," Tony finally answered. "Maybe."

He uncrossed his arms and leaned forward on the table. "Was that what you wanted to ask me?"

After having screwed up the courage to ask my question, I was now starting to lose my nerve. What if he blew up or totally freaked out? But we were in a public place, after all, so he couldn't react too badly, could he?

Do it, Sally—Miss Marple wouldn't be so chicken.

"No," I said. "I wanted to ask about something Javier told me the other day. About Letta. About what he told *you* about Letta."

Tony was looking at me, but I couldn't read his expression. He waited for me to go on.

"He said he told you about a woman Letta was involved with."

Tony frowned. "I thought that might be where you were going."

"Javier said you got really mad and slugged him."

"Guilty as charged." He held his wrists up together as if ready for handcuffs. "But in my defense, the little shit deserved it, using Letta like that to get at me."

I was surprised at how calm he appeared to be. So I pressed on, to see if he, like Kate, might be provoked. "You mean to tell me it didn't bother you that your fiancée was having an affair with someone else? With a *woman*?"

"Of course it bothered me." His voice was testy now, and he was starting to get fidgety and shift around in his seat. The subject was clearly making him uncomfortable. "But I sure didn't need Javier sticking his nose in our business. And I let him know what I thought in no uncertain terms." The hand-cuffed wrists became boxing gloves as Tony took a couple mock jabs at the air. But the levity seemed forced.

"So you already knew about her, about Kate?"

"Sure. You really think Letta would tell Javier before she told me?" Tony glanced around the restaurant, suddenly conscious that his voice had been rising. "Look," he said more quietly, "we'd already worked through it all before he even found out. Letta had told me about the affair, and yeah, we did have a fight about it. A big one. I was pretty pissed if you want to know the truth. But she told me it had just been a fling, 'an experiment,' she said. And she also promised me she was breaking it off, that she'd realized it was me she wanted to be with. That's when she agreed to get married, as a matter of fact."

"Oh."

He stood up. "I'm sorry, Sally, but I've actually got to get going. I'm supposed to meet a buddy at eleven to help out with an electrical problem at his house." He took his plate and can and deposited them in the bus tray and recycling bin, and we walked outside. "Hey, you want some sanddabs? My truck's just around the corner, and I'd be happy to give you a couple. I sure can't eat a dozen myself."

I never turn down freshly caught fish, so I gladly followed him to his truck, where he took out a cooler and showed me his day's catch.

"You want me to scale and clean 'em for you?"

Having grown up in a fishing family, I of course would have been able to prep the sanddabs myself, but it's a messy business, so I was happy to let Tony do it for me. He pulled a thin-bladed boning knife from a kit stowed behind his seat and deftly slit open the belly of one of the fish and removed its guts. Next, he used the flat of the knife and went backward, against the grain, to remove the scales. He made it look easy, but I noticed that the scales were flying all over the place, onto his clothes and into the gutter. "When I'm at home," he said, noticing my look, "I always scale fish under water in a dish pan—it's a lot less messy."

As he worked on the second sanddab, Tony told me how he prepares them. "I like to panfry 'em whole in some butter, with some garlic and maybe a little lemon and parsley. You don't want to overwhelm their flavor, which is pretty mild." He dropped the two fish into a plastic bag and handed it to me. "You want some ice?"

"That's okay. I'm on my way to work; we've got plenty there."

I followed Tony's advice about panfrying the sanddabs, and as I savored the delicate fish that night, accompanied by boiled red potatoes and a simple green salad with a Dijon vinaigrette, I pondered what I'd learned from him.

Not much, actually, when I really thought about it. In my mind, I'd built up this whole soap opera backstory about Tony and his reaction to finding out about Kate. So hearing his anything-but-dramatic account of it all was kind of a let-down.

Assuming he was telling the truth, of course.

Chapter Twenty-One

"There's one; there's a space!" I gestured frantically toward a car pulling away from the curb on the left side of the street.

"It's green," Eric replied.

"But it's Sunday. It doesn't matter if it's green or not."

Ignoring what I considered to be an astute observation, he drove on by the space, turning right once more onto Shattuck. I gazed glumly at the restaurant as we passed it for the third time, noting a group of people heading through the door with paper sacks in their arms.

"We're going to be late," I whined.

"No, we're not." Eric glanced over his shoulder, did a quick U-turn, and deftly pulled into a spot right across the street from La Récolte. "See?" With a smug smile, he switched off the engine and opened his door.

"I hate it when you do that."

Eric retrieved our brown paper bag from the back seat. "What did you decide on?" I asked. The website for the event had directed folks to bring Bordeaux-style wines, or Cabernets or Merlots, in order to match the menu. I'd deferred to

Eric for the decision, knowing he had a cellar full of fabulous wines, despite his government-lackey salary.

"Two of the same thing," he said, pulling one of the bottles out and holding it up for my inspection: a 2007 Storrs BXR.

"Sounds like the name of a dirt bike," I observed.

He gave a condescending shake of the head. "It's a Bordeaux-style blend, my dear. And, might I add, it's going to kick the asses of the Napa Meritages these Bay Area wine snobs will no doubt bring. I thought I'd show them just how good our Santa Cruz wineries can be."

We started across the street. "Now remember," I said in a hushed voice, "don't let on, when we see Kate, that I expected her to be there."

"Don't worry, I got it." Eric grabbed my arm as a car sped around the corner right at our feet. "We've been over it all ad nauseum. I'm not going to blow it."

The plan, which, I admit, we *had* spent a fair amount of time discussing in the car, was that I was going to pretend I'd found the tickets to the dinner among Letta's papers and had thought it would be a shame to let them go to waste. I'd act surprised to see Kate, gambling that she hadn't noticed her e-mail blunder and told Ted about it. That way, I could chat him up without him suspecting I knew about his secret identity.

And if Kate had noticed that she blew it with her e-mail message and if she figured out why I was really there? Well, then I'd just have to play it by ear. But I was really hoping that wasn't the case, because I totally suck at improv.

We walked in the door and were greeted by a woman seated at a card table. I gave her my name and, after locating me on the list, she handed us blank name-tag stickers to fill out. I scrawled "Sally Solari" as legibly as I could and handed the pen to Eric.

"You sure you want to use your full name?" he asked. "That Ted character will know who you are right away."

"That's the idea. As long as *he* doesn't know that *I* know who he is, I'm thinking he might think he's being really smart and try to get information out of me. Which could in turn give *me* information."

"Clever. I guess."

We turned to survey the room.

La Récolte—which I learned from Eric means "harvest" in French—had that stereotypical bistro feel. You know, with the black-and-white checkered floor, tables draped with white tablecloths and set with heavy flatware, lots of red plush and brass fixtures, old posters for Suze and Pernod, and a curved, zinc bar. It was almost too cutesy, but not quite.

Two long tables had been set up that ran the length of the dining room. It looked like they were expecting about forty people for the dinner. Along the far wall was another long table where folks were placing their bottles of wine and pouring themselves glasses. A waiter in a black vest and white apron was busy opening the bottles as they were set down. Spotting several platters of appetizers at either end of the table, I went over to investigate. Eric followed and set his wines next to the others.

"I was right. Just look at all these Napa wines: BV Reserve Tapestry, St. Supéry Élu, Ramey . . . Oh wow." He picked up a bottle to examine it more closely. "A 2011 Chimney Rock

Elevage, Stags Leap District. I've been wanting to check this out," he said and grabbed a glass to pour himself a taste.

I was more interested in the food. Wanting to save myself for what I was hoping would be a scrumptious dinner, I hadn't eaten any lunch, and my stomach had been complaining all the way up to Berkeley. There was a terrine of some kind of *pâté en croûte* and a basket of toasted bread rounds to go with it. Next to that sat a platter heaped with roasted vegetables: white and green asparagus, porcini mushrooms, spring onions, red and golden beets, fennel, and carrots in several flaming hues.

And finally, there was an enormous woodblock covered with different cheeses. Each one had a little sign stuck in it with a toothpick. I bent to examine them: Red Hawk and Humboldt Fog from Cowgirl Creamery, a blue from the Point Reyes Farmstead Cheese Company, San Andreas from Bellwether Farms, and Hollyhock from Garden Variety Cheese— all from Northern California, the signs noted. I cut a wedge from the Humboldt Fog and laid it on a piece of bread. It was a creamy white with a bright-white rind and was bisected by a layer of ash.

"Oh, yum!" I said to no one in particular.

"Have you tried the Hollyhock? It's from down in your neck of the woods." I turned, and there was Kate standing next to me, a glass of wine in her hand.

"Kate!" I was so startled to see her there that I didn't have to feign any surprise. "Wha . . . what are you doing here?"

"I helped organize this event. It's a joint effort between the Berkeley and Marin chapters. The better question is, what are *you* doing here?"

I saw Eric eying us. He had finished his taste of the Chimney Rock and was moving on to the St. Supéry.

Time for my story: "I found the tickets to the dinner in Letta's papers the other day and thought it would be a shame to waste them, so—"

"Tickets? There weren't any tickets to this dinner, at least not that I know of."

Oh boy. "Not tickets. I didn't mean tickets. I meant the, you know, the receipt thing you get when you register online and print it out . . ."

"Oh, right. Sorry, I didn't mean to jump on you. It's just that we'd talked about the idea of doing paper tickets, and I was sure that it had been nixed—to save the postage and paper. So I got confused when you said that, is all." Kate smiled at someone across the room and waved. "I didn't know Letta had been planning on coming to this. She hadn't told me. You said tickets, plural?"

Think fast, Sal. You know she's wondering if Tony was going to be her date. "Uh . . . I think she may have been planning on taking me, actually. She did mention something last month about a Slow Food dinner." I was amazed at how quickly the lies were springing from my tongue.

"Well, I guess it's good that you came tonight then," Kate said and finished off her wine.

I exhaled. It didn't seem like she was on to my game, and she sure wasn't acting like she was aware of her e-mail screw-up. But then again, I suppose you wouldn't know you'd sent a message to the wrong person unless you happened to check your sent e-mails folder, or the person it was intended for was expecting it and said something about it not arriving.

"Yeah, it seemed appropriate that I come." I reached over the *pâté* for a wine glass.

"You here alone?" Kate asked.

"Try the St. Supéry—it's fantastic," a male voice cut in. Eric had come up next to us at this last question as if on cue.

"No, to answer your question. This is my . . . friend, Eric."

He bent his head in salutation. "How do you do. Would you care to try a bit of the St. Supéry . . . uh . . . ?" Eric squinted at her name tag, pretending to read it.

"Kate," I said. "Sorry. This is Kate. Now where are my manners?" *Sheez.* Just because *I* knew Eric knew her name didn't mean *she* knew he did. Thank goodness he, at least, was doing his job.

At her nod of assent, Eric poured a taste of the wine into Kate's glass. I held out my glass, and he did the same for me.

"So how do you two ladies know each other?"

I would have kicked him had it been possible to do so without being observed. Kate saved me, however, from having to decide how to phrase an answer.

"I sell produce to Gauguin." Simple and truthful—what a concept.

"Ah. And is any of this beautiful produce yours?" Eric plucked a tiny purple carrot from the platter and bit off its end.

"As a matter of fact, it is. As will be the vegetables served with dinner."

He made a show of smacking his lips and swallowing with relish. "Delectable," he pronounced with a boyish smile.

I stifled a snort. Eric could be such a flirt. But I didn't think his charms would have much of an effect on Kate. He poured himself another half glass of the St. Supéry, killing the bottle. "Good thing we got here early," he said. Setting the bottle on the table, he turned back toward us, facing the now rather full room. "Hey, I think I know that gal over there. Will you excuse me a moment?" He strode across the room and struck up a conversation with a woman with short, red hair and a dress to match.

We'd agreed in advance that he'd make sure to leave me alone with Kate so I could ask her in private about the photo. But his chatting up hot, young babes—I knew he didn't really know her—had not been on the official agenda.

Whatever. I turned back to Kate.

"So since I've got you here, I wanted to ask . . ." I burrowed in my bag and came up with my wallet. I removed the picture of Tony and handed it to Kate. "Is this, by any chance, the guy who drove up to your farm that day?"

"No," she said. "I don't think so. The man in the Camaro, or whatever it was, was heavier set as I remember, with a broader face. And his eyes were different: more bug-eyed than this guy's." She studied the photo again and then looked at me. "So who is he, anyway?"

When I didn't answer immediately, she shook her head in disgust. "It's Tony, isn't it?"

"Yeah."

Kate handed the photo back. "I knew it. Yuck. Now forevermore, I'm going to have this picture in my mind of him—of *them*, together . . ."

It had been a good impulse to crop Letta out of the picture. "Sorry," I said. "I just had to make sure it wasn't him who came to the farm that day."

"Understood."

"So what else can you tell me about what he looked like?"

"As I said before," she answered with a hint of peevishness, "he had dark hair, was stocky, fiftyish, maybe older. I think he was wearing a T-shirt, but he didn't get out of the car, so I'm not really sure exactly what he was wearing. Oh, and that blue Giants tattoo on his left forearm—I saw that because he had his elbow out the window."

"*Blue*? Are you sure? 'Cause the Giants colors are orange and black."

"I'm pretty sure it was blue. A bright blue. But I'm not into sports at all, so I never really thought about it, whether the color was right or anything." Kate glanced over toward the door, and I saw her catch someone's eye. "Look, I gotta go relieve Patty at the door," she said. "But I'm glad you could make it. Are you a Slow Food member? If not, you should think about joining, especially now that you're the owner of a restaurant."

"Yeah, it seems like a great organization. I'll have to check it out."

I watched her make her way toward the front door, saying "hi" to various people along the way. It seemed like she knew just about everyone in the room. Looking around for Eric, I finally spotted him at the other end of the appetizer table. He was still talking to the redhead, pouring her a glass of wine and laughing at something she was saying. I grabbed a plate; loaded it with cheese, roast veggies, and bread rounds; and walked over to join them.

"Hey, Sal. There you are. This is Rebecca. She makes *charcuterie*."

We shook hands. "Like prosciutto?" I asked.

"Some. And other kinds of dry-cured ham, too. I also do several *pâtés*. That one over there is mine: it's a pork and chicken liver terrine with brandied prunes and juniper berries."

I glanced in embarrassment at my plate, which was noticeably lacking in *pâté*. I've never been a big fan of liver. "Sounds delicious," I lied. "I'll have to try some."

"But mostly I've been into sausages lately. I was just telling Eric about a new kind I tried making yesterday: turkey, chanterelle mushrooms, and dried apricots."

"Yum," I said, this time with conviction, and bit into a piece of bread slathered with creamy Red Hawk cheese.

"Yeah, they came out pretty good, but they were a little too dry. I was thinking the apricots would add more moisture than they did. I'll have to add a lot more fat if I'm going to start selling them. Did you know that most commercial sausage is between thirty and fifty percent fat?"

"I guess that explains why I like it so much," I said, taking another bite of the triple-cream cheese.

A woman started clinking a wine glass with a fork. As we turned toward the sound, Eric nudged me with his elbow and nodded toward a man standing to our right. On his name tag was printed, in large block letters, "TED."

"Dinner's about to be served," the glass-clinker announced after the room had quieted down, "so why doesn't everyone start getting seated."

Eric and I watched to see where Ted would sit. He chose a spot next to a woman he appeared to know and set a wine bottle down in front of his seat.

"What if it's the wrong Ted?" I whispered to Eric.

"What's to lose?" he answered. "It's not like there's another Ted we've seen here so far."

"Right." We followed Ted to the table; I took the seat to his left, and Eric the one across from me.

Chapter Twenty-Two

Ted had immediately turned to strike up a conversation with the woman to his right, so I had a good opportunity to check him out without his noticing. What was immediately clear was that he was *not* the guy who'd come into Gauguin to harass Letta. The man in the photo she'd taken was younger and with longer and darker hair. Oh well. So much for that theory.

But even so, Ted's looks didn't jibe with the rabid letter writer of my imagination. He was older than I would have expected: fifties, early sixties? It was hard to tell because of his fair hair. It could be natural, but I suspected it was a dye job. And those blond ringlets—could they be for real? In his vintage Hawaiian shirt and with that almost cherubic face, he gave the impression of an ageless surfer dude.

As I listened in on his conversation, however, I changed my mind: *No, not a surfer.* He had a sort of smarmy, low-key aggression that reminded me of a sales pitch—more like a real estate agent than a surfer. And he seemed a little tipsy, too.

He must have felt me staring at him, because he swiveled in his chair at that moment and graced me with a smile full of perfect, white teeth. "Howdy," he said. "I'm Ted. And you are?" He glanced down at my name tag, and I saw recognition appear in his eyes. He frowned briefly, then quickly smiled again. Nervousness?

I pretended not to notice. "Oh, hi!" I said, conjuring the most charming smile I could. "I'm Sally, and this is Eric."

Eric reached across the table to shake hands with Ted. "Glad to meet you."

"So . . ." I tried to think of something to say to put Ted at ease and convince him I had no idea who he was. "You know what's on the menu tonight? I hope whatever it is, it's soon, 'cause I'm famished."

His shoulders relaxed. "All I know is the main course is braised short ribs. But don't worry," he added, "it's grass-finished beef. The Slow Food folks are pretty good about that sort of stuff."

"Ah. Good." I picked up my glass and drained it. "That should go well with the Cab blends."

"Here, try the one I brought." Ted poured me a taste from the bottle sitting in front of him. I saw Eric squinting to see what it was.

"Estancia," I read off the label for his benefit.

"Yeah, it's the reserve," said Ted, "which is a lot better than their regular Meritage."

"Nice to see a wine from down in Paso Robles," Eric chimed in. "Most of the bottles here seem to be from Napa. Or Sonoma. We brought the Storrs BXR. Here, I'll grab the bottle so you can check it out."

Eric got up to retrieve one of our bottles from the wine table. When he returned, his path was blocked by a tray stand set up between the two long tables of diners. Three waiters were distributing bowls of soup, and Eric waited for them to finish and move the folding stand out of his way.

"What kind of soup is it?" I asked as a bowl was set down in front of me.

"This is a roasted shiitake mushroom bisque with wild rice and sherry," the server announced to the table at large.

I dipped my spoon into the nut-brown soup and blew on it. No reason to burn my mouth on the first taste of the dinner.

"Here you go." Eric sat back down and poured Ted a glass of the BXR. "Tell me what you think."

Ted swirled his glass and took a drink. "Not bad. It's from Santa Cruz, huh?"

"Well, the grapes aren't actually, but that's where the winery is."

Ted looked like he was going to say something but then didn't. He started in on his soup instead.

"So what brings you to a Slow Food dinner?" I asked him. "Do you work with food?"

"You might say that." Ted set his spoon down and took another swallow of wine. I noticed that the full glass Eric had poured was already half gone. "I'm sort of between jobs right now, but I've been helping out some friends who are experimenting with fermentation."

"You mean beer and wine?"

"More like sauerkraut and kimchi. And miso. It's amazing what I've been learning. Did you know, for example, that more than a *thousand* species of bacteria have been discovered *just in humans*—in our stomachs, intestines, and mouths and on our skins? We're like walking bags of microorganisms. And contrary to what you hear all the time about so-called 'dangerous bacteria' all over the place," he said, making quotation marks in the air with his fingers, "most of them are actually necessary for our survival. We need them to absorb and process the nutrients that we consume, produce our sweat, and combat infections."

He leaned forward, and I could see tiny beads of the aforementioned perspiration forming on his upper lip. "It's a little known fact that Captain Cook made sure to take sauerkraut with him on his trip around the world, and not one of his crew members died of scurvy."

"Wow" was all I could muster. I smiled but, at the same time, ever so slightly leaned back in my seat, away from his encroaching figure.

"And now there's this 'war' on bacteria. Those antibacterial soaps you see advertised on TV and chlorinated water and all the antibiotics they pump into the commercial meat we consume. What people don't realize is that by killing off bacteria, they're killing *themselves*." He was really excited now, and other diners at the table were starting to turn and look at him. "Did you know it can take *four years* for the bacteria in your gut to recover from a round of antibiotics your doctor prescribes for an earache?"

Ted glanced around, seeming to realize that perhaps he was being a bit too animated. "Anyway," he continued in a softer voice, "what's really cool is that by simply eating fermented foods, you can restore the proper balance of bacteria in your body. And they taste amazing. Think of cheese, sourdough bread, chocolate, *wine*." He finished off his glass with a flourish and poured another nearly to the brim. "They're all the product of fermentation. And best of all, fermented foods are really cheap to make. Just take a lowly head of cabbage, add some salt and a few seasonings, and prest-o, change-o: sauerkraut!"

He had to be the right Ted, I decided—the "Noah" Ted. I could totally see this ranting character as the author of those letters. But now that I had him here before me, drunk and clearly eager to talk, I couldn't for the life of me figure out how to make any use of it. What was I going to do? Just come out and ask him if he was the one who killed Letta?

The servers started clearing our soup bowls and replacing them with the entrée. Ted had been doing so much talking that he had to hurry to finish his soup. As he swiftly spooned up the last of his mushroom bisque, I took the opportunity to glance over at Eric, hoping maybe he could move the conversation to a more helpful subject. He was busy, however, chatting with the man next to him. Based on the little I could hear over the din in the room, the guy was apparently a winemaker. Oh, well, I'd never get Eric's attention now.

Ted handed his bowl to a passing waitress and excused himself to go to the restroom. As he got up, a large plate was set before me. On it sat two plump short ribs in a pool of thick, dark sauce, garnished with a scattering of slender chives. Next to the ribs were a few grilled vegetables and a stack of thinly sliced potatoes that resembled a short, round tower.

After we had all been served, the same waiter who had described the soup gave us a rundown on the entrée: "beef short ribs braised in Bison Imperial Brown Ale," he announced, "accompanied by grilled fennel and radicchio and potatoes Anna."

I dug in. When Ted returned, he offered to pour more wine for me, but I waved him off. I'd already had plenty for the night. Pouring himself another full glass, he too started in on his meal. "So," he said after swallowing a large mouthful of potato, "I wanted to ask you something. I noticed your name tag: Solari. Any chance you're related to Letta Solari? The woman who was murdered a few weeks ago? I only ask 'cause she was from Santa Cruz, and you brought a wine from there."

I stiffened. I'd of course been hoping my name tag would elicit some sort of reaction, but it was still a bit of a shock to hear him raise the very subject I'd been trying to figure out how to broach. My face must have showed my surprise, which he obviously read as grief.

"Oh my God," he said. "I guess you are. I am *so* sorry to bring it up like that."

Liar, liar, pants on fire. He knew damn well she was my aunt, since Kate had told him about me. But if he wanted to play this game, I was happy to go along with it.

"No, it's okay," I said. "The question just took me by surprise"—that much was true—"which is stupid, I suppose. Her death was, after all, plastered all over the newspapers. Even up here, I imagine."

"Yeah. But that's not the only reason I ask. I actually knew her pretty well. Years ago, when she lived up here in the Bay Area."

My beef-laden fork stopped halfway to my mouth. Now *this* was news. "Really?" I looked over at Eric to try to catch his eye, but he was fully focused on the winemaker.

"Uh-huh. I lost touch with her after she left the country. I guess she went off to Tahiti or some such place? But then I heard that she'd moved back to her home town and opened up a restaurant." He chuckled. "I totally cracked up when I heard what she'd named it. Didn't she know what a chauvinist pig Paul Gauguin was?"

I inwardly rolled my eyes at his use of this dated expression. I also noted that he missed a good opportunity there for more of his air quote marks.

"So what's going to happen to the restaurant now?" he asked and took a bite of short ribs.

"She gave it to me."

He just nodded while continuing to look at his plate and speared a piece of fennel with his fork. "You going to run it yourself or hire someone?"

I'd come to hate this question even more than people asking whether they'd caught Letta's murderer yet. But I knew I was going to have to come to some sort of decision relatively soon, and over the past few days, I'd begun to make the transition from studiously avoiding the subject to obsessing about it almost nonstop.

The problem is, once you've settled into a routine, the idea of any change can be unsettling, even if the routine isn't exactly the life you've dreamed of. Yes, I'd been growing increasingly dissatisfied with my life, managing the front of the house at Solari's. And yes, if I had any single passion, it was food and cooking. But over the years, I'd learned firsthand working at Solari's—and from watching my dad and aunt—just how hard a life owning and running a restaurant could be.

"I haven't decided yet," I answered Ted after a pause, during which all these thoughts flashed through my mind. But I didn't want to talk about me right now; I wanted to get the conversation back to him. "So how did you know Letta, anyway? Did you two work together?"

Ted shook his head. "Nuh-uh," he answered, mouth full. Cutting another piece of meat, he seemed to think for a moment as he dipped it into the gravy. Then, setting the uneaten fork-full of food back on the plate, he turned to face me. "We were lovers," he said, looking me in the eye.

What the—? No way.

"In fact, she left her girlfriend for me," he continued, a hint of a swagger in his voice, like he was bragging. Then again, it must have been quite the *coup* for a guy like him to snag a lesbian. But how could Letta—the sophisticated, confident, woman of the world—have fallen for someone like him, someone so narcissistic, so smug?

Maybe she wasn't, in fact, the sophisticate I'd always imagined her to be.

I wondered if Kate knew about Letta and Ted and then remembered what she'd said in that e-mail to him. *Ohmygod.* This was obviously the "betrayal" she'd mentioned. Ted must be the guy she'd found Letta in bed with all those years ago.

I looked around the room for Kate and finally found her at the far end of the other table. She didn't seem to have noticed that Ted and I were sitting next to each other.

"So why'd you break up?" I finally managed to ask.

"Oh, let's just say we had different perspectives—politically, I guess you'd have to call it."

Yeah. I can imagine. And thirty years later you're still angry enough to write virulent, anonymous letters to her. I wondered if maybe Letta had known all along that he was the one who had sent them.

"And you haven't seen her since then? You never stopped by her restaurant or anything like that?"

I thought I detected a brief pause as Ted's fork made its way to his mouth, but it could have been purely imagination. "It's been ages since I've been in Santa Cruz," he said, mouth full. "And no, I never stopped by Gauguin. I'm fairly certain Letta wouldn't have been all that crazy about seeing me again."

Ted chuckled as he scraped up the last of the gravy on his plate. He then licked his knife and fork clean and poured himself yet another glass of wine.

After the dessert course was served (molten dark chocolate cake with raspberry coulis as the hot lava), Ted lost interest in me and turned once more to talk to the woman to his right. He was really drunk by this time. So much so that I don't think his neighbor was all that thrilled to have his attention back. After a few minutes, she excused herself to go hang out with some friends at the other table. He too got up and wandered off.

Eric's new friend had also vacated his seat—folks were starting to congregate again at the wine table, where coffee urns were now set up—and Eric and I had the table almost to ourselves.

"How much of that did you hear?" I asked him.

"Some. Did I hear him say he was Letta's *lover*?"

"Yep." I filled Eric in on what I'd learned from Ted. "So how weird is that?" I said when I'd finished. "Him being the guy Letta left Kate for?"

"No wonder Kate's so pissed."

"Yeah. And not just at Ted, I bet. She must have been totally pissed at Letta, too. I mean, c'mon. Imagine if you were involved with a woman who left you for someone like Ted."

"Yuck," we said in unison and then both laughed.

But then I frowned. "Pissed enough to actually kill her?"

"I dunno," Eric said with a shrug. "But someone did, and I'm guessing whoever it was knew her pretty well. In my experience as DA, folks don't stab someone that many times unless it's personal."

I swiveled in my chair to look at Ted, who was helping himself from one of the coffee urns. "Speaking of personal," I said, jabbing my thumb in Ted's direction, "how weird is it, too, that he's the one who sent those letters? Someone Letta used to be involved with?"

"Maybe not so weird." Eric gave his wine glass a swirl and then drained its contents. "I mean, when you think about it, he must feel that her lack of food ethics, or whatever, is just as much a betrayal as Kate thinks his seducing away Letta . . . is . . . was. Is that even a proper sentence?"

"I better drive home, toots." I laughed and reached over to help myself to the lava cake still on Eric's plate. "But seriously, what a soap opera this all is. With Letta as the central character and everyone else revolving around her. Who knew my aunt had such a dramatic life?"

Eric stood up. "I'm gonna get some coffee. You want me to bring you a cup?"

"No, I'll be there in a sec." As I finished off Eric's cake, I pondered just how much Letta had kept from me. Would she have ever confided in me, told me about her secret past, had we gotten the chance to know each other better—had she lived to do so? With an impatient shake of the head, I pushed back my chair. Such morose thoughts did no one any good.

Eric and I drank our coffee and then found Kate to say good-bye. There was still no sign that she had noticed me sitting next to Ted or if she had, that she thought anything of it. Another bullet dodged.

As we made our way to the door to leave, we passed Ted, who had corralled the *charcuterie* woman into a corner. "I just found out about you selling foie gras," he was shouting at her. "So you think it's okay to make money off the torture of ducks and geese? How would you like it if I force-fed *you*?" Spittle was coming out of his mouth, and his eyes had a hard, scary look to them.

It was a reminder not to take smarmy Ted too lightly. For Noah was always there waiting in the wings.

Chapter Twenty-Three

The following Tuesday, Dad invited me over for dinner and, even though I was feeling completely beat, I accepted out of guilt. I wasn't much looking forward to the evening. It seemed like whenever we spent more than about ten minutes together, of late, we'd end up in some sort of squabble. And ever since I'd told him about inheriting Gauguin, it had gotten even worse. Pretty much the only things we talked about now were work-related issues and the weather. Even squabbling would be better than that.

But I figured he must be feeling pretty lonely these days, so it was my daughterly duty to hang with my dad. After all, other than Nonna, I was the only family in town he had left.

Plus, he'd promised to make his famous linguine with clam sauce.

Smiling at the sight of the pale-yellow T-Bird convertible sitting in my space, I walked briskly across the apartment's parking lot and climbed inside. It was probably too chilly to put the top down, but I couldn't resist the temptation. I zipped up my jacket, cranked the heater up to high, and jammed the stick into reverse.

As I slowed down to pull into my local liquor store for a bottle of wine to bring Dad—I figured a Pinot Grigio would go well with the dinner—I noticed a big ol' car right on my tail. *Jerk*, I thought as it just missed winging me and sped on past.

And then I did a double-take. It was metallic blue, all engine and tricked-out wheels. Your classic muscle car.

What color car had Kate said that mystery man drove?

I watched it disappear down the street and then shook my head and headed into the store. Allowing myself to slip into a state of paranoia was not going to help anything.

Dad was watching the news when I arrived. Grunting, he lifted himself out of his easy chair, shut off the TV, and then gave me a peck on the cheek.

"Hi hon, how are ya?"

I handed him the bottle. "Not bad. I'm looking forward to your linguine."

"It'll be a few minutes; I just put the pasta water on. You want me to open this?"

"That's why I brought it."

I followed Dad into the kitchen and watched as he uncorked the wine and poured us each a glass. He took a sip, nodded, and then handed me some papers that had been sitting on the counter. "Here's that surveyor's report you asked me to get. And a letter from her lawyer. Wanda stuck them in my mailbox today."

The attorney's language was full of bombast and threats—your typical demand letter. Rolling my eyes, I turned to the surveyor's report and flipped through its pages to the "conclusions" section. Yep, the fence was indeed on Wanda's property.

"Damn," I said.

My dad lifted the lid off the large stockpot steaming on the stove. "Yeah, I saw it too." He grabbed the package of linguine sitting on the counter and tore it open. "But maybe I can use that easement argument you were talking about. Prewhassit?"

"Prescriptive."

"Yeah, that one." He dropped a large fistful of the pasta strands into the pot and stirred them with a wooden spoon. "Now for the sauce." A large skillet was sitting next to the stockpot, and on the counter were all the ingredients, lined up and ready to go. Once you've cooked in a restaurant, this prep work and organization becomes second nature.

"I'll read through all this later and let you know if I think you should hire your own attorney." Walking back into the living room, I set the papers down next to my bag and then returned to the kitchen.

Dad was pouring a generous pool of olive oil into the hot pan. When the oil was shimmering, he dumped in some sliced garlic, cooked it for a minute, and then added a pinch of red pepper flakes.

"That's new," I said. "You didn't used to use hot pepper in your linguine."

"That's because your mother didn't like it. She said it overwhelmed the flavor of the clams."

"Right." Mom's family hailed from the Midwest, and the spices her mother had used when cooking had been pretty much limited to salt, black pepper, and the occasional oregano or parsley sprig. Marrying an Italian must have been quite the challenge for her taste buds.

Next went in about a cup of white wine and a bottle of clam juice.

"Gotta let this reduce a few minutes," Dad said, picking up his wine glass. "So what's new? How you been?"

"Busy—what with working and also dealing with Gau—" I stopped myself from completing the sentence, but it was too late: Dad was already frowning. "Also," I added quickly, hoping to distract him from the whole Gauguin issue, "I went to a Slow Food dinner up in Berkeley Sunday night."

But this just prompted a larger frown. "I heard about those food snobs."

"They aren't snobby. They just believe in real food. You know, back to the basics: using fresh ingredients rather than processed ones." I was on dangerous ground here, I realized, and had to be careful about what I said. Dad was touchy about anything suggesting Solari's wasn't about real, traditional Italian cuisine. "It's the same thing you believe in—food like this." I gestured to the sauce simmering on the stove. "A homemade dish rather than buying a spaghetti sauce in a jar. The Slow Food movement did start in Italy, after all."

"Huh." I could tell he wasn't convinced, but he at least seemed mollified. He reached for the bowl of clams on the counter next to the stove, dumped them into the pan, and covered it.

"By the way, I met this guy at the Slow Food dinner who used to be involved with Letta. You ever meet someone named Ted she used to date back in the 1980s?"

"Nope. We didn't hang out a whole lot back then."

I wasn't sure just how much to tell him about what I'd learned. Certainly not about her relationship with Kate. Letta wouldn't have wanted that. But the Ted thing seemed safe. "Well, it turns out this guy Ted had been sending Letta nasty letters—anonymously, that is—about her serving factory-farmed meat at her restaurant."

"I knew those Slow Food people were kooks. You should steer clear of them." He lifted the lid to poke at the clams, which were just starting to open.

"You're missing the point, Dad. I think it's possible that this guy might have been the one who killed Letta."

"Dammit, Sally!" He slammed the lid back down on the pan. "What do you think you're doing, poking your nose around into everyone else's business?"

"But I—"

"Sean told me yesterday he saw you a while back when he was down at the police station reporting his stolen bike. He said he overheard you talking to them about Letta."

Dang. He must have seen me when I dropped off those threatening letters.

"It's embarrassing. You have no business playing at being some kind of goddamn Columbo." Taking the lid off again, he started removing the clams with a slotted spoon and placing them in a bowl. "Why can't you just let the police do their jobs? They're the experts, after all." He cut a chunk of butter and dropped it into the sauce and then turned the flame up under the pot. We both stared at it in silence, Dad trying to maintain his glower and me pondering whether I preferred the comparison to Peter Falk's disheveled TV detective or to the prissy spinster, Jane Marple. Neither, I decided.

Proving the adage wrong, the saucepot came quickly to a boil. "We can eat as soon as it reduces by half," Dad said, breaking the silence. He turned and walked over to the fridge and brought out a bowl of baby spinach topped with red onion, orange slices, and pine nuts. "You wanna toss the salad?" He handed me the dish of creamy dressing sitting on the counter. I dipped my finger in it to have a taste.

"Mayo, balsamic vinegar, and Italian herbs?"

"Uh-huh. With black pepper and a dash of sugar."

While I tossed the salad, Dad set a plate of bread on the table and then caught a strand of linguine with a fork and lifted it out of the water to test. "Done," he declared and tipped the contents of the steaming pot into a colander sitting in the sink. Dumping the drained pasta into the now-reduced sauce, he stirred it all up and then added back the clams. After shaking in some salt and pepper, he served two large bowls and garnished them liberally with chopped Italian parsley.

"*Il tempo per mangiare!*" he announced with a broad smile, and we sat down to eat. Nothing beats food for, at least momentarily, setting aside one's differences.

Two hours later, I was back in the T-Bird, the ragtop now up, heading home. After dinner, Dad and I had watched the Giants clobber the dastardly Snakes, and I had now settled into a mellow mood, no doubt assisted by that glass of my dad's homemade limoncello during the ninth inning.

Stopping at a red light at Broadway and Ocean, I turned up the CD player to better hear Elvis Costello's hoarse, nasal voice. The red shoes in that song always reminded me of the Converse high-tops Nichole had worn her entire first year of law school.

When the signal changed, I fumbled getting the stick into first, prompting the person waiting behind me to lay on the horn. Resisting the urge to flip the bird—I try to do my part to prevent road rage—I studiously kept my gaze forward as the car changed lanes and came up next to me.

But when it stayed even with the T-Bird, not pulling ahead as I would have expected, I finally caved and glanced over. My gut tightened, and I was afraid my clam dinner might come back up to haunt me.

It was the metallic-blue muscle car.

Letting my foot off the gas, I slowed. The muscle car slowed with me. *Okay . . . Keep it together, Sal.* What to do? Maybe I could at least get a look at the guy.

I turned again. *Damn.* Wouldn't you know he'd have tinted windows. All I could make out was a lone figure in the driver's seat. But then we passed under a streetlight, and as the car finally raced ahead, wheels squealing, a silhouette was revealed. He was staring back at me.

* * *

I'd been dreading the advent of this phone call. But nevertheless, when it finally came the following morning, I was taken completely by surprise. I was at Solari's, counting out the starting cash for the register.

"Sally. It's me, Javier. The cops arrested me early this morning. I'm in jail."

"Oh my God, Javier!" I shut the drawer and headed for the office.

"They said I could make a phone call, and since you're a lawyer . . ."

"*Used* to be. I'm inactive now. But you did the right thing to call me. Are you all right? They treating you okay?"

"Yeah, they've been treating me fine. Not super friendly, but I guess they wouldn't be, since they think I'm a murderer." He coughed and cleared his throat. "But Sally, you gotta come down and get me out. *Soon*." I could hear the urgency in his voice. "It's really awful being here. You can't imagine."

"Look, I'll get down there as soon as I can, but I'm afraid it won't be for a couple hours." *And no one's gonna be springing you today*, I added to myself, though it was probably better to wait and tell him this in person. "I'm really sorry. It's just that I can't leave work right this instant. In the meantime, don't talk to them about Letta or the murder or anything, okay?"

"I know. They read me my rights and all that."

"Good. Just hang in there. I'll see you really soon."

"Yeah, okay. Bye."

As soon as he hung up, I called Eric.

"Hey, Sal," he said. "I just heard the news."

"So why now? What gives?"

"Look, I gotta tell you"—Eric lowered his voice almost to a whisper—"I'm obviously not going to be assigned the case, but Javier's arrest does make my position even more awkward than before. Here, wait a sec." In the background, I heard footsteps and then a door slam shut, and his voice came back on the line. "Okay, I'm in my office now. So anyway, I'm just gonna have to be super careful from now on. You know, making sure there's no appearance of conflict of interest and all that."

"Got it."

"But to answer your question, two things happened. First, the results of the fingerprint analysis on Letta's key to the knife cabinet apparently came back a few days ago. I only just found out today."

"And?"

"And it's not good," Eric said. "The only prints on the key are Letta's."

"Damn." This was bad news indeed. "And what's the second thing?"

"The tox report came in this morning, which I gather they think also implicates Javier."

"What? They did a toxicology test on Letta?"

"Sure. It's a normal part of the autopsy in a case like this."

I'd completely forgotten about the autopsy. It was so obvious how she'd died that I hadn't given it a second thought. "Did they find anything?"

"They did. I've got it here; the coroner's office sent a copy to our office. It turns out she was drugged before she was stabbed."

"Drugged? What kind of drug?"

"Here, lemme grab the report. Um . . . yeah, here it is: 'indole alkaloids,' whatever they are."

"Huh. Can you send me a copy?"

"I don't think that's such a good idea, Sal. If anyone gets wind of the fact that you've got it, I'll be the obvious culprit."

"C'mon, Eric, you can trust me. I swear I won't tell a soul."

"It's not that I don't trust you. But someone could see it or something. Or if you go snooping around based on what it says, then . . . I probably shouldn't even have told you about it."

"Look, I'll keep the report under lock and key if you want. And I promise I won't let on to anyone that I know what's in it." I was slipping into my whiney voice, which I knew would only serve to annoy him further.

"Jesus, Sally. You know Javier probably did it. Once the police get around to arresting someone for murder, statistically speaking, they're usually right. So really, what's the point? Maybe you should just let this whole thing go."

I took a few deep breaths. Losing my temper right now would not be a good idea. But it was taking all my control not to completely go off on the guy.

"Okay, Eric. I get what you're saying. And you may well be right. But I'm not going to give up on him yet. All I'm asking is that you do me this one favor, and I swear I won't ask for any more." I lowered my voice, hoping it sounded more like a request than a whine. "C'mon, Eric. *Please?*"

"Well . . ."

I could tell he was starting to waver.

"You know I certainly can't e-mail or fax it . . ."

"That's okay. I'm happy to come by and—"

"No way. I don't want you anywhere near the DA's office until this case is completely settled. Look, I'll tell you what: I'll swing by with a copy in a little bit. You at Solari's?"

"Right. And thanks. I owe you."

"You bet you do. So how did Javier sound when you talked, anyway?"

"He seemed pretty freaked out, actually. He asked if I could come down and get him released."

"Well, that's sure not going to happen today. He'll have to be arraigned and have bail set, which probably won't be till the day after tomorrow."

"How much do you think bail will be?"

"For a murder? Seven hundred fifty, I think it is now. Bail bondsmen usually charge ten percent, so he'd have to pay seventy-five grand up front. I'm assuming you don't have that kind of cash lying around to lend him?"

I didn't bother answering this. "He'll get a public defender, right?"

"I imagine so. I doubt he could afford the defense of a murder trial on a cook's salary. But don't worry: I'm friends with several of the local PDs, and they're top notch, I can assure you."

I asked about visiting Javier. Having been a civil attorney, I knew virtually nothing about the procedure and had actually never even been inside the jail.

"No problem for attorneys," he said and then stopped. "Oh, but you're not—"

"Yeah, I went inactive when I quit the firm to go back to Solari's."

"Dang. That makes it more complicated. 'Cause for lawyers, all they have to do is show up and present their bar card and driver's license, and they can see anyone there anytime. But for regular folks, it's a big deal. You've got to make an appointment and can only visit at certain times."

"Can't I just become active again? I mean, I am a member in good standing and all."

"Maybe."

"Look, I'm gonna give them a call right now and see. I'll talk to you later."

As soon as I got off the phone, I remembered I'd wanted to tell him about the blue muscle car. Oh well. It would have to wait.

The man at the State Bar office, after looking up my bar number on their database, informed me that, yes, all I had to do to become an active member again was send them the proper form along with a credit card payment for the prorated bar dues I owed, and I would be deemed active as soon as my payment was processed. Of course, I'd have to start completing my continuing legal education requirements again, too. But I wasn't going to worry about that right now.

I found the form on the State Bar website, printed a copy, and filled it out. As I was trying to remember how to work the Solari's fax machine, Elena came into the office holding a sheet of paper.

"A guy in a suit just dropped this off for you."

It was the tox report. "Oh, thanks," I said. "Hey, you know how to work this thing?"

Once Elena and I had finally succeeded in getting my form through to the State Bar, I sat down to study the report. There was this finding: "various indole alkaloids, esp. gelsemine, present in blood." Turning to the office computer, I typed "gelsemine" into the Google query box, hit "search," and clicked on the first entry.

Gelsemine ($C_{20}H_{22}O_2N_2$) is an extremely toxic alkaloid derived as a bitter, white, semicrystalline substance from *Gelsemium sempervirens*. It is easily soluble in alcohol, ether, and dilute acids. It is only sparingly soluble in water, though more easily soluble in hot water. If even a teaspoon is ingested, it can produce muscle weakness and general anesthesia.

I read on. There was lots of chemical jargon I didn't understand, but then this sentence jumped off the page at me: "It has a bitter taste and an aroma akin to green tea."

Green tea. That was what Letta drank every night after work. And a Chinese teapot and two cups had been found at the crime scene. Someone must have put gelsemine in her tea to prevent her from fighting back when she was stabbed. *Ugh.* It was a gruesome image.

I wondered who could have done such a thing. It had to have been someone she knew, someone she would let into the restaurant after hours, with whom she'd share a pot of tea. Ted sprang to mind first. He was, after all, suspected of having poisoned food before. And there was the violence implicit in those letters he sent Letta. Having seen his tirade against that *charcuterie* woman at the Slow Food dinner the other night, it wasn't too far of a stretch to imagine him actually attacking someone. I was guessing the tea habit went way back for Letta, so he would have known about it. And contrary to what Ted had said the other night, I could well imagine she would welcome in, with open arms, a long-lost ex who showed up like a stray cat on her doorstep.

Of course, Kate had demonstrated a penchant for violent behavior, too, and she certainly would have been invited in as well. Then again, I was starting to have doubts about her as a suspect—especially now that it looked like she'd been telling the truth after all about the guy in the muscle car. And about not knowing the man in the photo.

But what about those two mystery men? It seemed unlikely that Letta would have let the guy in the photo into Gauguin after hours, but I couldn't be sure. If he'd shown up with some apologetic story, she very well might have bought it and invited him in for some tea.

As for the man in the blue muscle car, it was becoming more and more clear that Letta had kept numerous secrets from everyone. For all I knew, he could be another one of her ex-lovers.

And speaking of lovers, there was Tony. I now knew he had enough of a violent streak to punch Javier in the nose, plus he'd also been a party to that tussle with the chef at the wake. And one thing for sure, he definitely had the knife skills to do the deed. I'd been impressed by how quickly and adeptly he'd eviscerated those fish.

Of course, if anyone was good with a knife, it was Javier. And not only was it his knife that had been used for the stabbing, but he was also known to drink green tea with Letta regularly after work. And to top it all off, he'd been the last known person to see her alive.

I leaned my head against my palms, thinking back to what Reuben had said about Letta comparing Javier to her dog. Humiliation can be a powerful emotion. Could I have been completely wrong about Javier all this time? As Eric had said, statistically speaking, the police did tend to be right when they got around to arresting someone for murder. The thought made me queasy.

Chapter
Twenty-Four

It's a little embarrassing being a lawyer who's never been to the jail, so I was feeling self-conscious as I pulled into one of the two-hour spots in front of the large cement building. What if I did something dorky, like touch Javier (was that allowed?), and had to be chastised by the sheriff like some schoolgirl?

I pushed open the heavy glass door and found myself in a somewhat shabby waiting room that could have graced any number of government agencies. A vending machine stood against one wall, and there were benches and chairs along the others. Spying a woman sitting at a window with a sign above it saying "Reception," I walked over, and she greeted me with a smile.

"Can I help you?"

"Hi. I'm here to see one of the, uh . . . inmates." That was the right word, wasn't it?

After a quick pause, during which I could tell she was sizing me up, she asked, "Are you an attorney?"

"Yes, I am." I handed her my bar card and driver's license.

"This says you're inactive," she said and started to hand the items back.

"I've only just gone active again and haven't received my new card yet. But here, call this number, and they'll confirm that I'm active." I pointed to the member services phone number on the back of the bar card.

With a shrug, she took the card, rolled her office chair over to the desk across from the reception window, and picked up the phone. After talking for a couple minutes, she rolled back over to me. "Okay," she said, keeping the card this time. "And who would you like to see?"

"Javier Ruiz."

She found him on the computer. "Here," she said and handed me a visitor's badge to hang on my lapel. "It'll be a couple minutes. One of the sheriffs will come out to get you."

"Okay. Thanks." I started to walk away, but she called me back.

"I'll need to check your purse. And you'll have to leave your keys and cell phone if you have one with you."

"Oh, sorry." I handed over my phone and keys, let her search my bag, and then wandered over to where a squat kiosk was sitting in the middle of the room. It took a minute, but I finally figured out that it was for depositing money to give to the inmates. The machine accepted credit cards as well as cash, the sign announced. Convenient.

Taking a seat by the window, I perused the stack of magazines sitting on the side table, curious as to what reading material one would find in the waiting room of a jail. There was a *Newsweek*, a *Sports Illustrated*, a *Redbook*, and at the bottom of the stack, one with the unexpected title of *Lucky Kids*.

As I was flipping through its pages, reflecting that any kids who happened to be in the jail waiting room likely wouldn't consider themselves to be all that lucky, a sheriff came out and said he was ready to take me on back. He was young, in his midtwenties, I guessed, and I saw that he had a yellow Taser in a holster on the front of his belt.

We passed through a double glass-door entry—the first one closing tightly before the second opened—and I followed the sheriff down a wide hallway. On our left was a row of little cubicles with phones and glass windows between them, but he didn't stop there. Instead, he showed me into a larger room on the right with a wall made of glass that faced out toward the hallway.

"You been here before?" he asked.

"No, it's my first time."

"Okay." He pointed to a metal box on the wall next to the door. "The one on the right is the call button for when you're ready to leave."

"What's the other for?" I asked, indicating the red one on the left. "The panic button?"

He smiled. "You got it. It'll just be a minute, and I'll bring Mr. Ruiz in." The sheriff closed the door, and I took a seat on one of the two red plastic chairs. There were no other furnishings. The room had a scuffed vinyl floor and white walls with an industrial-shade green trim. The plaster was cracked in spots and someone had scrawled "Marcus ♥ Trisha" to the right of my chair.

I started when the door opened again, and there was Javier in an orange jumpsuit with a brown T-shirt poking out from underneath. The words "XL Santa Cruz County Jail" were stenciled in black on his back and legs. I wondered why they hadn't given him a smaller size. The clothes looked sack-like on his slight frame. As he shuffled in, my eyes were drawn to the backless, brown plastic sandals he was wearing, which had a fake weave texture that reminded me of Mexican *huaraches*. I wondered if he, too, had noticed the resemblance.

He sat down in the other chair, and the sheriff left us alone.

"How you doing?"

Javier looked up at me. "How do you think I'm doing?" His face was drawn and looked pallid under the fluorescent lights.

"Yeah. Right."

"So I don't understand why they arrested me. Now, I mean. If they were gonna do it, why'd they wait so long?"

I told him about the fingerprint results, and he slumped in his chair. "That must be why they came by the restaurant again last week."

"And that's unfortunately not all," I added. I explained about the toxicology report and that I thought the tea had probably been drugged. "So I'm afraid it doesn't look good for you, Javier. You knew she liked to drink green tea after work, and they found tea cups at the scene. Not only that, but you were the last one there that night. And it was your knife."

"But—"

"I'm not saying I think you did it. But the cops clearly think so."

He leaned over, put his head in his hands, and started rocking his body back and forth in the chair. "So what are we going to do?" It was almost a moan.

I didn't have an answer to this. Although I had lots of suspects for the murder, as of yet, I had no actual evidence or proof that any of them had done it.

"I don't know, Javier," I said, sighing deeply. "I really don't. But you'll be getting a lawyer appointed for you—one of the public defenders. Maybe their investigator can do a better job than I've been able to do."

Javier sat up slowly, raising his head to look at me. "I don't mean to be ungrateful, Sally. It's wonderful, all you've been doing. I really appreciate it."

"Yeah. Too bad it hasn't done any good." *Useless, utterly ineffectual. That's what I've been.* Berating myself didn't help, but it was maddening to see him sitting there like that and to feel so completely powerless. "Is there anyone you'd like me to get in touch with? Let them know what's going on with you?"

He shook his head. "No, thanks."

I realized then that I knew hardly anything about his private life—whether he had any relatives in the area, any close friends. "'Cause I could contact your family—"

"No," he interrupted me. And then in a softer voice, "They're all in Michoacán, anyway." He sighed. "So what happens next? Can you get me out of here?"

I shook my head. "Not today, I'm afraid. You'll be arraigned probably on Friday. That's when they'll officially charge you with the crime. And that's also when you should be appointed your lawyer."

"But I can get out if I pay the . . . what's it called?" His voice was starting to have a frantic edge. "Right?"

"Bail. Yeah, probably. But I gotta tell you, Javier, it's going to be like seven hundred fifty thousand dollars for your case.

And you'd have to pay ten percent up front, nonrefundable, to get a bail bond—if they'd even give you a bond, that is. They'd most likely require some kind of security for such a large amount. You don't own a house, do you?"

His body slumped, and he shook his head. "No."

"Look, I'll see what I can find out about getting bail for you. But we don't need to deal with that right this second, since it's going to be at least a couple days before you could get out in any event."

As I said this, our eyes met, and I could tell we had both had the same thought: *the restaurant.*

I looked at my watch. It was a little after one. "You know anyone we can call to come in at a moment's notice and cook tonight?" I asked Javier.

"Well, Reuben will be there anyway. He should be able to act as lead cook. Just call him to make sure he knows to get there early. And Tomás can move over to head line cook. He's done it before." Javier did some mental calculations. "Let's see. That would mean Dave would have to help out with the *garde manger*, but I think he's up to it. And Amy can help too, if she's not too swamped with desserts. You'd still need one more person in the kitchen, though, and I don't know who we could get at this late notice . . ." He was looking at me.

"No way."

Javier shrugged. "It's your restaurant. If you want to be one short, that's your decision."

"But I've never worked the hot line. All I've ever done is help out in the kitchen. It'd be a joke!" Now it was my turn to sound hysterical.

Javier just kept looking at me. If he hadn't been sitting there in a jail interview room wearing a bright-orange jumpsuit, I swear he would have been enjoying this.

"Okay," I finally said. "You win. But just for this one night. We're finding another cook by tomorrow."

* * *

"Fire table seven!" Brandon poked his head over the pickup counter and caught my eye. "And I'm still waiting on that Tahitian sea bass for table two, Sally."

"I'm on it." I dropped the shrimp I'd been counting out for an order of scampi in orange sauce back into the hotel pan and went to investigate the missing appetizer.

After leaving a morose-looking Javier at the jail with promises of visiting the next day, I'd called Solari's to say I'd be missing in action *again* that night. I then headed directly over to Gauguin. Since Javier didn't know Reuben's number by heart and obviously didn't have his phone with him, I'd have to get it from the list in Letta's office. It was almost two o'clock by the time I got there, but fortunately Reuben picked up when I called and agreed to come in early and run the kitchen for the night.

"Actually, it will likely be for several nights," I corrected myself, "or more. I don't know how long Javier will be . . . unavailable at this point. But don't worry, you'll get compensated accordingly."

"No problem," Reuben said, no doubt pleased to hear this last bit. When I explained Javier's staffing concept to him, however—in particular that I'd be the extra cook, at least for this one night, until a real one could be located—he'd sounded dubious.

"It's okay," I said, trying to assure myself as much as him. "I've helped out cooking at Gauguin before." Which was technically true, if a little misleading. But I had forgotten just how frenetic it could be in a restaurant kitchen, especially during a dinner rush like we were experiencing at this moment.

Back in the *garde manger* area, I found Dave putting the last touches on the Tahitian sea bass, arranging rice balls around the plate and garnishing the marinated fish with grated coconut and twisted slices of lime.

"Sorry," he said as he handed it to me. "I'm totally in the weeds." He looked harried, and his station was in a shambles. But for someone who usually just broke down chickens and chopped vegetables, I thought he was doing a fine job.

"No worries." I rushed back to the pickup counter with the plate, tapped the bell, and called out, "Order up!" I then returned to my shrimp.

As I leaned over to check the thermostat on the deep fryer, a voice boomed out: "Behind you!" Tomás, bearing a small, round stainless-steel container, squeezed between me and the long work table running down the middle of the room. He set the container down near Reuben, who nodded thanks without taking his eyes off the four sauté pans he had going at the far end of the range.

I watched as Reuben picked up a pan in each hand and simultaneously flipped their contents. Reaching into the container Tomás had fetched him, he added a handful of dried apricots to each order, let them brown for a minute, and then deglazed the pans with a healthy glug from one of the bottles sitting behind him on the work table. Ah, seared pork chops with apricot brandy sauce.

A ding from the deep fryer brought me out of my reverie. Giving a final, quick stir to my batter, I started dipping shrimp and dropping them, one by one, into the hot oil. Once they were all bubbling nicely in the deep fryer, I grabbed a pair of deep plates from the warming oven and set about dishing up two orders of *coq au vin au Gauguin* for the deuce at table seven.

Just another average night in the restaurant business.

Chapter
Twenty-Five

Waking up at eight AM is not a pleasant experience when you didn't go to sleep until almost two the night before. I'd actually gotten home at around midnight but was too wired from the night's work to go straight to bed. Although cooking in a high-end restaurant can be crazy exhausting, it can also be a total rush. That feeling of synergy, when the whole kitchen is in perfect sync, like a finely calibrated machine, everyone at their different stations, elbows practically bumping in the cramped quarters.

And when the night is done—the last order sent out to the dining room, the perishables wrapped up and stowed away in the walk-in fridge, the pots washed and the rangetop wiped clean—you're left with a big-time buzz, as if shot up with some kind of strong stimulant.

So it takes a while to unwind. Alcohol helps and is commonly consumed by restaurant workers after hours. After closing that night at Gauguin, I hung out with the staff, drinking beer and shots of tequila till about eleven thirty.

But when I got home, I was still too hyped to go to bed, so I channel-surfed for an hour and a half and had another beer.

This lifestyle is all well and fine if you're young and if you don't have to show up for your next shift until four the next afternoon. But I am no longer in my twenties and was supposed to be at Solari's at ten thirty.

Groggy and slightly hungover (I should have skipped at least that last beer), I decided to stop by the jail before heading to work. I doubted Javier would be sleeping in, even if they let the inmates do that, and I figured he'd be thankful for the visit.

He looked a little better than the day before. The shock of yesterday's arrest and incarceration seemed to have been replaced by resignation. But I could tell he was depressed. Who wouldn't be?

"Well, Reuben did a good job as sous-chef," I said, trying to sound cheerful as he shuffled into the interview room once again in his soft plastic slippers. Were they purposely made backless in order to discourage thoughts of fleeing?

Javier nodded. He didn't seem too interested in the restaurant this morning, so I changed the subject. "How was it here last night?"

He shrugged. "My cellmate snores."

"That's no fun. I don't think I'm allowed to bring you anything like earplugs, but you could try wadding up some toilet paper."

"Yeah." He shifted in his chair. "What I'd really love is a cigarette, but there's no smoking in the jail."

"Any news on when you'll get arraigned?"

"Tomorrow morning, they said. Probably."

I wasn't sure why he was acting so different from yesterday, why he was so taciturn. Maybe it had just taken a day for it all to really sink in. That and shame, perhaps. The fact that he didn't want anyone to know he was here suggested deep embarrassment about his plight. I guess I couldn't blame him. I tried to keep the conversation going for a while longer, but after about ten minutes of me talking and Javier giving one-syllable responses, I gave up.

"Look, I gotta get to work. But I'll try to make it to your arraignment tomorrow." I stood up and pushed the call button. "Hey, Sally, can you do me a favor?"

"Yeah, sure. Of course."

"I forgot about it yesterday when I saw you, but I'm supposed to be feeding my next-door neighbor's cat while she's gone. She gets back tomorrow, but since the cat didn't get any food yesterday, it's probably pretty hungry."

I smiled. Depressed as he was about his own plight, Javier was still concerned about a neighbor's cat. "I can feed it. No problem."

He told me where his apartment was and that a bin of dry food was sitting right outside his neighbor's door. A pair of sheriffs came in and waited until he'd finished. Then one took Javier away and the other escorted me back out to the lobby.

*   *   *

I pulled up in front of Solari's and stripped off my wool blazer as soon as I got out of the car. These hot flashes were becoming truly annoying. As I tossed the jacket onto the back seat, I saw sitting there the letter and surveyor's report my dad had given me the other night. What with the chaos of yesterday, I'd forgotten all about them. Better take a look now, before he asked if I'd read them yet. I grabbed the papers and, after securing a much-needed cup of coffee, got myself settled in the office and pulled out the letter from Wanda's attorney:

Dear Mr. Solari,

Please be informed that this letter hereby serves as notice to you that the plants along the fence between your property and that of my client, Wanda Eldridge, are on the property of my client, as shown by the enclosed report performed by Hanson, Reilly & Assoc., Land Surveyors . . .

Blah, blah, blah. Typical overblown legalese. I was about to turn to the copy of the surveyor's report, but then my eye was caught by the word "toxic" in the letter. I read this paragraph:

As for the *Brugmansia*, a.k.a. Angel's Trumpet, this plant presents a serious hazard to the family of Ms. Eldridge, in particular, her young grandchildren. For notwithstanding that the flowers have a sweet perfume, they are in fact highly toxic. If only a small amount is ingested, it can be dangerous, even fatal. Because the flowers in fact look like small trumpets, there have been numerous cases of children being poisoned after putting them to their lips. Some municipalities in the US have actually banned the plant because of this danger.

I hadn't paid any attention to this when I'd first skimmed the letter at my dad's house, but now that the toxicology report on Letta had come back, it had a whole new resonance. That drug they found in her blood—what if it also came from a plant in someone's garden?

I grabbed my bag and pulled out the toxicology report I'd stuffed inside the day before. Unfolding the paper and smoothing it out, I scanned the page for the name of the toxin. There it was: gelsemine. I turned to the office computer and pulled the drug up again on the net.

Yep, I was right. The alkaloid was derived from *Gelsemium sempervirens.* Common name, "yellow jasmine." How could I have missed that before? I typed "yellow jasmine" into the browser search box and learned that it was a climbing vine with prolific, bright-yellow flowers and dark-green leaves. It bloomed in early spring. That would be now.

But did it grow in this area? Perusing several articles noting that yellow jasmine thrives in "temperate to tropical climes," I finally found one saying that it did fine in coastal California as long as it got good sun and received plenty of moisture. I took a good look at pictures of the plant on various websites in the hope that I'd be able to recognize it if I saw one.

A soft knock at the partly opened door startled me. "Sally, could I talk to you for a minute?" Giulia stuck her head into the office.

"Yeah, sure," I said and forced myself to pay attention as she explained about a scheduling conflict the following week.

Once the Solari's lunch crowd had finally thinned out, I headed over to Gauguin. Reuben had found us a new cook, which thankfully relieved me of further responsibility, but I needed to make sure he'd actually shown up and that all was going smoothly.

The new guy turned out to be a gal, Kris. She was already in the kitchen when I got there, being shown around by Reuben. They'd cooked together at another place some years back, and he was confident she'd fit in well with the Gauguin crew. My regard for Reuben bumped up a notch.

I left them to it and went upstairs to the office. I'd spaced out organizing the bills and invoices for Shanti the day before, and she'd be coming by for them in a few hours. Sitting down at the desk, I was about to open the receipts file Javier had left out for me when my eye was caught by a letter sitting at the top of today's mail pile on the desk.

It was a plain, white envelope with my name and "c/o Gauguin" typed on the front. There was no return address, but it did have a San Francisco postmark. I got a tingling sensation on my skin. Sure enough, inside was a sheet of paper with printed text that looked disturbingly familiar:

Sally—
So you've taken over Gauguin after the tragic demise of its previous owner. I suggest that this is a good opportunity to make some changes to the restaurant, which has sadly, up until now, been a *pawn of corporate agriculture.*

Not only are you supporting factory farming—in other words, ***the torture of innocent animals***—by serving industrial meat, but when you have farmed salmon and imported shrimp on the menu, you are a part of the systematic *decimation* of our ocean life.

It is time for you to switch to *humanely* raised meat and *sustainable* seafood! Do it **NOW**. I won't go away. Remember what happened to Letta.

Noah

I set the letter down and got up to yank open the window. A feeling of claustrophobia had overtaken me. My forehead was hot, and I was starting to sweat. It could have been a hot flash, and the lingering hangover also no doubt didn't help. But I knew those weren't the real causes.

That look in Ted's eyes as he'd raged at the *charcuterie* woman after dinner had come back to me, reading the last sentence of his letter. And now I was on his list.

I picked up the phone and called Eric.

"I'm scared," I said.

* * *

Eric advised me to take the letter straight down to the police station and talk with Detective Vargas. He became even more adamant after I told him about the blue car. "I may have my issues with the guy, but you should let the cops do their job. That's what they're there for."

"You sound like my dad," I said. But I knew he was right.

I couldn't leave Gauguin, however, until I'd organized the bills for Shanti. And then once that was finished, I remembered the cat. *Better stop and feed the poor, starving thing on my way over to the police station.*

Javier's apartment was downtown, a couple blocks from Neary Lagoon. I found a spot in his parking garage and climbed the stairs to the second floor. Following the walkway around the side of the building, I located his number. Sure enough, outside the next door down were two bowls and a Tupperware container of cat food. At the sound of the tub being opened, a large gray-and-white tabby came trotting down the walkway and brushed up against my legs. It started to eat as soon as I poured out the kibble.

Seeing that the water was also low, I picked up the other bowl and went in search of a hose or outdoor spigot. I finally found a faucet at the back of the building next to the garage. As I crouched down to fill the bowl, I noticed some yellow flowers scattered over the cement and looked up. There, climbing all the way up to the third story, was a magnificent vine covered in blooms.

I wasn't positive, but it sure looked like a yellow jasmine. Shaking my head in defeat, I picked a couple flowers and a sprig of leaves and tucked them into my jacket pocket.

It can't be. Please, no.

Water bowl in hand, I headed back upstairs, trying to decide what to do with this new evidence. Should I tell Detective Vargas about the flowers? On the one hand, it seemed wrong to volunteer information that could harm Javier when I had no proof at this point that it was even pertinent. For all I knew, the plant could be totally unrelated to yellow jasmine. And how could I even be completely sure that yellow jasmine was what had been given to Letta in any case?

But on the other hand, as a member of the bar, I knew I was considered to be "an officer of the court," which mandated the legal and ethical obligation to come forward with any possibly relevant evidence. Too bad I'd had to go active again, or I wouldn't be facing this moral dilemma.

The gunning of a car engine interrupted my musing, and I nearly spilled water all down my front. Turning at the sound, I was just in time to catch a flash of blue as a car entered the parking garage.

Was that the muscle car?

I set the bowl down and took several deep breaths, unsure whether this was paranoia or whether my ramped-up heartbeat was a rational response to the situation. I stood there on the walkway for a couple minutes, hoping that whoever was in the car would simply emerge from the garage and go into their apartment.

No such luck. *Damn.*

Removing Letta's can of pepper spray from my bag, I transferred it to my right jacket pocket and made my way back down the stairs.

At the door to the parking garage, I stopped and listened. All was quiet. I let my eyes get used to the dark and then scanned the place, searching for the metallic-blue muscle car. At this hour, when most folks were probably still at work, there were only a few cars in the building, and the only blue one I could see was a dinged-up Toyota Corolla—definitely not the muscle car that had followed me before.

I exhaled and released the grip I'd had on the can of pepper spray. The T-Bird was against the far wall, and as I crossed toward it, I could feel my shoulders begin to relax. After stopping by the police station, I was going to go home and pour myself a hefty Jim Beam on the rocks.

Once at the driver's side door, I set my bag on the hood and searched for my car keys. I rummaged around, cursing the propensity of keys to always sink to the very bottom of whatever clutter one might possess. And then a hand clapped over my mouth.

A second one immediately grabbed me around the waist.

I tried to yell, but the sound was muffled by the large hand pressing down more firmly.

"Don't struggle if you don't want to be hurt," a low male voice said.

I stood still. I'm tall for a woman and no weakling. But I could tell from the way he was bending over me that this guy was way bigger than me.

"I've been watching you," he went on, "and I'm gonna keep on watching."

So he must be the mystery man in the blue muscle car. But if so, where was the car? Why hadn't I seen it?

But mostly I was thinking, *Please let someone come into the garage—right now!*

"I seen you poking your nose where it don't belong, and I don't like it one bit." The man's voice was raspy, like he had phlegm in his throat that needed clearing. "But all you gotta do is lay off, and everything will be fine."

As he said this last bit, he squeezed even harder, pinning my left arm against my body. Painful as it was, however, it gave me an idea. With the way he was holding me, maybe I could get my right hand free.

He leaned down farther to whisper into my ear. "You understand what I mean?"

I nodded, using the opportunity for movement as cover to slip my right hand into my jacket pocket.

"Good. Because—"

My arm shot up, and a blast of pepper spray hit him square in the eyes. Doubling over, he released his grip and fell to the ground, hands over his face. A string of obscenities spewed from his mouth, all directed at me.

I grabbed my bag and dumped its contents onto the ground; snatched up my phone, wallet, and keys; and let myself into the T-Bird. He was still writhing about on the parking garage floor when I sped off.

Chapter Twenty-Six

It was only a few blocks to the police station, but I didn't want to waste any time, so I dialed 9-1-1 as I drove there, my shaking hands making it difficult to complete the call. The woman at Dispatch assured me they'd send an officer to the parking garage ASAP and then kept me on the line until I arrived at the station.

"It's okay," I told her as I pulled up in front of the building. "I'm here now." Grabbing the pile of papers sitting on the passenger seat, I jumped out of the car and ran up the steps to the double glass doors.

Dispatch had apparently already informed Detective Vargas of the situation, because he was waiting for me in the lobby. "Come on in," he said, and I followed his beefy figure once more upstairs to the investigation area.

After offering me a cup of coffee, which I declined, he motioned for me to take a seat on the same couch as before. "So why don't you tell me exactly what happened."

Unlike the last time we'd met, the detective seemed to be doing his best to put me at ease. He leaned forward as he spoke, and his brows were creased in a show of concern.

I thought back to all that had happened over the last couple weeks and decided to start by telling him about Letta's buying the pepper spray. "It was because of those letters she got, I'm sure, and that guy who was harassing her at the restaurant, the one in the photo Ruth Kallenbach sent you."

"Right," he said. "But we didn't know about the pepper spray."

I then recounted what Kate had said about a man in a muscle car coming up to her farm and told him how I'd seen a metallic-blue muscle car behind me twice the other day. "I'm thinking the car I saw might be the same one that guy—the one who came up to Kate's farm—was driving," I said, "and that he's been following me for some reason."

We were interrupted at this point by a call for Vargas. He listened for a minute; said, "Okay, thanks"; and then switched off the phone and returned it to his pocket.

"That was Dispatch. The officer who was sent to the parking garage saw no sign of the man who attacked you, but he did find your purse with all its contents spilled on the ground."

I nodded and then swallowed, trying to hold it together. *So he was still out there.*

"Why don't you go on with your story."

I picked up the papers I'd set down next to me and extracted the threatening letter I'd received earlier in the day. As he read through it, I explained how I'd met "Noah" and what his real name was. "It turns out he used to be involved with my Aunt Letta back in the eighties, so now there's way more of a connection between them than anyone thought before. And here, check this out."

I handed him the two articles I'd printed out about Noah's letters to Bay Area restaurants and the food contamination incident. "So it looks like he doesn't just stop at writing threatening letters. And I've got to say, having seen the guy in action, I'm not sure just how far he'd go."

The detective looked up from the articles he'd been skimming. "As far as murder, you mean?"

"Well, somebody stabbed my aunt in the chest multiple times, and now we've got several clear links between this guy, who's proven himself to be on the far edge of fanatical, and Letta. Not only that, but now he's turned his sights on me. Thank God he doesn't know that I know who he is . . ."

But as I said this, it occurred to me that maybe he *did* know. The thought was chilling, and I pushed it away. "So all I'm getting at is, I was wondering if you could look into him a bit—at least do a background check on the guy now that you know his real name."

Vargas gathered up the papers and secured them with a paper clip. "Sure, we can do that. But you wanna tell me about what just happened in that parking garage?"

"Okay . . ." I explained about going to Javier's apartment building to feed his neighbor's cat and was about to do my ethical duty as an "officer of the court" and tell him about the flowers. But then I realized that the only way I could possibly know of their relevance would be if I'd seen the toxicology report. Which would bust Eric big time.

"So on my way back upstairs with the water," I went on, omitting any mention of the yellow vine, "I hear this gunning of an engine, and I turn just in time to see a blue car go into the parking garage."

"Was it the same one you saw before?"

"I'm not sure. All I saw was a glimpse of the blue color. And when I got back down to the garage, there were only a few cars there, and none of them looked at all like the one that had been following me. The only blue one was an old Corolla, definitely not the muscle car. Anyway, so I was looking for my keys when it happened, when he grabbed me from behind."

I recounted what the man had said and then described how I'd managed to get free, at which point I kind of lost it and started shaking like crazy.

The detective started out of his chair, but I waved him off, so he just sat back down and waited till I composed myself. After a minute, he asked, "Can you describe your assailant? Or this muscle car that's been following you?"

"I didn't get a look at his face, unfortunately, but he was a big guy, well over six feet, and he had short, dark hair. He was wearing blue jeans, and a dark sweatshirt, and white running shoes. As for the car I saw before . . . I dunno. One of those big ones from the seventies. A Camaro? Or Duster? Like I said, it was metallic blue. Oh, and I do remember it had those old blue-colored license plates."

"Well, that's helpful, at least. You didn't get any of the license, did you? Even a partial would be helpful."

I shook my head. "Sorry. So anyway, I'm thinking it must have been that same guy—the one who drove up to Kate's farm—because of how she described it as a muscle car, just like the one that's been following me."

"But you said you didn't see that car in the garage."

"No, but I did see a blue car go in, and, I dunno . . . He could have hidden it out of sight somewhere. Maybe there's another exit I didn't notice."

Vargas drummed his fingers on his right thigh and chewed his lip. Then, leaning forward, he said in a soft voice, "Has it occurred to you that—given where this incident occurred—it's equally likely that it was an associate of Javier's who jumped you?" He leaned back in the chair and fixed me with a hard stare. "Especially if there was something you saw there that the associate knew could incriminate Javier?"

My face was burning, but with my olive complexion, I doubted the detective could tell. Of course the cops would already know about the yellow jasmine at Javier's building. That had to be one of the main reasons for his arrest. But how could Vargas possibly know that I'd seen the tox report? Or was this just a bluff?

I didn't answer and instead pulled the can of pepper spray from my pocket. "You want to keep this as evidence?" I asked.

"No, I think it's better if you hold onto it for the time being."

*   *   *

Javier's arraignment was set for nine o'clock the next morning, Friday. I got to court a few minutes early but needn't have rushed over, as it was almost an hour before his case was finally called. During this time, I tried to work on the scheduling snafu that Giulia had pointed out to me the previous day. But it was hard to keep my mind on it, as my thoughts kept returning to the guy who'd grabbed me in the parking garage and who was still out there somewhere. Plus, there was the threatening letter I'd gotten from Noah as well as the depressing discovery I'd made online that the vine at Javier's apartment did in fact appear to be yellow jasmine.

They finally brought Javier out in his orange jumpsuit, and the judge read him his rights, advised him of the charges against him—he visibly slumped upon hearing the words "murder in the first degree"—and told him that he was being appointed counsel. At this point, a man in a dark suit stood up and agreed to accept the case. He spoke quietly with Javier for a moment and then turned back to the judge. "Request to put the matter over, your honor, until I've had time to confer with my client."

"Granted. The matter will be heard"—the judge consulted her calendar—"a week from today, at which time Mr. Ruiz can enter his plea. Next case."

A sheriff escorted Javier out the side door through which he'd entered the courtroom. I waved, but I'm not sure he saw me. I would have liked to talk to Javier's attorney, but he remained sitting at the defense table after Javier was led away.

As soon as I got to Solari's, I went in search of my dad. He was at the six-burner range, sampling the sauce for the day's lunch special: chicken with tarragon-cream sauce.

"Tastes fine, Emilio," he said, smacking his lips, and dropped the used spoon into the sink behind the hot line. "Don't forget to sprinkle some chopped tarragon on top when you plate them up."

I was about to tell Dad that I thought he did need to hire a lawyer to deal with his property-line dispute and that there was a gal at my old firm who would be good for the job. But when he saw me come into the kitchen, he touched me on the shoulder.

"Hey, hon," he said. "I've been wanting to talk to you about something. C'mere."

We sat in the office, he in the folding chair and me on the corner of the desk—there wasn't room for a second chair—and he exhaled slowly.

Uh oh. What now?

He cleared his throat. "Look, I just want to apologize again for how I've been about this whole thing, you know, with Letta's restaurant." Dad ran a hand through his close-cropped hair, scratching his scalp. "It's just that after you came back to Solari's, after your mother passed on, I was so . . . I don't know. So relieved, I guess. 'Cause I didn't have to worry about the restaurant anymore—about who'd take it over after I was gone."

"Dad, I—"

"No, let me finish." He wiped both hands on the bar towel hanging from his chef's pants and then went on. "But I realize now that it's not fair to you. No matter what I may want, you gotta do what *you* want. I mean, really, that's pretty much what being a parent is all about: making sure your kids are gonna be able to make their own decisions, not forcing your own on them." He exhaled again and stood up. "So I just want you to know, if you want to take over Gauguin and run the place—if that's what *you* want, not what you think Letta or someone else would want—then I'm okay with that decision."

And before I could say anything in answer, he'd turned and walked out the door.

It was nearly impossible to stay focused on work during lunch, given all that had happened over the past few days. Plus, how unexpected was that about my dad? Not only what he'd said but also the very fact *that* he'd managed to say it at all. It was amazing but also daunting—because now I'd been given permission to do something that half of me desperately wanted but which filled the other half with unmitigated terror.

As I rushed about the dining room seating people, serving their bar orders, replenishing their bread, I couldn't stop thinking about how morose Dad had seemed as he'd essentially told me to leave the nest and go create my own new life. But I also kept seeing Javier's miserable face, standing there so alone in the courtroom that morning.

And then, while taking a phone reservation for Saturday night, my mind flashed on Ted's crazed expression at the end of that Slow Food dinner. After making an entry in the book (party of six for seven o'clock), I scrawled a note to remind myself to warn Reuben that he needed to be extra vigilant about checking the food deliveries at Gauguin.

At three fifteen, I'd had enough and sneaked out the side door without telling anyone but Elena that I was leaving. It had been ages since I'd gone for a bike ride, and I knew that rain was forecast for the next day, so I rushed home and changed into my cycling clothes. A trip up Highway 1 to Davenport and back before the busy Friday-night dinner shift seemed like a good way to clear my head.

I followed the bike path from the north end of town up to Wilder Ranch and then jumped onto the highway for the rest of the ten-mile trip north. It was tough going, as I was riding smack into a vicious headwind. To make matters worse, although there's a wide shoulder, cars were whizzing by at sixty and seventy miles per hour, which was rather intimidating.

But you can't beat the scenery: sandy beaches and rocky cliffs interspersed with cropland, old wooden barns, and stands of tall eucalyptus. And it was good to work up a sweat and feel my legs burn—the perfect thing to get my mind off Noah and Javier. And the guy in the muscle car.

When I finally made it to Davenport, I stopped at the bakery to refuel with a chocolate chip cookie, which I munched on the bluff overlooking the sea. Davenport is an old whaling town, and I squinted into the sun to see if I could spot any gray whales making their annual migration south. Must be too late in the season, I decided, brushing the crumbs off my jersey and standing up. Nary a whale in sight.

Mounting my bike and clipping in once more, I headed back down the coast. With the strong tail wind now pushing me along, the ride was an entirely different experience. I barely had to pedal, and it seemed like I was back in Santa Cruz in record time.

As I cruised down Delaware Avenue, I noticed several shrubs with yellow flowers. And then on the next corner, another tall bush dotted with yellow against a garage wall. Yellow plants were everywhere, it seemed.

That was it. With a quick glance over my shoulder, I took a hard left. Tony's house was just a few blocks over. I remembered lots of blooms in his front yard and had to see if any of them were yellow.

Negotiating my way through the labyrinth of the Circles, a Westside neighborhood confusing even to locals as it is laid out in almost—but not quite—concentric rings, I turned down Tony's street.

Damn. Not one yellow flower; the only vine in his front yard was the purple wisteria. Nor could I see any yellow plants along the side of the house.

Tony was out in front, sweeping the walkway. I stopped pedaling, and the clicking of the freewheel caused him to look up. He leaned on his broom. "Sally."

"Hi, Tony." I coasted up onto the sidewalk and clipped out of my pedals. "How you doing?"

"Okay," he said, leaning down to pick up a bottle of beer that was sitting on the walkway at his feet. "What brings you here?"

"Nothing. Just out for a bike ride. Before the storm comes in."

"Yeah. I hear you." Taking a long drink, he nodded toward the power mower sitting on his freshly cut lawn. "I wanted to get this done before the rain started."

"The yard's looking great," I said. "Those plants over there, especially." I pointed at the beds of flowers lining the walkway.

"Thanks. Just wait till next month, when the roses really get going."

"Speaking of flowers," I said, "are you familiar with a vine called yellow jasmine?"

Perhaps it was unwise to broach this subject with Tony. But I still hadn't gotten any closer to figuring out who had killed Letta, and with Javier now in jail, I guess I was feeling kind of desperate. Maybe I could learn something from his reaction upon hearing the name of the plant.

I studied his face, trying to discern any change in expression. There was a slight raise of the eyebrows, but I read this as curiosity as opposed to guilt. "Sure," he answered. "You see 'em all over Santa Cruz. Why do you ask?" Tony tossed the now-empty bottle onto the lawn, nearly hitting another that was already there and started sweeping again, piling the errant blades of grass into a mound.

"Letta's autopsy report just came back, and it looks like whoever stabbed her drugged her first, with something called gelsemine. It's a sedative that comes from yellow jasmine. *Gelsemium sempervirens* is its botanical name. But I probably don't need to tell you that." At his quizzical look, I added, "You know, being a gardening aficionado, an' all."

"Right." He resumed sweeping, brushing the pile of grass onto a dustpan and tipping it into the green waste container sitting on the sidewalk. "I'm done out here," he said, slapping his hands against his jeans. "You want to come inside for a beer?"

I considered for a moment before responding. I wasn't super keen on the idea of hanging out with Tony, particularly after he'd been drinking, but this would give me a chance to check out those photos on his fridge again. As I recalled, one was taken at the beach; it would surely tell me if he had a Giants tattoo on his forearm. Maybe Kate had been wrong, and it was Tony, after all, who'd visited her farm. "Sure," I said. "But can I put my bike around back? I don't want it to get stolen."

"No problem. Come on." He pushed the lawnmower over to the side of the house and unlatched the gate. As Tony stowed the mower in a little shed, I leaned my bike against the wall in the backyard and removed my helmet, taking the opportunity for a quick look around. No yellow vines in sight. We then went back out front, and I followed him up onto the porch, the cleats of my cycling shoes clunking on the wooden steps, and into the house.

"All I have is Negra Modelo."

"That's fine; I love dark beer." I leaned down to pat Buster, who had come running into the kitchen at the sound of our entry. As Tony got down glasses, I turned to the fridge and studied the pictures again. There was a shirtless Tony, arms displayed for all the world to see but completely bare of tattoos as far as I could tell. I glanced again at the photo taken at the ball game, but he had on a jacket in that one.

And then I did one of those classic double takes. *Whoa.* Tony's brother matched exactly Kate's description of the mystery man: stocky with dark hair, and it looked like he'd be around fifty now if the photo had been taken several years ago. Not only that, but he was a big guy, like whoever had accosted me in the parking garage. I looked to see if he had a tattoo on his forearm, but alas, he had on long sleeves.

And then I saw it: on the boys' jerseys, the letters *ny* stitched in lowercase letters right above the number ten.

What a dork I'd been. The tattoo was blue because it was the *football* team, the *New York* Giants, whose color was blue. Blue like the muscle car. Without thinking, I let out a little gasp.

Tony turned from opening the beer bottles and stared at me. "What is it?"

"Uh, nothing. It's just that, uh . . ." I tried to think fast what to say. "I thought I recognized the woman standing behind the kids in this picture, is all. But now that I look closer, I can see that it's not her."

Lame, lame!

"Huh." Tony turned back to the bottles and poured them carefully into our glasses while I pretended to study the woman in the bleachers behind Tony, his brother, and the two boys.

"Yeah," I continued with my lousy story, tapping the photo with my finger, "it's definitely not her. But they really do look alike. Funny."

"Yeah. Funny," Tony repeated. He set the bottles down on the counter next to a vase of tiny, bell-like white blossoms and handed me my glass of beer.

What a walking contradiction he was. The brash, sports-loving New Jersey macho man versus the tender boyfriend who'd bring Letta flowers from his garden for her restaurant and who worried about sea lice on salmon.

As we sat once more in his den, sipping our beer and making small talk, I tried to imagine Tony as the crazed maniac who murdered Letta. The clues did seem to fit, and I knew that most murders were recommitted by a family member or lover. But the idea of this guy, sitting here chatting with me calmly about spring bulbs, being someone who could stab his fiancée repeatedly in the chest until she was dead? It seemed way too surreal for me to accept as possible.

Tony was talking in a slightly slurred voice—I wondered just how many beers he'd had before I arrived—about bearded irises. There was a yard not too far from here planted with hundreds of them I should check out, he was saying, in a wide variety of hues: blue, lavender, yellow, cream, brown . . .

I pictured all those irises. *It would be like a Van Gogh painting. His are mostly blue and purple, aren't they?* The colors Tony described began to swirl about my head. *Nice . . .* I took another drink of beer. *Is it hot in here?*

My face was beginning to feel flushed and my hands cold and clammy. *Great. Another damn hot flash.* I tried to push the sleeves of my cycling jersey up, but they were too tight to go very far. Tony was still talking, but all of a sudden, my head started to hurt, and it was difficult to focus on what he was saying. Something about dividing the iris rhizomes every few years . . .

Oh my God. This can't be a hot flash; he must have put something in my beer.

I stood up.

"You okay, Sally?" Tony stood also and started forward. He was looking at me intently. Trying to decide if the drug had taken effect yet?

I had to get out of there.

"Uh, I just need to use the bathroom."

He watched as I walked unsteadily down the hall. Once inside, I locked the door and threw open the shower curtain. Thank God—there was a window. It was a struggle in my woozy state, but I somehow managed to hoist myself up and squeeze my large frame through, dropping clumsily down into the backyard.

I stumbled to where my bike was leaning against the house, wheeled it through the gate, and jumped on, pedaling off down the street as hard as I could.

My heart pounding, I turned to look back. No sign of him. Downshifting, I exhaled to get rid of the excess carbon dioxide that had built up in my lungs. And then I started to feel silly. Was this melodramatic or what? I'd obviously imagined the whole preposterous scenario. My dizziness must just be a combination of the strenuous bike ride up the coast, a half glass of beer on an empty stomach, and a general lack of sleep—plus maybe a hot flash, after all. No doubt, I was going to get home and take a couple Advil and feel just fine.

How embarrassing. Tony was probably wondering what the hell had happened to me and when I was finally going to emerge from the bathroom.

I turned left from the Circles onto California Avenue and into the wind. Feeling the breeze blow through my hair, I realized I'd left my helmet at Tony's house. Should I go back for it? Just then, I heard the squeal of tires from behind me. Glancing around at the noise, I almost lost my balance. So I wasn't imagining the woozy part. At the gunning of an engine, I looked back again.

It was Tony's blue pickup truck. And it was coming up on me fast. *Oh, shit.*

Leaning over and gripping my handlebars in the drop position, I shifted back onto the big ring and stamped down on my pedals. I took the right turn onto Bay Street way wide; luckily no one was coming up the other way at that moment. There was a fair amount of rush-hour traffic on the street, but I was able to go faster than it, passing on the right in the bike lane. By the time I got down to West Cliff, half a dozen cars separated Tony from me.

I bombed down the hill, passed the entrance to the wharf, and tore down Beach Street. The bad news was that almost all the traffic had turned left onto Pacific Avenue, so there was hardly anyone remaining to keep Tony from gaining on me. If only I could make it to the end of the Boardwalk, I could cross the river at the railroad trestle, and I'd be home free. Tony would have to either go all the way around to the car crossing at Riverside or ditch his truck and follow on foot. Whichever way he chose, I was sure that if I could make it to the trestle, I could beat him over the river and lose him on the Eastside—if I could just manage to keep my balance on the bike, that is.

So far, so good. I zipped by the beach volleyball courts and past the Cocoanut Grove and the arcade. Risking a look back, I saw Tony's truck just behind me, veering to the right to try to run me off the road. My heart pounding, I bunny-hopped the barrier into the bike lane to avoid him and rode on harder. Past Neptune's Kingdom. Past the Hurricane ride. Almost there.

A red light loomed ahead. I sped through it without stopping, narrowly avoiding a woman with a stroller. And as I turned to look for Tony, I saw him also run the light, swerve to miss the stroller, and crash head-on with a large delivery truck turning left off Riverside Avenue.

I breathed a sigh of relief and faced back forward—only to run smack into a kid on a skateboard who'd come out of nowhere from my right. The last thing I remember is me and my bike flying through the air, headed straight for a cluster of brightly colored beach balls.

Chapter
Twenty-Seven

"Where am I?"

"I can't believe you just said that. What a cliché." Eric was slightly out of focus, but I was able to make out the grin on his face. "Where do you think you are?"

"Uh . . ." I blinked a few times and looked about me. A room. Lots of white. Sheets. I was in a bed. *Ah.* "The hospital?"

"You got it."

I shifted my body, and a sharp pain shot through my left shoulder. "Ow!"

"Try not to move around too much. You broke your collarbone and your wrist. And you suffered a pretty severe concussion to boot."

That would explain the pounding headache. Leaning back against the pillows, I closed my eyes and tried to remember what had happened: Tony chasing me, the crash, the ambulance. *Right.*

"The kid on the skateboard—is he okay?"

"Yeah. He's young. Just a few bruises."

"And Tony?"

"He's also here in the hospital—just a few doors down, as a matter of fact. Though you fared a lot better than him. Looks like he might be partially paralyzed from a broken neck."

I nodded. *Instant karma*, I was thinking.

"He wasn't wearing a seat belt," Eric went on, shaking his head and making soft clucking noises, "and you weren't wearing your helmet, young lady." He took my good hand and looked at me, concern in his eyes. "You really scared me, you know? I'm not going to harp on you about it now, but sometime real soon I'm going to need to know what the hell happened out there between you two."

I jerked forward again and immediately regretted it. "My bike!"

Eric smiled. "It's fine. Well, other than the handlebars, which snapped in two. But the frame looks to be intact. Your dad took it home with him. He just left, by the way. Had to go deal with some restaurant thing but said he'd be back soon."

I nodded again. "Thanks. So what time is it? How long have I been here?"

"A few hours. It's a little after nine. They're going to keep you overnight just to monitor your concussion. But the doctor said you'd be released in the morning if it all looks good."

I closed my eyes but then immediately snapped them open again. "Buster!" I said, thankfully remembering this time not to jerk my body. "He can't be left alone again all night. Someone needs to go get him from Tony's house."

"Oh, right. Look, don't you worry about it. I'll make sure he's okay. I'll go get him myself if need be." Eric patted me on the arm. "You gotta try to chill, babe. You hungry?"

I was, actually. "Yeah."

"That's a good sign. I don't think the kitchen is still open here, but I can go out and get you a sandwich or something."

"How 'bout a burger, fries, and chocolate shake?" Hey, if now wasn't a good time for some classic junk food, when was?

After Eric left, I closed my eyes again and contemplated what had happened that afternoon. So it had to have been Tony, after all, who'd drugged and then killed Letta. And then I'd gotten too close to finding out, and he'd come after me. I shuddered at the thought of how stupid I'd been and how I'd almost suffered Letta's fate.

But at least it was all over. And I was pretty sure I now knew how Tony had done it.

The thing that was bugging me, though, was that I still didn't get exactly *why*.

* * *

I was cleared to go home at eight the next morning, my vital signs having been pronounced normal—but not until all the paperwork was done for my release, the doctor said, which could take a couple hours.

"Can I walk around the halls?"

"Sure. Just don't wander too far, so we can find you when we need to."

After a disappointing breakfast of overcooked eggs, cold toast, and watery coffee, I went in search of Tony. On hearing that he was down the hall, I'd been struck with the need to confront him. But I'd have to do so before talking to the police. Once he was arrested—and I had no doubt my statement would assure that—I wouldn't get the chance again.

I wasn't scared, exactly. From what Eric had said, I figured Tony was, at least for the moment, immobile from his injuries. So he wasn't going to leap out of bed at me wielding a knife or anything like that. He'd be a very captive audience. But I was feeling uneasy. I'd never knowingly been in the presence of a murderer before, much less accused one of his crime.

I found him down the hall. The door was open, and I could see him lying in bed, eyes closed, with some sort of contraption around his neck. His left leg was up in traction.

"Good morning, Tony." I came in and sat down, taking care not to knock my sling against his tray table. "Fancy meeting you here."

His eyes opened. He didn't say anything, but the muscles in his face tightened when he saw who it was.

"I just wanted to stop by and have a little chat. No need to say anything if you don't want. It can be a one-sided chat." He was eyeing my hospital gown and bandages. "Yep," I said. "I ended up here too, thanks to you. But unlike you, I'll be going home real soon. I think it's going to be a while—a very long while—before you get to go home."

Tony closed his eyes, but I didn't care. I just kept on talking. The anger was starting to come, and it felt good to have the upper hand. Cathartic.

"I think I've got it figured out, what happened." Was that a smile? I ignored it. "That night at Dixon's when Javier told you about Kate—that was the first time you'd heard about Letta's affair, wasn't it? You were lying when you said she'd already told you. And it surprised the hell out of you. So you had your brother—who'd been with you at Dixon's that night and also heard what Javier said—you had him go up to Kate's farm to check her out for you. How you found her, I'm not sure. But I'm guessing Javier told you her name and said something about her being one of the restaurant vendors. With that information, it wouldn't have been too hard to figure it out."

The smile was still there, but it seemed a little forced now.

"Once you confirmed Javier's story, that Letta was indeed involved with Kate, you fumed about it for a while and eventually came up with a plot to kill her. And at the same time decided that you'd frame Javier, the bearer of the bad news, thereby taking the heat off yourself."

A nurse came into the room to check Tony's monitor. "Oh," she said to him cheerily. "I didn't know you had a friend who was also in the hospital. That's nice." Tony didn't even open his eyes. I made polite small talk with her as she changed his IV bag and marked his chart and then continued with my narrative once she'd left the room.

"The first thing you did was snitch some yellow jasmine from Javier's apartment complex. You must have been following him, and I bet it felt like Christmas when you saw that vine growing at his place—the perfect final touch. And it almost worked too. It was only after the toxicology report came back that the police decided they had enough evidence to arrest Javier."

Tony opened his eyes briefly and then shut them tightly again.

"You showed up that night at Gauguin after everyone had gone but Letta. I imagine you just sat in your car or something, waiting. Once Javier left, it was a good bet she was alone. She offered you tea, as you knew she would, and it was a simple matter, when she wasn't watching, to slip some of the yellow jasmine into the pot along with the tea as it steeped. And she wouldn't have noticed that you didn't drink anything from your own cup."

I was getting to the hard part—not hard to figure out but hard to talk about. I simply couldn't fathom how someone could plunge a knife into the chest of another human being, especially one lying helpless, as she must have been, on the floor. You'd have to stab pretty hard for the blade to even go in. And he didn't do it only once but multiple times. Just thinking about it was sickening.

"The drug took effect after a few minutes," I finally managed to go on. "When she got weak, you took the key to the knife cabinet from her purse. Of course you knew which one was Javier's prized chef's knife; everyone who'd ever been in that kitchen did. So you got that one out of the cabinet, and . . ." I stopped.

The son of a bitch chose now to open his eyes and stare at me.

"You stabbed her. Over and over again. It was like fish in a barrel in her drugged state." I returned his look with one of disgust. "What a coward."

He shut his eyes once more.

"The thing that had everyone confused was the fingerprints on the key. But that was easy, wasn't it? With Letta dead, all you had to do was wipe off your prints, press her dead fingers on the key, and return it to her purse. Then you washed and wiped clean the cups and teapot, wiped the knife handle, and left, taking care not to leave your prints on the door knob. The fact that they would be found on other things in the room wouldn't incriminate you, since you were a frequent visitor. You'd been there that afternoon, in fact, to deliver the cherry blossom branches."

The image of him bringing flowers to Letta on the very day he knew he was going to stab her to death was especially disturbing. I tried not to think about it.

"And then, after I asked you whether you knew about Letta and Kate, you realized I was getting close to the truth, and you had your brother follow me and try to scare me off. How are his eyes, by the way?" Tony didn't respond, but I could see his jaw harden.

"There is one thing, though, that I can't figure out. I just don't get *why*. I mean, I certainly understand how you would get angry when you found out about Letta having an affair. But so enraged that you'd plot to stab her to death? And then actually *go through* with the plan? I just don't get it."

When Tony finally spoke, it startled me; I hadn't been expecting an answer.

"You could never understand," he said with a sneer. Opening his eyes, he fixed his gaze past me, toward the door. "I loved Letta; I really did. But when I found out she was with a *woman* . . ." The way he said the word "woman," as if it were the most distasteful thing imaginable, was unnerving.

He continued to stare at the door, jaw now working up and down. "I know they were mocking me," he went on after a bit, his cold eyes reminding me of those dead fish that had been floating in his cooler, "her and that bull dyke. And I couldn't get the picture out of my head—of the two of them lying in bed, laughing about me and then doing . . . whatever it is they do." He spat out these last words, and it was easy to detect the revulsion in his voice. "As if some broad could ever give her as good as *I could*."

Tony shifted in the bed and pulled his sheet up a little higher. "And Javier—he had to pay, too. For dissing me like that." Then, almost under his breath, "*No* one's gonna do that to me."

"Tell me, Tony. Were you really engaged to Letta?"

"No. I asked her, but she never did say yes." He grunted. "Now I know why. But I'm glad she said no. It would've been even worse if I'd married her."

I left him to his bitter reflections.

Chapter Twenty-Eight

It was good to see Javier back in his chef's whites again; they suited him way more than the orange had. He waved as I came into the kitchen and then went back to sorting through a box of cherries on the counter.

"The first of the season," he said, holding up a handful of the flame-colored fruit. "Kate dropped them off this morning along with her regular delivery—'a free extra,' she said. I'm going to take the best of 'em to go with my duck and then have Amy use the rest for a *clafoutis*."

It had been over a week since my—is it too dramatic to call it a "brush with death"? "A brush with beach balls" is what Eric would no doubt say. Ever the wit, he'd been quick to observe, once he knew I was out of danger, that my instincts had been correct. It was just too bad that the beach balls had been a decoration made out of concrete. He also couldn't resist pointing out that Tony and I had both crashed right in front of the bumper cars ride, which he found amusing to no end.

My collarbone and wrist still hurt. The doctor had told me I'd have to stay off my bike for at least two months, but the good news was that the pain should start to subside in another week or so.

Upon my release from the hospital, Eric had driven me straight to the police station to make a statement. Based on what I'd told them, they'd been able to get a warrant to search Tony's house and vehicle. On my advice, they'd confiscated the remains of my beer as well as the vase of white flowers sitting on the kitchen counter. I wasn't positive, but I had a strong suspicion they'd prove to be poisonous. In addition, they'd seized his computer, some clothes, and the smashed-up truck.

They'd hit the jackpot. Traces of a blood type matching Letta's had been found on a pair of Tony's shoes as well as on the floor mat from his truck. It would take a while for the DNA testing to be done, though no one doubted the blood was Letta's.

The beer would also take several weeks to analyze, but the flowers had been identified as lily of the valley, which not only is highly toxic but, when ingested, causes the very symptoms I experienced: hot flashes, dizziness, hallucinations, and headache. A website I found said that if enough is consumed, it can lead to coma and death from heart failure.

I also learned online that lily of the valley has a bitter flavor with a sweet aftertaste. No wonder he'd served dark beer. And even the water the cut flowers are kept in is poisonous. So he must have poured some of the water into my glass while I was distracted with looking at those photos on the fridge. *Oy*. Miss Marple would never have let that happen.

Tony's computer had provided incriminating evidence as well. Its browsing history turned up numerous searches over the past several weeks about poisonous flowers, including both yellow jasmine and lily of the valley.

The idea that he'd been planning to poison me in advance of my turning up at his house was disconcerting. But then again, maybe he merely had the flowers in the vase as a just-in-case? And then, of course, I had to go and show up, asking about that damn vine and reacting to the photo on the fridge. Great timing, that was. So I didn't know if they'd be able to prove that Tony's attempt on my life was premeditated, but it didn't really matter. Letta's murder clearly was. That, along with the fact that he'd used the lily water on me and then tried to run me down with his truck, would be more than enough to send him away for good. And his brother was likely to get some real time as an accessory to the crime, according to Eric.

I grabbed one of the cherries from the box Javier was picking through and popped it into my mouth. Sweet and juicy.

"Got a minute?" I asked him.

"Sure."

"Let's go upstairs."

He wiped his pink-stained hands on the towel tucked into his apron and followed me up to the office.

I'd been thinking a lot about "things" over the past week. Important things. Or at least things that should be important. Nothing like being poisoned and then almost run over by a truck to make you put stuff in your life into perspective.

And one of those things had been Gauguin.

"I've been talking to Shanti about our profit and loss statement," I said when Javier had gotten settled in the wing chair opposite the desk. "In particular, about how much play we have on the cost side."

Javier nodded, not sure where I was going with this.

"I've also been doing some research into the price of grass-fed beef, pastured pork, and free-range hens."

"Ah." He looked relieved.

"And really, it's not as bad as I would have thought. Look." I handed him the printout of a price list I'd gotten online. "If we raise our menu prices by just a few dollars, I think we can do it. And then we can advertise as selling only humanely raised meat and sustainable seafood, too. I want to become a part of the Seafood Watch Restaurant Program." I pulled the pocket guide I'd found at Letta's house from my purse and showed it to Javier. "This was in Letta's kitchen," I said, "so I'm pretty sure she was considering changing the menu. I want to honor her wishes. No more longline-caught tuna. No more imported shrimp . . ."

Javier was smiling.

"What?"

"You. You're talking real fast, you know?"

"Sorry."

"No, it's okay. I think it's great how excited you are."

I set the Seafood Watch card down. "Well, anyway, I just wanted to see what you thought about the idea."

"Hey, if you think we can do it, then I say let's do it. You're the boss."

"That brings me to the other thing I wanted to discuss." I'd thought about this over the past week, too, and had finally come to a decision. "As you can no doubt tell, I've made up my mind to keep Gauguin. Letta wouldn't have wanted me to sell, and the more involved I get with the place, the more I realize how much it means to me.

"But at the same time, I'm not ready to just up and quit Solari's, cold turkey. Even though my dad has said he can get on without me, I know it would be hard for him, more on an emotional level than anything else. And besides, the job brings in good, steady money. So here's the deal: I've talked with my dad, and he's agreed to let me go to part time—just work there a couple days a week—so I can have time for Gauguin, too."

Javier was looking at me intently.

"Don't get me wrong; I'm not a moron. I know it would be wildly unrealistic for me to take over the running of the restaurant, to try to step into Letta's shoes. Even working just part time at Solari's, I wouldn't have the time, and I certainly don't have the know-how, in any case. But I do want to be involved here in a real way—and not just with the front of the house, like at Solari's, but with menu planning, food costing and purchasing. Even cooking sometimes."

At Javier's look of mock horror, I laughed. "Okay, so maybe I'll need some extra help with that last one. But the point is, I'll never be able do it without your help. And I'm thinking a new title for you would be in order, and a salary to go with it. Maybe executive chef?"

He cracked a smile.

"So what do you say? You willing to team up with me? Be the Batman to my Robin, the Simon to my Garfunkel?"

His smile became a wide, toothy grin. "Sounds good to me, Tonto. So how soon do we change the menu?"